CW00410628

THE HIGHLANDER'S VIKING BRIDE

The Hardy Heroines Series (book #2)

By Cathy & DD MacRae

PRINT EDITION

PUBLISHED BY
Short Dog Press

www.cathymacraeauthor.com

Copyright © 2017
All rights reserved
ISBN-978-0-9966485-6-1

License Notes

This book is licensed for your personal enjoyment only. This book contains copyrighted work and may not be reproduced, transmitted, downloaded, or stored in or introduced into an information storage and retrieval system in any form or by any means, whether electronic or mechanical, now known or hereinafter invented, without the express written permission of the copyright owner, except in the case of brief quotation embodied in critical articles and reviews. Thank you for respecting the hard work of the authors.

This ebook is a work of fiction. The names, characters, places, and incidents are products of the writer's imagination or have been used fictitiously and are not to be construed as real. Any resemblance to persons, living or dead, actual events, locales or organizations is entirely coincidental.

Dedicated to Freki

Loyal companion,

Fierce protector,

And such a sweetheart.

OLD NORSE (NORN) WORDS OF INTEREST:

Afi – grandfather
Amma – grandmother
Beta – bite
Bjenk – dog
Bolli – darling
Borg – broch, an Iron Age structure peculiar to Scotland
Deg, Gud, til ære – To God the honor (a blessing)
Ek ann þér – I love you
Elkesdottir – Elke's daughter
Flatja – hold down
Fresta – wait
Ganga at – attack
Glene – clear patch of sky
Haar – sea fog
Halda – hold/halt
Hannja – come
Henta – fetch
Holm - island
Korrnorr – quiet
Kvala – calm
Lofta – rise
Niese – niece
Reginulfsdottir – Reginulf's daughter
Utgeng – go

GAELIC AND SCOTTISH WORDS of INTEREST

Buidseach - witch
Dreich – dreary (weather)
Fairetur – watchful tower
Loch Beaggorm – Little blue lake
Moonbroch – hazy halo around the moon signaling bad weather to come
Mumblecrust – toothless beggar
Roane – faithless faeries whose love for the sea overrode their feelings for their human lovers
Ruadhcreag – red rock
Siursach – prostitute
Snell – biting (cold) weather (wind)
Tanist – heir apparent to a clan chief
Trow - troll

THE HIGHLANDER'S VIKING BRIDE

Calder MacGerry, laird of an impoverished clan, has resolved to end the bitter feud between the MacGerrys and Sinclairs. He jumps at Laird Sinclair's offer of marriage to his only daughter, Katja, to seal the agreement between their clans—only to get more than he bargained for.

Katja's chance to escape her father's harsh treatment appears to be too good to be true. But becoming Lady of a clan that despises her because she's a Sinclair, doesn't make her life any easier. When the attacks turn deadly, she fights her way out, making a dangerous passage to the Shetland Isles for refuge with her mother's Viking family.

Calder and Katja's marriage, built on mistrust, rushes quickly into disaster. As Calder seeks to repair the damage, Katja discovers not another enemy, but a husband who pledges a new beginning.

Chapter One

1445 AD
Caithness, Scotland

Robert MacGerry's gaze locked on his son's, his voice cracked and twisted with pain, his gnarled hands clenched tight on Calder's arm. "Promise ye'll keep the clan strong."

Calder swallowed his grief, his chest burning with shock and dismay as he gently rested his father's head in his lap. Applying pressure with a wadded length of woolen cloth to the jagged belly wound, Calder watched his father's eyes as the spark of life ebbed.

"Aye, Da, I'll do all that I can." Calder choked on his anguish, his da—his hero, his protector—lying in his arms, forever broken, mortally wounded in a raid gone awry on Sinclair lands. Calder rubbed the rough, twisted wooden cross hanging about his neck and prayed fervently to trade places with his da. He shuddered as a biting wind wrapped ice-laden fog and the acrid smell of a nearby bog around them.

"Did ye take care of the bastard who did this?" Robert rasped.

Calder glanced at the lifeless body of the man who'd dealt his father his death blow, crumpled against a large rock. "Aye, Da. I did."

Robert gripped Calder's shirt, his eyes searching his son's face. "Take care of yer brother and sister."

Harsh reality dug its talons deeper at his father's request. Calder glanced at his Uncle Finn standing next to him. Finn settled a heavy hand on his shoulder, nodding his support. Calder swallowed hard before answering. "Aye, ye can trust me to see to all that needs doin'. When ye get to heaven, tell my older brother I miss him."

Grief seared Calder's throat and eyes as his father drew his last ragged breath. Time stood still, waiting desperately for the exhale that never came. Silent tears dropped onto his da's torn shirt, mixing with the final pulse of dark red blood. Several minutes passed before anyone spoke.

"What do ye command, laird?"

Calder jerked with surprise. He stared blankly at his uncle before he understood what Finn asked. With his older brother, and now his father dead, he was the new MacGerry laird.

Calder cleared his throat. "Prepare to leave."

They gently wrapped Robert's body in his cloak, securing him to his horse for their return to Fairetur. The few sheep stolen this night came at too high a price. Whatever had begun this feud with the Sinclairs had cost the MacGerry Clan dearly.

Finn pulled his horse alongside, breaking Calder's thoughts. "What will ye do, laddie?"

"'Twill be as we discussed these past months," Calder replied stonily. "I will seek a truce with the Sinclair. We dinnae have enough food to survive the winter. This damnable feud has gone on long enough. No one knows the why of it anymore. Fighting has cost the lives of too many good men, making too many women widows whilst still in the bloom of youth. I willnae see more lives wasted on a blood feud started by the dead long cold in their graves."

Finn nodded. Calling a lad over, he sent him ahead of the group to prepare the clan for the grim news of Robert's death.

The gates of Fairetur swung slowly open at their arrival. Two riders drove the stolen sheep inside to join the small herd they already possessed. Calder handed his horse to a waiting lad. He spotted his sister, Torri, standing at the front of the crowd, bunching her skirts in each fist, one word, one glance away from crushing despair. He would give anything to cushion the blow for her soft heart. She must have read the truth in his expression. Tears burst forth and flowed silently down her cheeks as she ran to him, throwing herself into his arms.

"Och, now. 'Twill be well." His voice sought to soothe, but Torri stiffened and drew away.

Her eyes sparked at him through her tears. "How will it be well, brother?"

He had no ready answer, so he hugged her again and slowly walked her toward the great hall, holding her upright as she sagged against him. Word of their laird's death filled the keep with the thick flavor of mourning and a deep melancholy overtook the normally warm-hearted inhabitants. Lively voices fell to whispers, and the normal clatter of feet on the stone floor became a muted shuffle. Calder guided Torri into the comforting arms of their grandmam and the two huddled together in shared pain.

He strode to the hearth inside the great hall, settling into the worn oak chairs with his uncle and younger brother, Robbie.

Robbie perched on the edge of his seat, his face grim. "How'd it happen?" he murmured, scarcely meeting Calder's gaze.

"The Sinclairs waited fer us." Finn's pain-filled voice rode barely above a whisper. "'Twas as though they knew we were comin'. Yer da and Calder covered us as we retreated with the flock we seized. The Sinclairs dinnae have too much fight in 'em over a handful of sheep, but one bastard struck a lucky blow. Yer da took a sword in the gut." His voice cracked. "He died in yer brother's arms."

"What did Da say, Calder?" Robbie's words, heavy with anguish, renewed Calder's torment, and he paused before answering.

"He asked for my vow to keep the clan strong," he finally replied.

When no more explanation came, Robbie pressed further. "No demands of vengeance? No words of hatred for the thrice-damned Sinclairs?" His voice rose in challenge.

Calder waited for his brother to calm. "Nae. He claimed no vows of vengeance. I dinnae think his last thoughts were on killing, but rather on his family and clan."

Robbie sucked in a deep breath. Calder sensed part of the darkness hanging over them lift a fraction. Perhaps there would be a chance for something more than blood and death in their future.

"What will ye do?" Robbie asked.

"We will see to Da's burial on the morrow. After I am installed as laird, I will offer a truce to the Sinclair. Then we prepare for a hard winter. Too many crofts in the village arenae ready. I dinnae want the deaths of widows and bairns on my hands. Those whose homes we cannae repair in time will move into the keep when the snows hit."

A serving woman brought them each a tankard of ale. Setting down their drinks, the buxom lass draped her arms around Calder from behind to whisper in his ear. "I'm sorry for yer da, Calder. I will fill yer bed if ye need comfort tonight." The warmth of her breath tempted.

Calder gave her a small smile. "Thank ye, Lorna, but I wish to be alone this eve. I have too much on my mind and dinnae want ye to think I am a neglectful lover."

"We have too much experience together for me to think that. If ye only want a fierce ruttin' to ease yer pain, I can live without yer tender touch tonight."

The enticing purr of her voice recalled images of their shared pleasure, but his heavy heart did not respond to her promise of temporary relief. Calder dropped a chaste kiss on her cheek. "Thank ye. Nae tonight."

Lorna hugged him once, pressing her soft bosom into the back of his neck before retreating to the kitchen. Calder watched the exaggerated swing of her hips as she left. The scent of roses lingered in the air.

Finn sent a nod in the woman's direction. "Ye know the lass fancies herself the laird's woman now, aye?"

Calder glanced at his uncle. "I have greater things to worry about than the schemes of my leman, Uncle."

Finn shook his head, but said no more.

After receiving sympathies from members of the clan and family, Finn and Robbie left Calder to his thoughts. Calder knew sleep would not find him as he rolled the situation fate placed him in over and over in his mind. After more than twenty years as the second son, he found himself laird of the MacGerrys with a feud to end and a difficult winter ahead. His gut clenched at the many tasks before him. Long hours passed before his mind stilled and sleep came.

Thick fog hung over the moors the next morn, which seemed appropriate given the mood of those who surrounded Robert MacGerry's grave. As the last of the clan filed past to pay their respects to the old laird and give their greetings to the new one, Calder led the procession into the great hall to accept his new title. His father's title. The title that should have gone to his older brother. After a brief ritual, he bade everyone sit and break their fast. He stood and raised his mug of cider in a toast.

"To Robert MacGerry. A good laird, a good father—and a good

man."

All raised their mugs in salute. "MacGerry!"

Calder stood, his determined stare sweeping the room. "The last words my father spoke were of ye, his clan. He made me swear to keep ye strong. I intend to do that verra thing. Henceforth, there will be no more raids or attacks on Sinclair lands. Tomorrow, I will send a message to the Sinclair offering a truce."

A collective gasp of surprise spread into disgruntled murmurs, sparking a few looks of outrage. Calder did not flinch.

"Hear me! No one has lost more than Robbie, Torri, and I. We lost our da and brother Ewan to this feud, and Grandda before them. No one remembers why we raid and fight the Sinclairs. 'Tis only that we always have—an insufficient cause to keep the blood flowing. Clan MacGerry willnae long survive if all our men are killed. 'Tis not vengeance or justice, but madness. I will call a truce so we can see to surviving the winter. Come spring we will work toward making the MacGerrys stronger."

Uncle Finn, Peadar the Red, and Ramsey stood with Calder. Auld Liam rose reluctantly to his feet. A hiss of dissension swept the room, but Calder could not mark its source. The elder council, along with Robbie, gave no doubt of their support of the laird's decision. He could only pray Sinclair would support it, too.

* * *

The outer doors creaked and the thud of boots striding purposely across the stones grew louder. Calder raised his head to find the man he'd sent out two days before offering peace to Sinclair crossing the hall. His swift return could be either a very good or very bad thing, as the Sinclair was known to be quick to say *aye* or *nae*. The fact Niell appeared hale seemed an encouraging sign.

Clearly pleased with himself, Niell approached the high board.

"The Earl of Caithness' response, laird." He bowed and handed over the letter.

Breaking the dark red wax seal, Calder scanned the contents. In disbelief, he read the missive twice more before he allowed a smile to creep over his face. "'Tis good news, lads. The Sinclair invites us to come and enjoy his hospitality whilst we negotiate an accord." He handed the parchment to Finn seated next to him.

Auld Liam scowled. "'Tis a trap. Ne'er trust a Sinclair. They be a treacherous lot."

Calder gave the older man a nod. "Aye, it may. But we willnae know without going. 'Tis what we hoped for."

"To treat with the devil in his own lair is madness." Liam's scowl deepened and he shoved back in his chair, arms across his chest.

Calder passed the note around the table as they lingered over the evening meal.

Finn rubbed his grizzled chin. "Auld Liam is right. It could be a trap, laddie."

"'Tis why Robbie stays here whilst you and I go, Uncle, with half a dozen men-at-arms," Calder explained.

Peadar spoke up. "I dinnae like it, but if we truly want peace there's little choice but to chance it."

"If Sinclair springs a trap, Robbie will ride to the king's man at Wick and report what happened. With this note as evidence, Sinclair isnae fool enough to risk his reputation and prove a man who doesnae keep his word." Calder glanced to each man, seeking their consent. Heads slowly nodded agreement.

"'Tis settled then. Finn and I will ride to Ruadhcreag on the morrow. We'll take young Cole with us. When we see what the Sinclair offers, he will return with the news."

The next morning, Calder and Finn, along with several MacGerry men, set out for Sinclair land. Passing through the forests to the south, Calder caught a glimpse of Loch Beaggorm, recalling the girl he'd seen while hunting two years ago when he'd ventured close to the loch where their lands bordered with those of clan Sinclair.

His lips tilted up in fond memory of the young woman sitting on a rock warming in the sun, wearing little more than her skin. So affected by her beauty he couldn't breathe, couldn't move, he could only watch from the shelter of the forest. Her long, lithe body lay gracefully along the rock, blonde hair twisted into a thick braid reaching the curve of her hips. Her skin, the color of cream, seemed flawless. She appeared both innocent and provocative with small breasts riding high on her chest. A dusting of fair curls nestled between her legs, easily seen through her short, thin chemise. Unable to see the color of her eyes, Calder guessed them to be of the deepest blue.

She slipped from her rock and into the water, swimming effortlessly for a time before climbing out again. After drying in the sun, she donned trews and a tunic over her abbreviated chemise. Mounting a blue roan gelding tethered to a nearby tree, she headed deep into Sinclair lands. Calder had lingered for several minutes, bewitched by the scene he'd witnessed. Moved beyond reason, his world had shifted in an unseen and unfamiliar way.

Returning home, he'd asked about, seeking to learn who she might be, to whom she belonged. To his frustration, he learned his siren of the loch was the Sinclair laird's daughter. It was completely out of the question he would seek out the daughter of his enemy, much less an earl's daughter whose rank placed her far above him. His disappointment, however, did not keep him from thinking of her often. She invaded his sleep many nights. Even now, two years past, she never strayed far from his thoughts.

The possibility he might see her again raised his pulse and nervousness fluttered in his belly. Always at ease around the lasses, Calder couldn't understand what it was about this one that made his heart race like a skittish colt. Whatever the reason, her image rolled through his mind, thickening his blood and hardening his body.

Chiding himself for youthful foolishness, he forced himself to concentrate on the task at hand, not some youthful dream beyond his reach. Certainly she was another man's wife by now. Yet he was unable to completely banish the hope he would lay eyes on her while on Sinclair land. He pushed hard enough to force the small yearning into the back corner of his mind. Still, she continued to taunt him, refusing to be ignored. Calder gained a sliver of understanding of why Adam dishonored his vows to God for the love of a woman.

Sinclair guards greeted the MacGerrys cautiously at the gate though their arrival was expected. Peasants leaving the castle on their way home eyed the MacGerrys with fear and suspicion.

Up close, the Sinclair stronghold loomed impressively, dwarfing the scope of the MacGerry home. Blocks of red stone stood in contrast to the green of the surrounding landscape, hence its name, Ruadhcreag. The high, thick curtain walls protected four stone towers riddled with loopholes designed to accommodate either long bows or crossbows. These, along with multiple iron gates, made this fortress all but impenetrable. Any hostile force would fare better waiting for the Earl to surrender, exhausting his supplies over time, rather than to throw themselves hopelessly at these walls.

Leaving their horses with the stable lads, Calder and his men followed the guards who escorted them to the great hall as distrustful eyes shifted their way. The Sinclair laird was seated at the raised table with three young men. Taking notice of their arrival, he rose.

"Welcome. I am Henry Sinclair. These are my sons, Bjorn, Christer and Patrik. Come. Join us as guests at our table." Sinclair's stout frame and burnished auburn hair contrasted sharply to his taller blond sons, though the eldest appeared more the coloring of his sire.

Exchanging a glance, Calder and Finn joined the laird while their men accepted seats at a lower table. Calder immediately noticed the abundance of food and the comfort of the hall.

Elaborate tapestries covered the stone walls. Windows were fitted with glass. The room glowed, well-lit from innumerable candles in stands against the walls and in chandeliers hung over the tables. A great hearth blazed at one end, adding light and warmth to the room. The table and chairs they sat upon were of an ornately carved dark wood. Silver *quaichs* rested in front of each chair, awaiting wine or ale.

A servant poured ale into the drinking bowls while two others brought out platters of game fowl, fresh baked bread, and soup. Bowls of honey and butter graced the table. Calder's stomach rumbled at the smell of hot meat pies. He could not recall seeing so much food at one time. Everything about the room and meal spoke of wealth and prosperity.

As one of the serving women poured Calder's ale, she bent over enough to allow him a full view down her bodice. After filling his cup, she caught his eye and gave him a smile promising a warm bed should he be interested.

The Sinclair's voice boomed from the high table, disrupting Calder's subtle decline of the woman's services.

"Allow me to express my sympathies on the loss of yer father. I dinnae know him, but all said he was a good man. This feud has been costly for both clans. I welcome the offer to end hostilities between our people. No one here can remember why we are at odds."

"'Tis the same for us," Calder replied.

"Then let us toast to new beginnings," Sinclair offered as he raised his *quaich* in a toast. Around the tables, the others followed their laird's example. So far, their welcome was more than Calder could have hoped for. A prickling sensation down his spine cautioned him something was afoot.

* * *

Katja reluctantly heeded her father's summons to the great hall. She much preferred taking meals in her chamber, as constant criticism and scorn from her father made for poor company. Her only regret was not spending the time with her brothers. She remembered the days before her *amma* died when mealtimes were pleasant, even enjoyable. She did not remember the days when her ma was alive.

Everyone in the keep knew guests had arrived—rumored to be the hated MacGerrys. Her father would likely use the opportunity to dangle her as bait again for some sort of alliance, her hand in marriage as part of the bargain. She grimaced. The MacGerry laird was as old as her sire—as were all the men her da had presented as prospective husbands.

"I willnae marry a man thrice my age. Why does he keep bringing such old relics about, Freki? Has the man not made the acquaintance of anyone younger than two score?"

Her companion did not answer.

Katja hurried to the great hall with Freki at her side. If she allowed her sire to wait too long, he would add to her humiliation by displaying her like a freshly caught trout in front of his guests. Much as she disliked appeasing him, flaunting her disdain was far worse.

When they reached the door to the hall, she raised a hand, whispering a command for her companion to wait outside the door as she perused the people seated in the great hall. Pale auras of color surrounded each man, giving the room a festive look were it not for the unsettling tale each told her. The reds of anger and lust, the brown of dishonesty, gray and sulphur of dark thoughts and pain. From long practice, she ignored the pale green of pity she knew were aimed at her.

Skirting the red auras, Katja moved silently into the room, attracting no attention. Years of avoiding her father gave her the skill to move about the castle like a wraith, finding tremendous value in being invisible when the need called for it. It wasn't until she stood near the foot of the lower tables that anyone noticed her. Laird Sinclair's eyes gleamed.

"Ah, here is my daughter. Katja, meet the new MacGerry Laird."

* * *

Calder glanced at the young woman who'd entered the room as silent as a ghost. Though the Sinclair men did not stand in respect at her introduction, Calder, Finn, and the rest of the MacGerry men rose immediately from their seats. She offered a small curtsy, her gaze dropping to the floor, seeming uncomfortable with the attention.

Calder stood stricken as if struck by a smithy's hammer. He could do nothing but stare at the lass in front of him who'd haunted his thoughts and dreams for so long. To his amazement, she appeared even more beautiful than he remembered. Grey. Her eyes were grey, not the dark blue he imagined. If he'd been told she was an angel come to earth he would not have doubted the claim for a moment.

Finn tugged on his sleeve and inclined his head toward the girl. Calder retrieved enough of his wits to speak. "'Tis a pleasure to meet ye, Lady Katja."

* * *

The sight of a young man instead of the old laird she expected startled Katja. Tall, lean of muscle, with dark brown hair and fair skin, his deep blue eyes were the color of sapphires or perhaps the ocean on a calm day. A high forehead, strong jaw, and full lips made for a very handsome face. Lips which curved into a kind smile at her.

His eager blue eyes stared, as if caught in a pleasant dream. Katja's stomach twisted in a way she'd not experienced before. Heat scorched its way from her head to her shoulders, tingling along her breasts and descending lower. She didn't recognize or understand the strange awareness. Her breathing picked up its pace as her heart beat tripled. How could one look from a man inspire such a reaction?

She averted her gaze in an effort to wrestle her body and emotions under control. Inhaling deeply, she raised her eyes again only to find the same sensations slamming into her anew. She needed a distraction.

Use the sight. It doesnae lie.

Looking past her normal ability to see, she glanced first at her father. The darkening gray aura surrounding him reflected his greed, his nature growing more corrupt with time. A band of deep brown layered on top of the gray was new today. She knew it as a sign of deceit and wondered what he was up to. Scanning the rest of the table, the light blue surrounding her brothers Bjorn, Christer and

Patrik reflected confusion. Whatever her father contrived with the MacGerry, they knew nothing of it.

Yellow surrounded MacGerry's older companion, apparently happy about the circumstances of this meeting. Finally, looking upon the man introduced to her as Calder MacGerry, he seemed awash with color. He wrestled with strong emotions, the red of lust mixing with the yellow of happiness. Dark blue rode over the top of all, the fear of speaking the truth. Suspicion flowed through her as she considered what MacGerry might be hiding. Her father addressed her again, interrupting her thoughts.

"Daughter, have chambers prepared for our guests. See to it all their needs are met. They will experience the fullness of our hospitality whilst here." Sinclair sent Calder a sly smile.

Calder's eyes widened, clearly taken aback at her father's words. "Many thanks for your hospitality, Laird, but after this fine meal we will have no needs beyond a bed this eve."

Mortification filled Katja at her sire's brazen suggestion, pulling her back to the purpose for which she'd been summoned. It was bad enough he kept serving women around who openly flaunted their favors toward anything male. To make her responsible for having these women brought to his guests proved more than her temper could bear.

Grateful their guest rescued her from further humiliation, she exited the room quickly, daring her sire to rebuke her abruptness. As Katja crossed the doorway, Freki rose, following close behind. She made the necessary arrangements with the housekeeper, then headed for the respite of her bedchamber.

She slammed the door and threw the bolt as soon as she and Freki entered the room. Her father was clearly up to some deception. No matter his generous words, his brown aura said everything she needed to know, guaranteeing he would try to trick the MacGerry in some manner despite his seemingly warm hospitality. Though the MacGerrys and Sinclairs had been bitter enemies longer than she could remember, she couldn't help feeling sorry for them. Even the MacGerrys deserved better than betrayal at the hands of her father.

After tonight's encounter, she vowed to avoid her sire more than ever. Unsettled by her reaction to the new MacGerry laird, it was best to stay away until they concluded their business. She wasn't sure she could stomach watching whatever duplicity her father planned, and she didn't want their visitors to think she played any part in the treachery.

Chapter Two

After consuming a better meal than Calder could remember—perhaps ever—pleasant conversation followed as they retired to chairs before the hearth. The sweet smell of rowan burning filled the hall instead of the peppery scent of peat to which Calder was accustomed. Over spiced wine they spoke of news of the area, naming allies and enemies, drawing their informal meeting into the late hours of the night.

At last, Laird Sinclair rose from his chair, indicating the evening was at an end. "Follow the maids to yer chambers." He waved to a couple of serving girls in the hall.

Sinclair tilted his head, a half-smile stretching his lips, his hands spread before him in a placating manner, though the look was disconcertingly predatory instead of reassuring. "Because of our history together, I have placed two guards in the hall for yer protection more than to keep ye confined. We shall commence negotiations after we break our fast on the morrow. I bid you good sleep."

The man strode from the hall, leaving the MacGerrys to follow the two maids to their respective rooms.

Both women made unspoken offers of companionship by briefly touching and brushing against the MacGerry men. With a subtle hand gesture, Calder warned the others they wouldn't be enjoying female company this eve. After the chambers were issued, several men gathered in Calder's room.

"All appears as we hoped thus far. Sinclair's a good host and seems honest in his desire for a truce," Finn said.

Calder reclined in a chair in front of the small hearth, musing the evening's events. "Aye. I detect no deceit in his words or actions, albeit 'tis troubling and something tells me all is not as it seems. However, we've yet to hear his terms. Seek yer beds. We need our wits about us on the morrow."

Finn gave him an odd look once the room cleared. "Is there something you need to tell me aboot the lass?"

Calder pushed deeper into the chair, considering how much to reveal to his shrewd uncle. "I saw her a long time ago and have been bewitched by her since. Once I found out she was Sinclair's daughter, I tried to forget about her. I hadnae laid eyes on her again until tonight."

Finn smiled. "Will the lass be a distraction? Sinclair certainly noticed yer reaction to her."

"Nae. I will not allow it to affect the reason we are here," Calder declared with more conviction than he felt.

Finn touched a knuckle to his forehead as he rose. "Good sleep, Laird."

Calder returned his uncle's nod, his mind already on other things as the door latched shut. Sitting before the small fire in his chamber, Calder took a drink of wine and glanced toward the bed. If he turned in early, he would have a good five hours of slumber. But sleep proved to be elusive. Thoughts of the beautiful Katja Sinclair overrode any possibility of a restful night.

The next morn, they met for a meal of hot oat porridge, honey, cream and fruit. The smell of baking bread filled the hall, causing even a full stomach to growl at the prospect of another well-cooked meal. The earl rose from his seat, drawing Calder's attention.

"Let us discuss our future." He opened the door to his solar through the wall behind the high table. The room contained more of the rich furnishings they'd seen throughout the castle. An ornate desk stood in one corner while a table with cushioned chairs around it sat to one side. As everyone settled, Sinclair began. "My sources say ye will have a difficult winter."

Calder shot Finn a glance and scooted forward in his chair, wary of the direction of the conversation. In spite of his hope for peace, something about this man pricked at Calder. He had learned long ago to trust his instincts. It had kept him alive more than once in the past.

The Sinclair cocked his head. "Easy, lads. I mean no disrespect. Is this not the truth?" He raised his hands in mock surrender.

Calder eyed their host.

Sinclair's black tunic with silver embroidery was made of the finest wool. The cost of the man's garments would feed the MacGerry clan for a month.

With a curt nod, Calder admitted to the unfortunate circumstance.

Sinclair seemed satisfied with the response and he clasped his hands before him on the desk. His eyes glittered as he turned his attention to Calder alone.

"I believe I have a solution to our mutual problem. My sources also tell me ye are unwed, Laird MacGerry."

Again, Calder nodded his assent, his unease growing.

"I noticed yer . . . interest in my daughter last eve."

Calder looked Sinclair in the eye, his gaze narrowing. A chill skittered across the back of his neck as if the cold unearthly breath of a *Sìth* touched him.

"I have had a devil of a time marrying her off. When we draw up a treaty between our clans, ye must agree to wed my daughter. Marriage will strengthen our accord and finally put an end to the raiding."

Calder's eyes widened, stunned by the demand. He couldn't

have heard him correctly. "I dinnae understand. She is a beautiful woman. Why is she not married already? She is of marrying age?"

"Aye, she is, but she refuses any match I make for her. I grow weary of trying to please her. Her reaction to ye last night was the closest I've seen to acceptance. She comes with a large tocher. 'Twill give yer clan the coin ye need and a sizeable tract of dower lands. The two *davochs* lie on your northwest border and the crofts with them. The people tending them will move elsewhere."

Calder sat speechless. He knew the area, as they'd raided there more than once. So much land along with gold—all for marrying the man's daughter? Unable to make sense of what Sinclair placed on the table before him, he remained silent. He glanced at his uncle. Finn twisted his neck until it popped, fidgeting in his chair. Something didn't feel right. It was too rich an offer.

Finn recovered his voice first. "Aye, we are familiar with that bit of land. 'Tis verra fertile, verra fine. Why would ye wish to part with it?"

Sinclair's predatory smile flashed briefly. "When her grandda died, he left specific provisions for his only granddaughter. The gold and lands can only be released upon her marriage." Disdain saturated the earl's words.

"What does she say of the match?" Calder asked.

Sinclair's face hardened. "She willnae be told until the wedding. I willnae have her running away or saying nae yet again. An agreement of peace is too important to both our clans."

Calder shook his head, stunned. "I'll nae have an unwilling bride in my bed. 'Tis a sure path to misery."

Sinclair's expression darkened. "We both know the likelihood of yer clan surviving the winter hearty and whole. I offer peace, a large amount of gold to feed yer people this winter, and lands to keep ye from starving in the future. I will include enough sheep, cattle, and grain to sustain yer clan through the next few months and from which to grow new herds. In exchange, we will have peace, but ye must wed and bed my daughter, and depart at the end of this day. I dinnae wish to lay eyes on her again. Those are my terms. They arenae open to negotiation."

Too astonished to form a coherent answer, Calder stared, transfixed.

Finn spoke first. "'Tis a generous offer, laird. Might my nephew and I go for a wee stroll whilst we discuss it?"

Sinclair waved his hand in response. "Take as much time as ye need. I notified the priest this morn. He awaits us at the kirk. My offer expires once the sun sets."

Finn grabbed Calder by the arm and dragged him from the chair, nodding politely to Sinclair before departing the room.

Once in the bailey, Calder glared at Finn as he paced. All around them, large and well-maintained outbuildings stood in tribute to Sinclair prosperity. The ping of a hammer and anvil drew his gaze to a blacksmith as he cajoled a piece of metal into the shape of a horseshoe.

Calder fumed. "How can a man do such a thing to his own daughter? She will have no wedding dress, no time to prepare, no celebration with friends or family. What kind of man is this Sinclair? Something is amiss. There must be something verra wrong with the lass."

"Or something verra wrong with her da. She is the woman ye have been dreaming of, aye?"

"Aye."

"Ye know we will nae get such a generous offer without ye agreeing to the marriage?"

"Aye."

"Then where lies the problem?"

Calder spun to face his uncle. "The problem is, I'll have a wife who doesnae wish to be married. 'Tis a sure way to a cold bed. As the daughter of an earl, she is too far above my touch. I am nae a man who marries a woman of noble blood. There is a reason why Sinclair wants to rid himself of his daughter. I need to know why."

"Excuse me gentlemen, may I ask about yer argument?"

Caught in their discussion, Calder hadn't noticed Christer Sinclair's approach. He stared at the man with suspicion. A sidelong glance at his uncle's countenance proved Finn wary as well.

"I take it from yer lively conversation father has offered my sister to ye."

Calder studied Christer for a moment longer before answering. "Aye, along with all the gold and lands in her tocher. He willnae tell her till 'tis time to be wed, nor give her a choice in the matter. I dinnae wish to take home an unwilling bride, no matter how bonny she is."

Christer grimaced as he rubbed his chin. "I understand. Did my da tell ye why he wishes to proceed in such a fashion?"

"He said she refused every match he's made for her," Calder replied.

Christer snorted. "I'll wager he dinnae tell ye all those matches were to men his age or older?"

Finn spat on the ground, his disgust clear.

"As I thought," Christer said with a nod. "Our sire has never treated my sister with the respect she deserves. I have done what I can to protect her, but for reasons of his own, he resents her. Katja serves faithfully in keeping our home. She is a good lass, though a bit headstrong and lacking refinements expected of an earl's daughter. She would make ye a fine wife."

Calder leveled a skeptical look at the young man.

"Our mam died when we were young," Christer explained.

"Katja was raised by our grandmam. *Amma* passed when Katja was but ten and two summers. She grew up around brothers rather than women who would teach her to be a lady. Ye have seen the kind of women my father keeps about the castle." Christer paused, eyeing Calder, compelling a response.

Calder nodded, remembering the less than subtle offers by the serving women since their arrival.

Christer gave Calder a hard look, then continued. "The MacGerry have a reputation of being a close-knit clan. Such warmth is the verra thing Katja needs after so many years of scorn. If ye favor her at all, ye would grant her a boon by taking her to wife. Even if she dinnae see it now, she will if ye're patient. Otherwise, my father will continue to seek those matches which most benefit him, rather than seeing to her happiness. As her brother, I want what's best for my sister and the clan, but have little influence with the earl."

"Yer da wants her wedded, bedded, and out the gates by the end of the day. Otherwise, the transaction is cancelled." The contempt in Calder's voice was palpable.

"Sweet Mary!" Christer spat, shaking his head. Silence hung in the air while the gravity of the situation sank in. He stared into the distance before his gaze returned to Calder.

"Ye have little choice if what we hear of yer clan is true. I will speak with her, make her understand the situation. I will tell her of yer reluctance to agree to the earl's plans. She knows she must marry. Ye are by far the best choice she has been presented with. She will agree with that. I willnae lie, Katja will be angry. But if ye treat her well, she will come 'round, ye have my word. Will ye do it?"

Calder leaned a shoulder against the rough red stone wall forming the Sinclair keep and furiously rubbed his forehead, trying to ward off the pain rising behind his eyes.

Finn's urgent voice rose. "Laddie, ye must. When we ride out those gates today ye will have gained the fortune we so desperately need, the peace we have lacked for three generations, and the woman ye have been thinking on for years."

Christer's eyebrows shot up. Calder noticed his reaction and waved him off. "I'll agree, but I'm holding ye to yer word. Explain the circumstances to her. I dinnae wish to worry about my wife gutting me in my sleep."

Christer and Finn both smiled at his answer. Christer clasped Calder's in rough reassurance, then strode to the keep.

"Weel laddie, let's dinnae keep yer new father by marriage waitin'." Finn's mouth widened in a grin.

Calder shook his head. "Have Cole travel home with the news. Send two of the men with him. Tell them to prepare a welcome for our new lady."

"Aye, my laird." Finn winked, his eyes full of mischief as he clapped his nephew on the back, hoots of laughter trailing in his wake.

A sense of dread filled Calder's gut as he considered the web he found himself caught in. Every possible reason why the man would want to rid himself of his daughter in such a shameful way rose to his mind—each more distasteful than the next. With jaw clenched in determination, he strode in Finn's wake.

When they arrived at the great hall, the midday meal awaited them. Joining Sinclair and his sons at the high table, Calder met Sinclair's gaze. "I agree to yer terms."

The man's face broke into a toothy smile as he gripped Calder's shoulder. "Wise decision, Laird. We shall be kin today. I took the liberty to draw up the contract."

At their sire's words, Bjorn and Patrik glanced at the two of them, surprise on their faces. Christer wore a grim frown, but kept his silence.

Studying the agreement, Calder noted the terms were as generous as discussed. Something about seeing in writing all the MacGerrys would gain confounded him, increasing his suspicion. The amount of gold, land, sheep, grain—it was all too much. All this to relieve the man of a long-standing enemy and his only daughter? Something felt very wrong. However, he had no time to ferret it out.

Calder reminded himself he'd made the best possible decision for his clan. He was doing Katja a favor by taking her away from a man who barely deserved the title of father. She might come from noble blood, but at least *he* knew how to properly care for a lass. That he would wed the woman of his dreams this very day? There might be a good chance his dreams would become something much darker.

He agreed with this cruel plan against his better judgment. For being forced to marry the laird of her father's enemy, he could only hope she would forgive him. If not, they were both young enough to look forward to a long, miserable marriage.

* * *

"I hear the MacGerrys have been shut up in the earl's solar since the morning meal."

Katja glanced at the older woman beside her. She could always count on the Sinclair cook as a source for gossip. All the women bent over the table slicing vegetables turned their attention to hear more.

"What are those thieving curs doin' here, anyway?" Mab, a kitchen maid, asked.

"The way my man tells it, they're here to seek a truce," Dora, wife to one of the laird's guards, answered.

"Humph. The day those low-born outlaws abide by a peace agreement is the day ye'll bow to me as queen." Cook placed a fist on her ample hip, waving a cleaver like a scepter with her other hand. The women laughed at Cook's prediction.

Katja glanced at the women as they returned to their chores. With the fall harvest complete, there was plenty to keep them busy. It had been a prosperous season, which would ease the harsh winter storms drawing near.

This morning they cooked, preserved, and stored the last of the harvest for the coming change of season. Pickled vegetables and fruit preserves lined the storeroom shelves. Grains and legumes lay drying and would today be placed in secure bins to keep out vermin. The scent of fresh cut vegetables filled the air and the sound of chopping pounded out an unsteady rhythm.

Incessant gossip kept everyone close and attentive. At the end of the long center table, some of the women salted recently butchered meat and fish for drying and smoking. Katja moved among them, keeping a detailed account of the amounts and their storage locations. It was her job to see to the food supply, making sure it lasted through the harsh months. She also created lists, prioritizing tasks to be done once the cold drove everyone inside.

Katja noticed the serving women bringing the remnants of the midday meal into the kitchen. She hadn't stopped to eat, grazing instead on the food while they prepared it. Christer waved to her from the doorway.

"Come, sister. Father wishes to speak with ye in his solar."

The fine hairs on the back of Katja's neck rose at this ominous request, but she dragged the kerchief from her hair and followed him into the passage, unrolling her sleeves as she went. Freki rose from his spot by the door and ambled a few feet behind. "Why his solar,

Christer? What is it?" Apprehension crept up her spine.

"I cannae say, but promise me ye will hold yer tongue this time." His stern expression melted into one of concern.

"So ye know, but refuse to tell. 'Tis bad if ye are asking me to hold my tongue." She lifted her chin, daring him to deny it.

Releasing a heavy sigh, Christer tugged her by the arm further down the passage to a private alcove. "Katja, ye know I dinnae approve of father's ways nor his schemes. Believe me when I say the situation at hand will be to yer advantage. I cannae say more." He met her eyes with a look imploring her to trust him.

She stared intently at his face, seeking the meaning behind his words, then gave him a short nod, ignoring the apprehension creeping through her limbs. She braced herself, muttering, "I will not lose my temper, I will not lose my temper," all the way to the earl's solar. Laying a hand on her companion for strength, she drew a deep breath.

Katja knocked on the door. Her father's rough gruff call came through the thick portal. "Enter."

Opening the door, she quietly uttered a command for Freki to stay behind and slipped inside the room.

"I have told ye nae to use that curst language in my home," Henry snarled. Katja grimaced. She hadn't realized he'd heard her speak. Since her mam's death, Henry forbade the Norn language, though her mam had spoken it to all of her children, teaching them of their Norse heritage. It enraged Katja to know her da scorned her mam's beautiful legacy, declaring it tainted her Scots blood. She knew why he thought so, but refused to give him reason to reconsider.

"'Tis why I only use it with my animals," she murmured. Averting her gaze, Katja waited to hear his plans for her.

"'Tis past time for ye to wed." Henry's harsh voice and

expression carried no fatherly affection. "Too long now ye have avoided yer duty of marrying for an alliance to benefit yer clan."

Bracing herself against the familiar tirade, she gritted her teeth, knowing she'd done her duty without a kind word for years. She refrained from answering, remembering her promise to Christer.

Her da rose to his feet. "Ye will defy me no longer. Ye shall marry the MacGerry laird."

It was as she thought. He used the offer of her hand as an incentive for a new alliance. She chewed her lower lip. At least the MacGerry wasn't an auld man, but a braw, handsome one not many years older than she. Marriage to forge peace between clans was something Katja could embrace, though it galled her to submit to her father's demands. She knew this wasn't the whole of it. Meeting his gaze evenly, she waited for the rest.

"Ye will be wedded and bedded this afternoon, leaving with the MacGerry before nightfall."

His words struck her like a blow to the stomach. She struggled for a moment to speak. The repercussions of his demands bested her normal stoic obedience. "But I have no wedding dress. The banns havenae been called. There is to be no feast or celebration?" She faltered, upset by his declaration, defying tradition and canon law.

As soon as she spoke the words, the answer appeared in his mocking smirk. He wanted her married and out of his sight as soon as possible, and the ability to thwart her in the bargain pleased him. Katja knew her grandsire left written instructions for her dowry in both coin and lands. She'd endured her sire's bemoaning about it for years, complaining the tocher was too good for the likes of her. If her sire could manipulate the provisions of the old laird's will claiming the coin and land for himself, he would. But her *afi* had been respected by all, and the clan elders would see his wishes carried out as requested.

There would be no celebrating her wedding with friends and family. No days of planning and anticipation. He would take advantage of this situation to inflict as much hurt and humiliation on her as possible. This, his final punishment for not being a son, or at least not being a daughter he could use to deceive others. Not for the first time, Katja was glad she'd kept her ability to *see* to herself.

"So I am to be married off hastily, in shame as if I were a fallen woman?" Katja leaned forward, hands clenched, her stomach roiling as though she had eaten something foul. The promise to Christer flew from her mind.

Her sire's sneer deepened. "Ye have ever been a disappointment. I grow weary of the daily reminder of yer lack and wish to be rid of ye. Generations of Sinclair women have inherited the *sight*." Contempt thickened his tone. "But ye, with yer mam's Norse blood, have failed me." He rose from his desk and moved to perch on the front edge. His expression turned to one of gloating.

"Since ye have said nae to all others I have so diligently offered as a fit husband for ye, ye willnae have the opportunity to say nae again. Ranald stands outside this door to escort ye to yer chamber. Ye have one hour to prepare. If ye dinnae come to the kirk, ye will be married by proxy. Either way, ye will be another man's burden after today."

Chapter Three

Her da's implied insult that she would act cowardly and not go to the kirk pushed her temper beyond her control. "Ye are a horrible man. I dinnae know why my mam ever married ye," she spat, glaring a challenge. Anger thrumming in her gut, she did not react swiftly enough to escape her sire's wrath. The next moment she lay on the floor, lights sparkling in her vision, a burning pain emanating across her face.

Henry stomped to the door and called for Ranald. "Get her out of my sight!"

Freki's body catapulted through the air as Sinclair opened the door, a growl rumbling in his chest. Katja's hand fumbled at the hem of her skirt, reaching for the dagger strapped to her calf, only to remember she had left her blade in the kitchen, pinning a hapless fowl to the table. Catching her breath, she quieted Freki with a word.

The strong hands of the earl's captain gently grasped her arms, lifting her upright. "Come, Lady Katja, ye must prepare."

Freki nuzzled his head against her arms where Ranald held her. She scratched him behind the ears to let him know all was well.

"I am honored to escort ye to yer wedding, milady." Ranald tipped his bonnet. His sympathetic expression tempted her to struggle for a smile, though her face hurt. He was as a beloved uncle to her, one of the few among the Sinclair clan she would miss. He'd always been kind, looking out for her as much as possible when her sire never did. Yes, she would miss him.

Once in her chamber, she walked to the mirrored glass mounted on the wall and took in her appearance. Her hair straggled loose from its braid, her gown stained and disheveled from working in the heat of the kitchen. Her eye and cheek merited concern. Blood already rose to the surface of the skin above her brow and her eyelid and cheek showed signs of swelling.

Seeing her reflection brought the weight of the earl's hatred down on her, and she collapsed onto the bed and wept. Tears for the loss of those few who truly cared about her, and grief for the love she'd never received from her da. Freki crawled onto the mattress with her, nosing her until she hugged him close.

A soft but insistent knocking pulled her from her sorrow. Rising from the bed, she padded to the door. Morag entered, offering her arms. Katja did not hesitate to wrap herself around her old nurse.

"Hush now, child. I've heard the news. I knew ye'd need help gettin' ready for yer weddin'." The old woman gently wiped the tears from Katja's cheeks, carefully avoiding the tender area flowering into what would no doubt become a vivid bruise under her left eye. "I think yer blue gown makes ye look yer best."

Katja nodded and turned so the older woman could unlace the gown she wore. Using a basin of water and soap scented with bluebells, Katja washed away the perspiration of the morn. Once clean, she donned the chemise Morag handed her, followed by a sturdy wool gown dyed the color of a deep blue sky.

With little time left before they were expected in the kirk, Morag released Katja's hair from its thick braid. "We dinnae have time for fancy, but with yer hair, ye will look bonny even with somethin' simple."

She created two thin braids on either side of her face then wove them together in the back, forming one long, slim plait down the middle, leaving the rest of Katja's thick blonde hair loose, flowing almost to her hips. After Morag finished, she offered Katja a goblet of mulled wine. "Here, my sweet lamb. This will ease yer fears and sufferin'.""

Katja took the cup and drank deep. The warmth of the wine seeped into her stomach, spreading throughout her body. In two long gulps she drained it, welcoming the calming effect. The old woman sniffed and wiped her eyes. Katja gently laid a palm on the woman's withered cheek.

Morag patted Katja's hand. "Dinna fash over an old woman's sentiments. I recall the day ye were born as if 'twere yesterday. Now look at ye, a beautiful woman grown. Yer new husband is a verra lucky man, my bonny lamb."

Katja gritted her teeth. Husband? How could she give herself willingly to a man who went along with her father's shameful plan? She recalled the colored auras about him when she'd met him earlier. Accustomed to the lustful atmosphere of her father's castle, she understood the red haze about Calder. Yellow? Could he possibly be happy to be here? She shook her head, dismissing the thought as she recalled the last color. Dark blue—he feared to speak the truth. In front of her father? Or was he normally a man who kept his thoughts to himself—or lied?

Morag tucked a curl behind Katja's ear, interrupting her reflections. "There now. We cannae keep them waitin'."

"But how can I bear a husband who would allow such an insult to my honor?" Katja demanded, her lips thinned with anger. "What must he think of me and the reasons behind my da's haste—if he's told him any reason at all?"

Morag's expression softened. "We dinnae know why he has agreed. 'Tis said his clan suffers terribly from the feud. We do know his da recently died because of it. Mayhap he had nae choice in the matter. Ye know the earl. He's a hard, cold man when it comes to ye. Would he be any less with an enemy?"

Katja chewed her lip. What did Christer say earlier? This

situation would be to her advantage. She'd dreamed for years of escaping from her sire's harsh grip. Leaving the only home she knew would be worth not having to live in fear of the earl any longer. But how could it be any better to be thrust into the possession of a man who would allow such shame to be brought upon his new wife? Would her husband be no better than her da?

* * *

Calder strode the top of the outer wall. He would be married in two hours. *Two hours!* The fact his marriage was a gift beyond any he could have hoped for steadied the indecision remaining. As laird, it was his duty to marry to benefit his clan, rather than for his own desire or heart. Such was the way amongst people like him and Katja. That he would accomplish both this day went beyond what he could grasp.

He couldn't help but believe his da would be happy at how the Fates smiled on him and their clan. Though armed with this knowledge, he still battled a creeping sense of dread. He tried to replace his misgivings with thoughts of the bonny Katja lying naked beneath him, moaning his name. Those images caused him to harden, quickening his pulse. He entered his chamber to prepare for the wedding. A hasty wedding aimed at shaming his new bride.

As he finished washing, a knock on the door pulled him from his thoughts.

"Come," he called.

His uncle sauntered into the chamber, a grin lighting his face.

"How fare ye, laddie?"

"I'm fine, Uncle." Calder did not look up from dressing in his newly brushed plaide, leine, and doublet.

"Any doubts?"

"Nae. 'Tis best for the clan."

"Aye, and a bonny prize thrown in to boot." Finn chuckled.

"Did ye have something on yer mind other than goading me, auld man?" Calder shot him a look of irritation.

"Nae. Since my brother is at his eternal rest, I thought to stand in his place with ye." Finn's expression changed to one of affection.

Calder smiled at the man who'd always been a second father to him. "Aye, I would be honored to have ye take his place." It was a sad reminder his da wouldn't see his three remaining children wed, nor ever hold one of his grandbairns.

Finn looked him over. "Are ye not nervous? Ye seem as composed as if ye were aboot to go down the stairs to sup."

"A wee bit, but more still in shock. Part of me thinks 'tis the best thing that could happen. Another part of me warns 'tis a mistake, and I'm laying a poor foundation for marriage. As the second son, I'd always hoped to find love the way my parents did, rather than marry for an alliance."

"Aye. But as her brother says, she's a smart lass. She'll see the truth of our situation soon enough when she arrives at her new home. She will understand the why of it. By the looks of the way she tends her da's keep, mayhap she will be able to ease yer burdens in many ways. We've been without a true mistress since yer ma died."

Calder winced at his uncle's words. "There's the other part. As an earl's daughter, she should be beyond my reach. How can I make her happy when this is what she's known all her life? True, we'll accomplish much with what this agreement brings, but Fairetur will never be this grand." Calder ran his hands through his hair with a frown. For all he and his clan gained, it seemed his bride faced nothing but loss.

"What makes Fairetur home? Is it the walls, or the number of towers, or the tapestries in the hall?" Finn demanded, his hands fisted at his waist.

Glancing out the window, Calder considered the question. "Nae, 'tis the people. Not the stones or stairs."

"Aye. From what we have seen, Lady Katja hasnae been treated well by her father. If we only think on what we saw last night when she entered the hall, 'tis clear she doesnae receive the respect she deserves. Her sire's example seems to be followed by all. If ye treat her with kindness and honor, do ye think she will care how many towers ye offer?"

Calder heard the truth in his uncle's words and blew out a breath. Still, guilt gnawed his gut. How could this present path be kind or honorable?

"Aye, I cannae replace the finery she's surrounded with, but I can offer more caring and respect than she's known here. But what of our people? Will they accept the daughter of the Earl of Caithness as their new mistress?"

Finn rubbed his whiskers and had no answer for him—or quite possibly feared what the answer would be.

* * *

Standing at the door of the kirk, Calder swore a herd of wild horses thundered in his chest. He'd never felt his heart work so hard while his body stood idle. Ever a patient man, today the waiting rubbed him raw like sand in his trews. Dread grasped him by the throat, whispering that he reached too high with this marriage. Leaden fingers of doubt constricted his breathing. He wondered again how much time would pass before his wife forgave his actions of this day—if ever.

He spied Katja approaching and his fears immediately

evaporated. At least she came of her own volition, no matter how coerced. On the arm of one of her father's guards, she was a vision in blue, her pale hair shimmering in the sunlight. If he didn't know better, he would believe her to be one of the fae.

Her hair hung loose about her, flowing like a pale golden waterfall. Graceful, she glided toward him. The deep blue of her gown accentuated the golden tanned flesh of her neck, with a hint of her breasts showing at the top of the bodice. He lifted his eyes from the tempting sight and found her face etched with defiance—and bravery.

His bride possessed spirit—that much was certain. Feelings of gladness, of a dream come true, coursed through him along with visions of what they would be doing soon—very soon.

As she approached, he glimpsed a stain at the side of her face. She'd been recently struck? Previous pleasant feelings spiraled into rage. Who would dare strike the earl's daughter?

Immediately the answer flew to him. Her father. The man must truly be a fiend to add one more injury to the list on this of all days. Calder struggled to rein in his urge to leave his bride for a moment while he taught Sinclair a lesson about how to treat a woman. He forced himself instead to center only on her.

"Are ye well, my lady?" he whispered in her ear as she arrived at his side.

"Well enough, m'laird." Her eyes stayed fixed on the priest, her face a mask of inflexible composure.

He drove away thoughts of aught else, reducing the world to his bride and the priest as they stepped inside the small kirk. Pride rose in his chest when he took in her strength and courage as she recited her vows in a clear and forceful voice. No wilting flower, his Katja.

His Katja.

Wanting to reward her courage, to let her know he was greatly pleased with her, he faced her when it came his turn to speak. He repeated the vows, each word filled with as much meaning and sincerity as he could summon.

When the priest announced them wed, Calder put all the promise of caring and protection she would find with him into that one kiss. He wanted no misunderstanding that she now belonged to him. He would take care of her with honor and affection, and looked forward to the day she could put her past behind her.

* * *

Katja's new husband wrapped one arm around her and cupped her chin gently with his fingers, tipping it toward him. Slowly lowering his head, he placed his mouth on hers. Her heart lurched, her breathing tripped in her chest. Who knew a man's lips could be so soft, so heated? Though brief, the burn of his kiss lingered. She resisted the temptation to place a finger to her mouth, to see if it felt as hot to the touch as it seemed. She was torn between railing at him for going along with this insult of a wedding, and grabbing him to resume their kiss.

When she'd approached the kirk, she'd spotted Calder at the door with the priest. He'd worn the same kind smile she'd seen last night in the hall. She'd immediately sought the thin colors surrounding him, using the *sight* as she always did when she needed reassurance of a person's thoughts. The yellow aura of happiness encircling him told her he wasn't being forced into this union. Or, if forced, he was glad of it.

What kind of man agrees to begin his marriage thus? How can he abide marrying me in shame? She gritted her teeth with knowledge. Gold and land, that's how.

She allowed her humiliation to fire her anger as she strode to his side. That they expected her to lay with this stranger immediately following the ceremony added more fuel to the flames rising within.

His yellow aura soon blended with the bright red of lust. *Typical of a man to look past all happening around him, thinking only with his cock.* Ignoring that image, she took in his appearance. He was handsome in his white leine, woolen doublet and plaide. Though she knew not what kind of marriage they would have, at least her husband was pleasing to the eye.

His charming smile faded into something hard and dangerous, his eyes narrowing as his gaze snapped to the side of her face. The yellow and red aura around him darkened until the muddied red of anger swirled around him. She took satisfaction in knowing he angered over his new bride wearing a bruised face on her wedding day. At least he proved capable of understanding a portion of her humiliation. Once she arrived at his side, Ranald kissed her hand and placed it in MacGerry's. A transfer of property. Her life now his to direct. Katja's chest tightened. Together, she and Calder stepped inside the kirk, followed by those who would witness their blessing by the priest.

As the ceremony began, Katja tried not to consider how different this day would have been were her ma still alive. How they would have planned together for weeks. There would have been the ritual of the women closest to her coming together to make her wedding dress, sharing tales of married life. Music, dancing, feasting, and drinking would have gone on until the wee hours.

Their bed would be blessed by the priest, with friends and family escorting them into their chamber, bestowing wishes of happiness, long life, and many bairns. It would be her perfect day, her best day. Instead, she wedded in haste as if guilty of fornication—or worse, already with child. She glanced quickly at the man beside her. Surely, he did not suspect that of her?

No, it would not do to dwell on such maudlin thoughts. The blood of Vikings flowed in her veins! She would not cower behind the dreams of what would not be. She'd concentrate on what lay before her, meeting it head on as was her custom. He would soon know she carried no man's child.

Stealing another glance at the man next to her, she wondered again what kind of husband he might be. She only knew he possessed a kind smile and she saw none of the disturbing grey or brown colors of her deceitful sire about him. She also knew something unexplainable flowed between them. She canted her head sideways, almost expecting to see sparks arcing between them.

When it came time to say her vows she steadied herself, speaking in a clear, loud voice. No one could claim she was a coward. When it was MacGerry's turn, he faced her to speak the words of binding, as if he wished her to know he took his vows to her seriously, to tell her this meant more than uniting one clan to another and an exchange of wealth. Her stomach fluttered at his simple gesture in spite of the hurt and anger still swirling around her heart. The dark timbre of his voice curled about her like a warm blanket on a cold winter morn.

At the priest's pronouncement, her brothers each hugged her, shaking her new husband's hand. Christer pulled her into his embrace with a whisper for her ears alone. "MacGerry had naught to do with this. In fact, he voiced opposition to the timing. Howbeit, he isnae opposed to wedding ye. He seems a good man. Ye might do well to trust him, sister. I wish ye happy."

She smiled for the first time that day, kissing him on the cheek in response. Trust? She would give no man her trust. She spotted Morag in the back of the crowd, wiping her eyes with a tattered square of linen. Her father strode past, a smile of victory on his face. Now bound to this man by God, Katja couldn't escape the feeling of a sheep being led to the butcher.

Chapter Four

A passion Calder didn't see coming unexpectedly set him afire. He'd certainly sampled his share of feminine delights over the years, but no single kiss ever moved his ardor or enflamed his emotions as this one did. Now, before a priest and surrounded by a clan he'd only known as hostile, he struggled to find his wits, stunned by the brief touch of their lips. His heart pounded, his lungs sucked air like a smith's bellows.

Keeping an arm around Katja's waist, he faced the few well-wishers who witnessed their union. The first slap on his back forced him out of the bliss he'd fallen into with her in his arms, her mouth on his. The earl slunk out the door, reminding Calder of the tawdry circumstances in which he found himself.

Katja's brothers were present, along with a small number of people from the clan. Ranald, a handful of Sinclair soldiers, and the MacGerry men rounded out the rest of those in attendance. It was an embarrassingly small gathering for the wedding between the earl's daughter and a neighboring laird. Particularly since their union marked the end of a long and bloody feud.

Allowing the few who came to see their lady's wedding an opportunity to offer their blessings, Calder considered the next step in her father's harshly contrived plan. He needed to win her trust quickly, to gentle her, assuring her he had her best interests in mind, put their wedding *night* behind them.

Boar's bollocks! He'd never had an unwilling woman in his bed before. And a virgin at that. He owned no skills of wooing. But woo her he must, and with haste.

He found himself shaking the hand of brother after brother, and then the Captain of the Guard, along with several other servants in attendance. Each crushing shake, each hard look seemed to blame him for her situation. Apparently, all knew how poorly her father regarded her. No one uttered a word about her injury nor gave any looks of surprise—as if seeing the earl's daughter with the beginnings of a blackened eye was a common occurrence.

Saint's blood! What did I agree to?

With their unspoken messages, her kin let him know his handling of her had damned well be better than what she knew here. He gripped her hand possessively, as if offering proof of his good intentions. The warmth of her flesh on his brought a sense of calm he didn't have time to contemplate.

Finally passing through the gauntlet of brothers and surrogate brothers and uncles to the door, Calder wanted nothing more than to get her alone. He had a burning need to explain, to distance himself as much as she would allow from her father's schemes. Worried she would neither accept his explanation nor that of her brother.

He would find out soon enough.

His wife's old servant opened the door of the kirk and Calder rocked back on his heels, confronted by a mountain of fur growling menacingly at him, with shining teeth that would make a *Cù Sìth* envious. Momentarily frozen, Calder heard his bride murmur something in a rough language then offer the hands they held together for the beast's perusal. After a few sniffs and one wet swipe of the tongue, the monster uttered a whine of reluctant acceptance before taking his place at Katja's other side.

"Freki willnae harm ye now, unless ye make an aggressive move toward me," Katja said matter-of-factly, a cold edge to her voice.

Still taken aback by the size of the creature, Calder asked,

"Freki? What is he?"

Katja scratched the beast's ears. "Freki is a wolfhound—a gift from my uncle. According to Norse legend, he is one of Odin's wolves." She gazed at the russet-colored behemoth with an expression of adoration on her face, as if he were her very own bairn.

One of Odin's wolves? *Freki* was an appropriate enough name, then. The monster was certainly large enough to be the pet of a war god. "I've never seen a dog his size." Calder still didn't trust her beast had taken him off the list of potential meals.

"Ach, well, my uncle says his bloodline is found in Ireland. Wolfhound, sometimes called a deerhound."

Calder looked at the beast askance. More like *devilhound*.

Her tone warmed as she spoke of her dog and he struck for a way to keep her talking, if for no reason other than to hear the sweet sound of her voice. Though clear as chimes in the wind, it possessed a seductive quality that stirred his lust.

"What were the words ye spoke to him? I've not heard them before."

Katja's cheeks darkened. "Norn. My mother's language. I am Scots on my sire's side, Norse on my dam's."

Calder recalled Christer saying their mother no longer remained among the living. But proof of Katja's bloodline resonated in her pale blonde hair, her slender, proud posture, and the fearless way she met his gaze. Viking blood ran strong through her veins.

"How many years have ye, my lady?" Calder wondered. Two years ago at the loch it didn't matter to him how old she was. Now he wondered if his lustful thoughts that day were aimed at a lass too young for his carnal fantasies.

"Eight and ten, m'laird. And ye?"

Relieved he wasn't as much a lecher as he feared, he answered her question. "A score and four, my lady."

They continued into the keep and up the stairs. As they approached Katja's chamber, Freki growled, baring his teeth. The earl stepped into the passage from the recess of a darkened doorway.

"I see no wounds or cuts on ye, son by marriage."

Calder tilted his head, furrowing his brow. "No wounds, Laird. Why do ye ask?"

"Ye seem to be a gallant, honorable man. I wouldnae have ye supplying the blood our agreement demands."

The implication he'd supply the blood to prove Katja's purity struck like the blow the earl had delivered earlier to his daughter. Calder sucked in a ragged breath, fighting the urge to trounce the man before him, his body hardened, his eyes narrowed.

"As ye say, Laird, I am an honorable man holding always to my word. That means I will abide by our agreement and see no harm comes to my wife in any form." Calder glared at the bastard he now called father by marriage.

Sinclair's lips curled upward, though it was hardly a smile. He nodded and moved aside, allowing them to continue.

When they arrived at her door, Katja commanded Freki to sit outside the bedchamber. Calder stepped into the room, pacing to and fro in front of the blazing fireplace, his nostrils flaring, fists clenched. On a final pass, he realized where he stood, what he was doing there. Ceasing his march, he closed his eyes, took a deep breath, and forced his body to relax.

When he opened his eyes again, his new wife stood before him. She stared at him as she might a rabid animal, assessing how dangerous he could be when angry. Realizing his display of temper placed him in the same category of man as her father, a stabbing pang of remorse pierced his chest, flushing out his remaining rage and recalling him to the task before them.

"Forgive me, lady, but your father would try a saint's temper."
He saw one corner of her mouth twitch at his words and her eyes
glittered. "Now that we are alone, may we sit and talk?"

Katja nodded once and moved warily toward the small table and
chairs in the corner, as if she didn't believe the storm truly over. She
grasped the pitcher of wine resting on the table and poured his
goblet, followed by one for her. Calder stood and held out her chair,
earning him a wrinkled brow and look of confusion—or was it
distrust?

She allowed him to seat her and placed herself on the edge of
the chair, back stiff, poised to flee. She glanced at the door as if to
assess the distance, appearing to remain seated only by force of will.
Calder took another deep breath as he sat, feeling as though he was
about to kneel before a confessor after a lengthy season of
debauchery.

Taking a long drink to steady himself, he tried for an
explanation, an apology, something to clear the way between them.
"Lady Katja, I must beg yer forgiveness. 'Twas never my intention
to cause ye distress. When my da died a few days past, the lairdship
fell to me. I wished to put an end to the strife between our people
and approached yer father a sennight ago asking for a discussion of
peace. Today, he offered resolution, but at the price of yer hand in
marriage. His terms were that it be done and consummated before
sunset. He left no choice."

She stared at him a few moments. "The coin and dower lands I
bring with me—they figure into this decision?"

Calder glanced at the worn tabletop, wincing at her accusation.
Guilt rose to the surface threatening to spill over. What could he say,
what could he do? If nothing else, she deserved his honesty. Placing
his elbows on the table, he rubbed his face, running both hands
through his hair once, then twice.

"Aye, the coin, lands, sheep, and grain the earl included are what persuaded me to accept the terms that shamed ye," he admitted, avoiding eye contact.

"Sheep and grain?" Her voice rose an octave in disbelief.

He reluctantly nodded. "Yer da knows our clan is poor. We will have a hard time feeding everyone this winter. 'Tis why I needed to pursue peace. We cannae continue as we have. His offer includes enough grain, sheep, and other foodstuffs to get us through the winter and help reestablish our herds this spring."

Her expression changed from disbelief into something harder. She turned away, folding her arms over her chest. "Ye truly had no choice and my sire knew this. He made ye an offer ye couldnae turn down. And in turn, he arranged it so I couldnae say no, either."

Calder's head tilted, brows angling downward in silent question.

Katja's chin lifted. "He threatened to marry me by proxy if I refused to meet ye at the kirk today."

Calder's guilt took another leap forward. He swallowed hard before asking the question he needed an answer to. "Aye. But what I cannae understand is why he would be so cruel to his own daughter?"

Pain crept across Katja's features and she lowered her eyes before answering. "I have ever been a disappointment to him. He has tried to rid himself of me by marrying me off for over two years now."

"It doesnae make sense. Yer brother says ye are a good woman and will make a fine wife. I look around and see how well ye run his home." Calder stared at her, knowing he wasn't hearing the whole of it. "I know this match isnae of yer choosing. I cannae offer ye what ye are accustomed to. I am sorry."

Katja's long fingers traced the rim of her cup. "Ye and yer men have already given me more than I am used to by standing in respect when I enter a room."

For the first time, Calder saw her smile. It wasn't big, more like a shooting star—a bright flash then gone. However brief, its beauty brought a bit of hope, inspiring him to acknowledge what she offered up against her will. To credit her bravery.

"Sometimes we must make difficult sacrifices for the sake of our clan," he murmured in platitude. To his surprise, her cheeks flushed and her body tensed. Her eyes narrowed as she leaned toward him.

"I am sacrificing my *virtue*, my *family*, my choice of husband and the only home I have ever known. Tell me, my laird, exactly what are *ye* sacrificing?" Her biting tone flowed thick with contempt.

Calder offered a weak smile and nod, then gazed out the window. She'd earned the right to be angry. He rubbed his chin. He hadn't explained himself well. She didn't understand his situation as clearly.

"I buried my most recent *sacrifice* a sennight ago. Before Da, 'twas my older brother Ewan, my grandda, several cousins, and many kinsmen over the years. I dinnae mean to belittle the cost of this treaty to ye, but believe me when I say ye are not the only one who risks much." He offered her a mournful smile he hoped reflected some of the loss he described.

She ducked her head, the stain in her cheeks darkening. "I beg yer pardon, my laird. I dinnae realize so many of yer family have died in this feud." She glanced at him, apology rounding her eyes.

Calder tried to assure her with another warm smile. "Dinnae fash. I would gladly take the burden from ye if I could, or pursue another path if I saw one."

Katja released a sigh. Calder took a sip of his cup. "And no more, *my laird* from ye. I have only been laird a matter of days and find being called by my father's title, which should have been my brother's, leaves a bitter taste. We may yet be strangers, but we are married. My name is Calder. It would please me if ye used it."

She nodded again, her only response.

They sat in silence, drinking from their goblets. The wine served as a distraction while they each chewed on what had passed between them in such a short time. Calder knew he needed it as much as she did to prepare for the next step. After a long silence, he noted the position of the sun in the sky through the window. The sooner they consummated their union, the sooner they could begin their life together.

Calder wanted away from this place. More than that, he wanted to take *her* away from this place. He took one last sip of wine, then rose from the chair. Katja's gaze locked with his, her stare tunneling through him to peer into his soul. His skin prickled. He offered his hand. She hesitated before rising to take it. Slowly, he pulled her in close and wrapped his arms around her, anticipating the act that would bind them together forever.

He savored the softness pressed against him. Even though a part of him still disbelieved the beautiful lass of his memory was now his bride, he struggled with the mounting desire threatening to break free from his command. Too many wounds had been inflicted this day. He would not add to them by acting a brute. Her body quivered against him as she allowed him to hold her.

He spoke low but clearly. "Ye have my word I will never raise a hand to ye or knowingly harm ye. I will care for ye, treat ye like a lady and protect ye." He ran his fingers slowly through the golden silk of her hair to gently rub the back of her head. "I couldnae have chosen a more bonny lass for my bride. I am verra pleased to have ye as wife, with or without yer dowry."

Katja drew back and caught his gaze. Her angry expression faded to uncertainty, but he detected no fear. As she hesitated, Calder lowered his head, covering her lips with his in a slow, gentle kiss. Never before had he bedded an innocent, though he knew enough to go slow. She needed to be wooed, but his knowledge of seduction was lacking. His experiences in a woman's bed had always been of mutual consent, a good-natured tumble. He hoped his meager skills were enough to please his virgin bride.

Tasting her, he became awash with the flavor of wine and woman. She smelled of flowers and something else, something he couldn't place. She exuded an element of sweetness that wrapped around his senses, pulling him into her.

His control slipped, the desire to lift her skirts and take her rising with each breath. He fought the urge, needing to continue to gentle her. She softened under his kiss, inviting his next step. He gently drew her bottom lip into his mouth and the soft mewl that escaped her nearly undid him. Taking advantage of her parted lips, Calder slipped his tongue into her warmth, slowly exploring her. She stiffened before easing into the kiss, tentatively following his lead in their dance.

He continued his seduction of the woman he'd thought of, dreamt of for so long. He drew small, calming patterns on her back with one hand and pulled her closer. She lifted her arms, wrapping them about his neck, slowly threading her fingers into his hair. He couldn't suppress an inward smile at her shy acceptance. He kissed the line of her jaw, the long, smooth column of her neck. Katja's breathing labored, her body softened and further pressed against him.

After a few moments, Calder drew away, studying his new bride. Her eyes darkened, and her chest heaved with each rapid breath. He turned her about, moved her hair over one shoulder, and encircled her waist with one arm. She bent slightly forward, allowing his kisses better access to the soft, sweet skin of her neck.

He continued the small circular movements with the hand trapping her against him. As he touched the underside of her breast, she stilled, sucking in a startled breath. Giving her time to get used to his hand, Calder brought it up further, cupping her breast. He rubbed lazy circles around her nipple with his thumb and another gasp escaped her lips as the flesh grew to a hardened tip beneath his hand. When he switched to the other breast, her small whimper heated his blood, his erection growing painful as it pushed against his plaide.

Taking her responses as permission, he worked the laces on the back of her gown with his free hand. She pressed the softness of her perfect bottom against his arousal, almost calling an early end to his seduction. Calder sought to put his mind on other things in an effort to keep control of the lusty beast threatening to take over.

Distracting himself by running his tongue lightly along the sensitive flesh of her neck, he managed to unlace her gown, though the task seemed to take an eternity. Desire caused his fingers to fumble as if he were an untried lad. When at last he finished, he moved slightly back, allowing the gown to fall to her hips. She stiffened on a sharp inhale.

Calder resumed stroking her breasts. They easily fit into the palms of his hands. This time, only the thin cloth of her chemise remained between them. As he nuzzled her neck, breathing in her sweet scent, his hands caressed her breasts with the lightest of touches. Her whimpering noises drew him taut with desire like a minstrel tuning the strings of a lute. He tempered his response. *One step at a time.*

Her innocent reactions quickly sheared through the bindings of his control like the sharpest honed blade. Untying the ribbons of her chemise, he eased the gown and chemise over her hips. They dropped to the floor in a graceful heap. Calder paused, startled. Strapped to her thigh was a well-used dagger.

* * *

"Ye come armed to yer wedding, lady wife?" Calder cocked an eyebrow and nodded toward her leg.

Keenly aware of his gaze and how vulnerable she was, Katja made to cover her naked breasts. Calder pulled her into his arms. She leaned back to make eye contact, titling her head a bit.

"Aye. I never go about unarmed," she replied, striving for honesty.

Her answer inspired the first real grin she'd seen from him and heat bloomed inside her at the sight.

Before her sense of modesty could protest, he swept her into his arms and carried her to the bed, sweeping aside the coverings to place her on the sheets. The play of hard muscle against her skin increased the heat within her. Unsure how to surrender herself to the husband she scarcely knew, she pushed her panic aside, staring at him, leaning on the only truth she could rely on. The bright red of lust glowed about him as she expected, but Katja found herself surprised to see an equal amount of yellow. He did not lie when he said he was happy to have her. Her heart beat a little faster. Perhaps she could trust him . . . in this.

Calder unbuckled his broad leather belt, sending his plaide and sporran to the floor next to her gown. He quickly removed his boots, then moved back to her and slowly unrolled her stockings, unfastening the sheath, consigning it to the growing pile of garments. Tightness in her chest blossomed into a languorous heat that set every nerve alight as he kissed, licked, and nipped his way down first one leg and then the other. An intense throb began within her core. Flustered by her body's reactions, she ducked beneath the sheet and blanket. She stared at his muscular legs and the front of his leine, tented forward with his arousal. A slight gasp escaped her as she observed him with wary fascination.

He slowed his movements, climbing calmly onto the bed. She released her grip on the sheet, rebuking herself for acting craven. She was a Sinclair. She would do what generations of Sinclair women did. Unfortunately, without her mother or grandmother to advise her, she wasn't quite sure exactly what that entailed.

"I dinnae know what to do." Her tone was brittle as she sought to hide the fear and anticipation in her voice.

He favored her with another smile—she was beginning to look forward to those—before slipping beneath the coverings with her.

"'Tis yer first time. Yer job is to relax and enjoy as much as ye can. Ye know there is pain with the first joining, aye?" His voice flowed as smooth and sweet as the finest mead. The colors about him did not change. The yellow did not muddy into the brown of deceit. *Trust him.*

Katja nodded. She knew there would be pain and blood—her blood.

"We will take our time. I want to offer ye a taste of pleasure first. Mayhap I can soothe some of the sting from today." He whisked off his leine with a quick movement then settled next to her.

His warm hands caressed along her arms, causing the fine hairs there to rise and prickle. His mouth found hers again, gliding, tasting, caressing. His tongue outlined her lips and she opened for him. As their kiss deepened, his hands stroked from her hips to her ribs then shifted to her breasts once more. Her body moved upward into his grasp, as if pulled on a string. She moaned into his mouth.

His lips curved into a smile.

Breaking their kiss, his mouth closed over first one nipple, then the other. His hot lips and tongue pulled and teased, creating sparks that flared into her lower belly. His hand lightly stroked her stomach, tracing lazy circles that dipped to the top of her thighs.

He suckled her breasts until she was breathless, her body beyond her control. Her hands traced the curves of his back and sides, sliding apace with an urgency rising within. She wanted more, more of his touch, more of his taste, more of his smell.

When his fingers deftly glided through the downy hair between her legs, Katja's breath fled. Never before had anyone dared touch her in such a manner. His caress floated over the skin of her thighs. Her hips moved without any sensible thought on her part. He skimmed the sensitive skin over and over, rising higher until he touched her core.

"My lord!" she cried breathlessly, half in protest.

Calder raised his head from her breasts. His deep blue eyes glimmered. The calloused pad of his finger, slick with her moisture, rasped lightly, rhythmically around the nub of flesh, lighting her entire body on fire.

"Aye, that's it. Relax and enjoy the pleasure I can bring ye." His whispered encouragements stirred her almost as much as his touch.

He increased speed to match the movement of her hips as she pressed harder against his hand. Her body struggled to keep up with his maddening movements. Katja grasped his hair, tangling her fingers in the long strands. Her legs seized, arching her hips in one final thrust as she sucked air into her lungs. She cried out as a dizzying sensation seized her and wave upon wave of pleasure poured over her. After a few breathless moments, she settled back onto the bed and her lungs took in air once again.

Her husband hovered over her, nudging her body's opening

with his erect cock. Instinctively, she opened her legs wider to give him better access. He entered her a fraction and her awareness came rushing back to the present.

"I will go verra slowly and ease the way." His eyes held a mixture of barely restrained desire and concern.

Beyond speech, she nodded her assent and grabbed his hips. He'd sought her pleasure before his, earning her trust all the more. The scent of her arousal blended with his muskiness and she reveled in the feel of his bare skin. With each careful stroke, her channel burned as it stretched to accommodate him, until at last he sheathed himself deep within her. Her jaw clenched, she willed herself not to cry out.

Calder paused, buried completely within, the muscles in his arms trembling beneath her fingers. His face contorted, sweat forming on his brow. Something else crossed his expression but Katja was too caught up in the moment to question him.

"Are ye ready, lass?" His question a hoarse whisper. He did not move. It appeared he awaited a response from her.

"Aye." The word came out as a husky plea for him to continue, to do something about the ache in her body as the pain receded. She moved beneath him, seeking relief from the rising tension.

"Ah Katja, ye feel so good, so tight. Ye're mine now, only mine."

She almost didn't recognize his voice, low and gravelly with pleasure. She raised her hips to meet each stroke, ignoring the burning sensation that caught anew. A sense of expectation built slowly and a mewl rattled in her throat. Calder groaned and shook above her, then stilled.

As they lay entwined, she drew meaningless patterns on his back, her thoughts scattered as she sought something just beyond her grasp. Calder dropped a light kiss on her cheek and rolled off her.

Katja clenched her legs together against the lingering sting and a peculiar sense of loss.

"Do ye have something to tell me, wife?"

Chapter Five

Katja's eyes flew open at the change in his voice. Gone were the soothing tones of her lover. In its place was the harshness of suspicion. He lay next to her, still under the coverings, resting his head on an elbow, a faint drift of dark green jealousy twining the yellow aura of lust.

"What do ye mean?" Fear she'd done something wrong doubled her heart rate. Uncertainty crept into her voice. She knew nothing of lovemaking and wondered if he would now voice his displeasure with her. After being a disappointment to her father, she should have known her husband would find fault in her, too.

"Ye werenae a virgin."

His words stung like a slap to the face. She sat bolt upright, clutching the blanket to her, covering her nakedness.

"What a thing to say!" she gasped. "Of course I was a virgin. Why would ye make such a terrible accusation?"

His face softened. Without a word of answer, he slipped from the bed and she looked her fill at his lean, naked body. He bent and retrieved her chemise from the floor, offering it to her. Uncertain what he was about, she accepted the garment and slipped it over her head before taking his hand to join him beside the bed.

He pushed back the coverlet, indicating the bed where she'd lain beneath him.

Snowy white linens!

Katja covered her mouth with a hand, but not before a gasp of horror escaped. The wet spot from his seed was plain to see, but there was no blood. Panic threatened to steal her wits. How could there be no blood?

"Just so, lady. As I said, do ye have something ye wish to tell me?" His eyes turned cold.

Katja found her voice. "I assure ye, I've been with no man before! Ye are the first man I've even kissed much less . . ." She didn't finish, but merely pointed a shaky finger at the spot on the center of the bed.

Calder dressed as Katja reeled in horror. He obviously didn't believe her. What would he demand of her sire in satisfaction? From her?

"Without blood, I amnae sure how yer da will react. I dinnae wish to see ye shamed further." His words rolled as casual as the motions he used to settle his plaide about his hips.

A bolt of fear jarred her as she considered the earl's response to her lack of maidenhead. It only took a moment to decide. She reached for her bare leg. "What did ye do with my blade?"

Her husband gazed at her as if she'd asked for the Stone of Scone. She tossed her head. "'Tis my blood he wants, 'tis my blood he'll get."

Calder retrieved her dirk from the jumble of skirts on the floor.

Setting a leg upon the mattress, Katja bit back a gasp as she made a small cut on her calf. A rivulet of blood ran across the muscle and pooled onto the damp sheet below. After what she deemed an appropriate amount, she cleaned her leg and the blade in water from the basin on the table. Wrapping her cut with a strip of linen, she sheathed her weapon and strapped it to her leg once more.

She gave him a brittle look, tremors of shock still resonating. "Yer honor is intact. We willnae have to lie about it being my blood."

A knock on the door interrupted any further discussion. The door cracked open, and a head full of grey hair appeared. Katja recognized her old nurse.

"Come, Morag."

The old woman bowed her head to Calder and met Katja's gaze before darting a look at the stained sheets. A smile crept over her face as she turned to the task of packing her mistress's possessions for the trip.

Fear and shame collided in Katja's chest as she struggled to find the words to form a question. "Morag. How can it be I came to my marriage bed with no maidenhead?" Heat washed over her upper body, her head ducking to avoid words she wasn't sure she wanted to hear.

With a hiss of breath, her old nurse met her charge's stare. There was no mistaking the questioning glance at the linens and back at her. Katja raised her chemise so Morag could see her bandaged leg.

The old crone gave her a look of compassion before turning a defiant look toward MacGerry. "I will swear on my own life this lamb came to ye pure as the day she was born." She turned toward Katja. "'Tis the ridin' astride that took yer precious maidenhead. I warned it could harm ye, but ye're too headstrong to listen to old Morag."

She pointed a boney finger at Calder and narrowed her eyes. "Dinnae get to thinkin' ye've been cheated, laird. This one ne'er came near any man here. Her sire threatened death to any Sinclair who touched her. As a bargaining tool, he would stand interference from no man. Every potential suitor he trotted her in front of only met her in the great hall. I made certain of that meself."

She sniffed. "Besides, most of them were so ancient they couldnae stand at attention with a stiff wind assistin' them . . . if ye get my meaning." She stepped between the two of them, her fists resting on ample hips, hardened eyes daring MacGerry to argue with her.

Another wave of heat flowed over Katja and she tore her gaze away from Morag and her bold words. Before her gaze met the floor, she saw her husband's lips twitch upward into a smile.

* * *

Calder recognized he'd been outmaneuvered. In truth, it didn't matter to him if she had taken a lover in the past. She was now his wife, and anything that happened before this day would remain in the past. He'd certainly been no saint, so he could excuse Katja's indiscretion if indeed it ever happened. Their lovemaking exceeded any expectations he'd held, certainly far from the cold bed he'd feared. As long as she remained faithful, he foresaw no complaints.

He raised his hands in surrender. "I believe ye, madam. Her reactions to even the gentlest of touches were of an innocent, nae a woman who'd tasted passion before. Whether or nae she was a virgin at the start of the day, she isnae one now. She is my wife, and I am well-pleased with her and all she brings."

Morag bobbed her grey head once, seemingly pacified he would not reject her mistress. "My bonny lamb is a well-born lady and will make ye a fine wife. I would only ask that ye treat her with the kindness she rarely knew here."

Calder fought to keep a smile from his face, giving a short bow with what he hoped appeared to be a solemn expression.

Gathering the stained sheet in one hand, he headed to the door. "I will see this to the earl. Bring only what ye can carry on yer horse. The rest will be brought by wagon with the supplies and sheep a few days hence. We will depart within the hour." He offered Katja a smile of assurance before leaving the room. Once again, Calder wondered what the hell he'd gotten himself into.

* * *

Katja finished packing her meager possessions as Morag left to accomplish other tasks. Eighteen years of life packed into one middling trunk. She found the fact liberating, though with a hint of bitterness. Aggrieved she had no more to show for so long a time in this place. Though, not being tied to possessions, unlike her sire, gave her the freedom to enter her new life without hesitation.

A new life. She mused the words. Her husband so far proved handsome, well-spoken, and kind. The secret place at her core throbbed. The act itself had been painful, abrupt. But *before*. Heat bloomed in her belly at the memory of his hands on her. Caressing, licking, touching. Welcoming her to a new season with him. Heat crept up her cheeks and she forced her mind to the task at hand.

A familiar square of linen lay atop the neatly folded stack of clothing. With worn edges and faded bluebells delicately embroidered in the center, this scrap of linen and love never failed to recall the touch of her mother's arms around her. The smooth texture of the finely woven cloth gave way to the raised silk thread of flowers.

If she closed her eyes and concentrated, Katja could imagine her mother's scent lingering on the cloth. After ten years, the rational part of her knew no scent remained. However, the little girl within who desperately missed her mother, missed the arms that once held her, and the tender kisses freely given, still smelled bluebells.

Freki laid near the small hearth, his massive head resting on big paws, expressive eyes following her every move. Katja gave the beast a wan smile. "We leave for good today, my braw laddie. We have a new home now, with new places for ye to discover. Have ye heard? I'm to be the new Lady MacGerry. I think the MacGerrys willnae be pleased to hear the Sinclair's daughter is their new mistress. Nae pleased at all."

Freki groaned and shifted his weight.

"Aye, and the worst is, the man I married thinks I came to our marriage bed unchaste." The words stabbed her heart, leaving a jagged wound behind.

Changing her gown for trews, tunic, tall boots, and leather jerkin, Katja opened the door to find Ranald and another guard waiting.

"Are ye ready, Lady MacGerry?" Ranald asked.

Uncertainty unfurled inside at the sound of her new title. She wondered how long it would be until the gossip in her new home began over the circumstances of her disgraceful wedding.

* * *

Ranald stepped into the room and picked up Katja's saddlebag. Spotting the sheathed broadsword propped in the corner, he grabbed it as well. "Ye are Lady MacGerry now, but there may be those who willnae take kindly to the earl's daughter being set above them. Keep yer weapons handy, milady. Remember our lessons, and keep Freki close."

Katja nodded. She knew marriage and a peace agreement wouldn't erase nigh on a hundred years of strife overnight. Perhaps the wealth and lands she brought might ease the way, if only a wee bit. If the loss of family Calder suffered proved typical of all MacGerrys, she'd go to bed each night with a dirk in hand.

Ranald handed her a small bundle as they exited the keep. "'Tis a wedding gift from Terric. He says this new design will fly true, replacing the blade at yer nape."

Katja unwrapped the rough hemp cloth and found a small

dagger within. Like others the old blacksmith gave her, he'd crafted it for her hands. The flat design made it easy to throw with accuracy. The Sinclair crest was carved on the bone handle, their clan motto, Commit Thy Work To God, etched on the other side. She shook her head at the irony of the words.

All the work around Ruadhcreag was committed solely to its laird. The Almighty received naught. Her tireless efforts to run her father's house would ever remain thankless. Soon she'd take up whatever position awaited her on MacGerry lands. Yet another unknown about the situation she found herself in. What would be the extent of her duties, her authority? She'd wait until her new laird and husband chose to tell her.

She withdrew the dirk nestled in the hidden sheath at her nape and replaced it with the latest gift from the blacksmith. The old dirk joined the others she kept atop her boots.

Patrik and Christer met her outside the doors to the great hall, opening their arms to her.

"Be happy, sister. Ye deserve to be." Patrik placed a kiss on her uninjured cheek and gave her a gentle squeeze.

Christer took her by the shoulders, making sure she met his gaze. "Aye, ye do. 'Tis time for ye to have yer own family. I expect to become an uncle next summer. 'Twill give us an excuse to come visit and know all is well. If something should happen, send word and we'll come. Promise me ye will write and tell us how ye fare."

Katja blushed at the thought of becoming a mother, but thrilled at the idea of having someone to care for and love her in return. She smiled and nodded. "I promise. I wish ye both happy, also, though I dinnae know how it can happen if ye both stay here."

Christer grabbed Patrik around the neck and scrubbed his head with his knuckles. "I'll have a constant job keeping this fool out of trouble and away from the kitchen lasses."

Katja managed a smile as she left her brothers, twisted though it was against the bitter-sweet tang of farewell. No doubt it was their intention. However, the most difficult farewell lay ahead. Morag met her in front of the stables wringing her hands, distress crowding her features.

"Milady, are ye sure ye dinnae want me to come with ye?"

Conflict and tears from her old nurse pulled at Katja's heart. "Nae. Yer place is with Edeena and Ranald. They need ye, and the bairns need their grandmam."

Morag gripped her in a fierce hug. "I've looked after ye every day ye've drawn breath. In all that time, we've ne'er been apart. What will I do without ye, my bonny lamb?" Morag's voice thickened.

"I will be fine," Katja replied, forcing confidence into her voice. "Ye have plenty to keep ye busy. My husband will see to me now." She forced back the tears threatening to take over, knowing once she gave in, there would be no stopping the flow.

Katja glanced away to regain her composure, swallowing hard. She noticed Calder checking the saddle on his horse as he secured his bags. He met her gaze, giving her a look of such compassion her heart stopped. Rarely had she seen such expression from the people of Ruadhcreag, and only occasionally from her brothers. Never from an enemy. Not merely an enemy anymore—her enemy husband.

Calder approached her horse and took her things from Ranald, sharing a few brief words she couldn't hear. Her new husband secured her belongings then offered Katja his hand. With a last kiss to Morag's frail cheek, she strode to him and reluctantly accepted his offer, allowing him to help her into the saddle.

Falling into line with the rest of the MacGerry men, she allowed herself one final look over her shoulder. Though she longed to be shed of the daily fear and scorn she suffered from her sire,

Ruadhcreag was the only home she knew. For the first time in her life, she didn't know where she belonged.

As loss and longing collided with fear of the unknown, tears trickled down her cheeks. She dashed them away before anyone observed her weakness. If she was to be their mistress, she couldn't allow these men to think her cowardly. She'd been their enemy for far too long.

Every few moments a MacGerry man glanced her way. Dark red anger danced around them like wisps of fog on the moors. With each seething stare, Katja retreated further inside, pulling the hood of her cloak over her head. She suspected their laird and perhaps her tocher were the only things keeping them from venting their spleen. In spite of being their laird's wife, she would never cease being the daughter of their lifelong adversary.

She attempted to ignore the hatred rolling off them. Hostility thickened the air around her, suffocating until she forced herself to breathe slowly, warding it off, shielding herself from those around her.

* * *

As soon as he'd handed the bloody sheet to the earl, Calder itched to be away from the foul man. Sinclair gave him an assessing look before offering his hand as a final gesture to seal their pact. Taking one last glance at the sheet, Calder wondered again if his bride spoke the truth about her chastity. Every word she uttered, every reaction she made to his lovemaking supported her claim.

Even her old nurse's explanation made sense. He'd heard that particular warning before. How many times did their grandmam scold Torri over the same thing? Luckily, he possessed enough of his wits not to make more of an issue of it. As he said, it was in the past now. No need to address it further. They would move on from here.

But move on to what?

Though he greatly enjoyed their joining—and hoped she had as well—Calder knew Katja would not easily dismiss the part he played in agreeing to the hasty marriage. The bruise blooming on her bonny face remained a reminder of his role of co-conspirator. What would the MacGerrys believe of their new lady?

His bride took less time than he imagined a female could to prepare for the journey. Less than an hour had passed since she lay in his arms, but seeing her slender form in men's clothing stirred his desire, tempting him to take her again. He sighed. She would need time for the soreness in her body and the ache of her heart to wane before they coupled again.

The tearful farewell from the old crone pulled at his sympathies. He knew about loss. Katja would bring no one with her to her new home. No one except her wee beastie who stood obediently next to her horse. The two animals sniffed and nudged each other like old friends. It was then Calder noticed no matter where she went, the rust-colored monster's eyes never left her. His stare grew more intense, his body more taut the farther she stood from him. Even with her gelding nibbling playfully at his ears and fur, Freki's gaze never broke.

Calder motioned for them to depart. "We travel till dusk and should arrive by midday on the morrow."

With a gesture from him, the men grouped around her mount, a rider on either side. They allowed her dog enough room to run alongside, their horses tossing their heads and stamping their hooves in distrust of the great beast.

They crested a hill and Calder caught Katja wiping away a few tears as she turned to take a final look back. Her courage continued to impress him. He suspected most women leaving home to take up residence amongst an enemy clan would weep and wail endlessly. With a shudder, he sent up a silent prayer of thanks for Katja's forbearance.

Calder surveyed his bride and his trained eye noticed she near bristled with blades. He counted the two dirks in her belt, three in her boots, and one she slid under the plait at the back of her neck. It would have remained hidden had he not seen her place it there.

Based on the way the cloth bunched on her left arm, he suspected a seventh lay tucked in a sheath attached to her forearm. Include the sword strapped to the back of her horse and the curved bow in its leather case, and she was better armed than he and his men. That didn't include the great mound of fur and fang at her side. If she had the skills the Sinclair captain had suggested, with the weapons she carried, he needn't worry about her safety at Fairetur.

Chapter Six

The riders stopped at Loch Beaggorm on the edge of MacGerry lands to camp before evening. Some tended the horses while others gathered wood for a fire. Katja busied herself unsaddling her horse.

"'Tis a beautiful horse. What's his name?"

The small hairs on the back of Katja's neck prickled at the sound of Calder's voice behind her, his warm breath tickling her skin.

"Skündi, which means *swift* in Norn." She fussed with the girth, lingering over her chores, unwilling to show that their joining—and the past few hours in the saddle—had left her sore. Uncertain she could walk without staggering about like a drunken fool, she garnered time to allow the tenderness to ease. She did not wish to embarrass herself by giving the men a reason to laugh at her discomfort. Nor did she wish to reveal her failings to her new husband.

Calder placed his hand on hers as she reached to pull the saddle off Skündi's back. "I have men who will tend to yer mount, Katja."

"Thank ye, Laird, but I prefer to care for my own horse."

He released a sigh. "Ye agreed to call me Calder."

"Aye, but to do so in front of yer men would be ill-mannered."

"Unless we entertain important visitors, I'm always Calder to ye. As yer husband I will see to yer needs."

She nodded though she pleaded with her eyes for him to relent in this case. With a smile, he squeezed her hand then walked toward his men. Her breath caught as the heat of his touch and the warmth of his smile brought visions of their lovemaking—the part before he'd consummated their union. Her heart raced as she wondered if he would approach her again this night. She wasn't sure if she could endure another coupling so soon. The hours in the saddle hadn't been kind to her tender flesh.

Tethering her horse with the others, she gingerly ambled to the edge of the group, acutely aware of the resentful stares aimed her way. Their animosity grew thick, threatening to choke her again. She spread a plain woolen blanket on the ground outside their circle near a fallen tree. She'd purposely left her Sinclair plaide and pin at Ruadhcreag with Morag, certain such a reminder of her heritage would earn her no favors from her new clan.

Freki remained at her side as she glanced about for something to do. The men worked silently, each with a prescribed task, but she had no job assigned her. She gathered a few fallen branches and placed them beside those already lying by the freshly dug fire pit.

The man she knew as Calder's Uncle Finn handed her chunks of bread and cheese with a grin, a gleam of playfulness in his eyes. Other than Calder, he was the only MacGerry she sensed no hostile feelings from. His steady blue aura bespoke his relaxed nature.

"Here ye are, milady. 'Tis not grand fare, but 'twill keep yer belly from rumbling."

She accepted it with a tentative nod of thanks. Finn sauntered back to the fire with his peculiar bow-legged gait. Katja settled on a fallen tree, keeping an eye on those in front of her. Freki nudged her hand with an expectant look. She loathed being without his protection even for a few minutes, but he needed to eat as well.

"Freki, *henta*." She swept her arm across her body and pointed in the direction of the woods. Ears alert, he scanned the immediate area, then sniffed the ground and loped off into the gathering darkness.

Every pair of eyes watched him leave.

"What did ye send him off to do, milady?" Finn voiced what everyone clearly wondered.

"I sent him to hunt his supper. He will return in a wee bit." Katja didn't glance up for fear of what she would see now that her protector no longer sat beside her. She eased a dirk out of her belt, using it to slice the hard cheese as well as bolster her confidence. The time before Freki's return seemed an eternity.

She dropped onto the blanket and pulled her cloak around her. Freki settled next to her with a satisfied huff. She tucked in, curling against his warm body and wiry fur, wanting nothing more than to give in to sleep after such a life-altering day.

Lady Katja Sinclair, the person she awoke as this morning, no longer existed. Though never happy, at least she'd known her role, knew those around her and knew what each day would bring. A stranger she could scarce come to grips with now occupied her skin. She'd experienced the heights of passion and depths of humiliation within the span of a few hours. More importantly, she possessed a new title, a new husband, and a new clan.

Busy enough with the swirl of thoughts wending through her mind, she tried not to listen to the conversations over the fire. Hearing the contempt she'd observed and sensed all day voiced aloud held no appeal.

* * *

"Do ye wish to invite yer new wife over for a wee bit of the water of life?" Finn handed the flask of whisky to Calder as they sat beside the fire.

"Nae. Let her sleep if she can. She's dealt with more than a lass should in one day."

"Aye, and with nary a word of complaint nor tears. I never

knew a Sinclair to be brave without the advantage of numbers. This one appears to have a full measure and then some. Mayhap their women are fiercer than their men."

Chuckles rumbled low.

"She's a bonny sight, though she carries more blades than a tinker. Do ye think she knows her way around a dirk?" Finn asked.

Calder spotted the mischief in Finn's eyes now he'd had more than a few pulls on the flask they passed around. Often, he would get on like this and target his favorite nephew or some other poor soul. Calder didn't mind the teasing, but had no intention of letting his bride suffer any more disrespect, good-natured or not.

"Sinclair's man says she does. Says he trained her together with her brothers since they were weans. The way he tells the tale, she's a fair hand with the bow, too, and trained the horse and dog herself."

"Speaking of her furry brute, he seems to have taken yer side of the blanket, laird."

More laughter followed until Calder motioned for them to keep quiet. He had to admit, seeing her lying cuddled next to her massive guardian provoked a bit of jealousy. How long would it be until she desired to lie at his side seeking protection and warmth?

"Laird, what of her face? 'Twas all we could do to hold our tongues each time we looked at her. Me and the lads will gladly ride back and teach that bastard a lesson. Just give the word."

One side of Calder's mouth angled up at the offer. In spite of being the earl's daughter, a Sinclair, his men were ready to defend her after being around her only one day. It was a good sign. Of course, Quinn always was a bit headstrong.

"Willnae be necessary. Remember, we agreed on peace. The worst is behind her. We'll make it a point to show her how true Scotsmen treat a lass, especially a noblewoman. I would rather look to the morrow when we introduce everyone to the new Lady

MacGerry, and the reason why we willnae starve this winter."

His words sobered everyone. The men nodded agreement with more than one grateful glance aimed toward Katja's now sleeping form. Though pleased these men saw it the way he did, Calder doubted the rest of the clan would receive his new wife as easily.

* * *

Katja woke as the first streaks of a new dawn pinked the sky. She stretched her legs, soreness between them and down her thighs and calves reminding her of the previous day's activities. Though not as bad as the day before, she knew another half-day in the saddle wouldn't help. Startled, she realized her companions were up and about, some readying the horses while others broke camp.

An oatcake and waterskin sat on the blanket next to her. Staring at it like she'd never seen a bannock before, Katja tried to recall a man ever fetching her meal. An odd sensation thickened in her chest as she reached for the still-warm oatcake.

How did she sleep through the sounds of their activity? She'd heard rumors the MacGerry moved like shadows, neither making noise nor leaving a trace while raiding. It seemed 'twas more than rumor. With hand gestures and nods, they moved together, using only silent communication.

The unmarked, dew-laden grass next to her blanket declared Calder had slept elsewhere. Though she'd chosen a spot away from the men, she'd wondered if he would seek his rest with her. A flicker of memory stirred low in her belly, reminding her of the pleasure he'd given her before he'd taken his own. Mayhap she could ignore the uncomfortable stretch and burn if he cared for her needs first. The thought both excited and embarrassed her. How could she long for his touch after such a short time in his arms?

Deprived of affection since her grandmam died, mayhap he awakened a hunger of the skin she didn't know existed.

Katja's thoughts turned sour. With the peace agreement firmly in hand, along with her tocher, he no longer needed to worry himself over a soiled wife. Would he insist they continue on as strangers as her parents had, interacting only when necessary? A man as handsome as he likely kept a MacGerry lass about to slake his lust. She was no longer necessary until he wanted an heir.

She shook her head to clear it against such dark notions and the despair that threatened to overwhelm her. It would do no good to worry about what might be. She would meet each day as it came.

Katja rose, shivering in the cold air, noticing her breath fogged. She stepped stiffly to the loch and tended to her morning needs, probing the tender skin around her eye and cheek, wondering how bad she appeared.

"How do I look this morn, Freki?" She turned, giving him a good view of the left side of her face.

He cocked his head and whined.

"Bad, aye? I feared such."

Sighing, she decided there was nothing to be done. She'd be presented to the MacGerry clan bearing the mark of her sire's displeasure. She changed into a clean chemise and light green gown of thick wool before returning to camp to fold her blanket and pack her horse. As she strolled toward the group, the hard stares returned, though each man touched his bonnet in a respectful manner. She dipped her head in response, not knowing what else to do. Her brow wrinkled as she wondered what the two conflicting actions meant. Muddy red mingled with a light green aura around the men. Anger and dislike coupled with pity—for what she would face as an outsider? Katja lifted her chin and strode to her horse.

Again, Calder stood, waiting to help her mount.

"How did ye sleep, Katja?"

The warmth of his hand and the rumbling of his deep voice invited her to lace her arms around his neck and take one of those kisses she dreamt of the night before. A kiss he no doubt shared freely with other lasses since he saw no reason to gift them to his new wife. The thought tightened her stomach, threatening the oatcake she'd eaten earlier.

"Well, my la...Calder, and ye?" Her gaze tangled with his, leaving her feeling like a doe caught by the stare of a hungry wolf. Her burst of anger slipped away as a warm tingle spread through her body, centering on the place most sore.

His appraising look reminded her of her father's men as they watched the serving women. His naked hunger sent a shiver darting through her body. Her heart beat a slow, thick cadence.

"Aye, well enough," he replied. "No trews today?"

The question took her by surprise. She cocked her head to study his features, wondering at the playful quality evident in his half-smile. The twinkle in his eyes.

"Do ye jest with me?" she asked, perplexed.

His lips parted, showing off a set of white teeth. "Aye, I do. As much as I enjoy seeing ye in trews, ye look verra bonny today. Dinnae fash. The clan knows I bring home a Sinclair bride with a tocher that will give them all full bellies this winter. They will be lining up to kiss yer hand in thanks." His grin widened.

Katja arched an eyebrow. "Even when they discover I am the earl's daughter?"

The lighthearted gleam in Calder's eyes faded a bit. "Ye should know this feud has left no MacGerry untouched. Everyone has lost loved ones. Yet all know a daughter has naught to do with her sire's decisions. Some may nurse hard feelings and stay clear of ye, but the clan will know the sacrifice ye made for them. 'Twill be a period of adjustment, but ye are their new mistress."

She let his words settle. It was as she thought. Their clan lost more than she ever imagined. Certainly more than her own in terms of lives. The man must be daft, though, to think they would line up to thank her. A full belly and fertile lands made a poor exchange for the life of a father or brother. A poor exchange, indeed. Still, she couldn't help but be thankful for his respect and care. Given his absence at her side last night, she wondered what his intentions were.

"If ye dinnae mind overly much, I would rather not assume the position of mistress right away. I think it best to work amongst the women for a wee bit whilst I learn their ways and earn their respect." She wondered if he would rage at her for choosing a path other than what he wished.

Calder tipped her chin with his fingers and brushed his thumb across her bottom lip. The rough pad gently scrapped against the sensitive skin, causing her knees to weaken and her breath to hitch. She wanted to purr from the sensation and wrap herself around him, even though part of her remained wary of his intentions.

"Aye, 'tis a sound strategy. Infiltrate the enemy before taking over. Seems I need to be studying yer tactics." He winked, hoisted her into the saddle, and gave her bottom a gentle squeeze.

Katja gaped at him. The provocative way he rubbed her lips and touched her, coupled with his making a jest of her entreaty left her breathless. In spite of its soreness, her body desired his touch again. She'd never thought twice about a man before, but a look and a touch from this one left her hungry.

He belongs to me now.

The thought echoed across her heart with the power of a crashing wave. Caught within the group of riders, she was swept away by men and horses as surely as Calder swept away her emotions with his touch and playfulness. As the immediate spike of longing eased, she realized she would have to guard her heart.

It was not hard to imagine herself chasing this man like a child chases sweets. But the danger of giving him such power over her loomed as a genuine threat. She shuddered at the unpleasant idea any man could control her heart. She would not end up like her mother, loving a man who treated her like any other possession. A despised one, at that.

Katja turned her attention to the moorlands, enjoying the fall colors as they traveled east. The crisp smell of the changing seasons drifted in the air. Only a few weeks remained before snow announced the coming winter. She thought of all the things left to ready Ruadhcreag for the harsh days ahead. Knowing the MacGerry were not as prepared, she wondered what remained to be done at Fairetur.

"Och, my wife will welcome me with open arms when she sees me," a red-haired man she'd been introduced to as Quinn announced with a grin.

"Only because she needs yer help with the six bairns ye've bred on her," Finn replied. The men roared with appreciation.

With each furlong covered, the other horses and riders acted more at ease but anxious to be home. She hadn't considered how difficult the past two days had been for them. To be housed behind the walls of their enemy, vastly outnumbered, must have been harrowing. Swallowing a dose of guilt, Katja realized her thoughts had lingered selfishly on her own troubles. The role of mistress required putting the needs of her new clan first rather than her own discomfort and uncertainty. Two qualities she held in abundance—and with good reason.

* * *

By midday, a fortified keep came into view. A combination of curiosity and dread slid through Katja as she spotted the large rectangular structure with towers at two corners atop the hill overlooking the valley and nearby river. Its height and location gave the MacGerrys an advantage of viewing miles of hills and valleys from all directions. The curtain walls surrounding the keep were not as tall as those at Ruadhcreag, but looked to be thick and effective. A single portcullis and sturdy iron-studded wooden gate stood between the keep's inhabitants and their foes.

As they approached, Katja noticed many empty crofts in various states of disrepair. Even the occupied ones appeared to be in poor condition. For every cultivated field they passed, at least two lay fallow. The few people working outside waved enthusiastically at their group and hastened toward the keep. Twice as many women and children than men worked outside. Did the men hunt or work elsewhere?

The sound of pipes rose from the keep, playing a rousing victory song. As they entered the gate, a throng of people met them in the yard. She spotted an old man atop the steps gripping a bagpipe, filling the air with the lilting music of triumph. Surrounding Calder, the crowd ushered him into the keep like a conquering hero, separating him from her and carrying him away on a tide of excitement. Bemused at the sight of such a joyous homecoming, it was a few minutes before Katja realized she was still mounted and alone. She glanced down to see a lad of no more than twelve summers staring at her with wide-eyed curiosity, a nervous eye on her dog.

"D'ye need assistance, milady?" He spoke slowly, as if worried she was simple, glancing at her and back toward her companion.

"His name is Freki. He willnae hurt ye."

Slipping from her saddle, she smiled and placed the reins into the lad's hands. "Thank ye for caring for my horse." She rubbed Skündi's nose lovingly. He nuzzled her, a light snort warming the side of her neck.

The lad grinned widely, displaying crooked teeth. "Aye, milady. I'll treat 'im as if I were 'is mam."

Katja stretched her palm to him. "Give me yer hand. What's yer name?"

The lad tentatively placed his hand in hers. Freki stepped forward to sniff the lad's fingers, a quick lick with his pink tongue wiping away the lad's worried expression.

"I'm Jamie, milady. Ye be the laird's new wife, our mistress?"

"Aye Jamie, I'm the laird's new wife. 'Tis a pleasure to meet ye." She patted his shoulder. Jamie tore his gaze from Freki, his eyes wide with excitement.

"That's the biggest dog I ever seen!"

"Jamie! Stop pesterin' the lady and take care of her horse." A hobbled old man beckoned from the entrance of the stables. He doffed his hat and bowed stiffly. "Sorry, milady, but Jamie here talks more than he works." Worry lit his eyes and he bowed again.

"No bother, sir. He's only being friendly. And yer name?" Katja tried to put him at ease with a small smile.

"Titus, milady. Jes' like in the Bible." He bowed a third time.

"'Tis a pleasure to meet ye both." Glancing about, she realized few people remained in the yard and the doors to the hall had closed behind her husband and the rejoicing clans people. She grabbed her saddlebag and headed to the door, Freki at her side. Running a hand across his coarse fur for confidence, she opened the door.

She entered the hall, the smell of food and sounds of celebration rising around her. A crowd of people surrounded Calder. He stood taller than the rest and she instantly recognized his dark hair. Feeling abandoned, she hung back, unsure of her surroundings and what to do. After a few moments, she chided herself for being timid. She was Elke Reginulfsdottir's daughter, descendant of warriors, trained to be a shield maiden. Without her there'd be no celebration. Smoothing her gown, she approached the crowd.

Head high, she drew closer, Freki padding beside her. A few people spotted the two of them and allowed her into the crowd, giving her escort distance aplenty. Katja halted a few feet away from the men as they shook her husband's hand and slapped his back, waiting for him to acknowledge her. A buxom woman with dark red hair threw herself into Calder's arms.

"Calder I've missed ye. My bed has been cold without ye." Pressed against him, her ample breasts threatening to squeeze from the low neck of her gown, she planted a kiss on his cheek.

Katja stared in shock, her bags slipping from nerveless fingers. Laughter rang out and the foul wench shot Katja a knowing glare as she rubbed against Calder's shoulder.

"When ye've drank yer fill, I'll see to yer bath and a proper welcome tonight." She turned back and claimed Calder's lips. Stares fell on Katja and no laughter followed the brazen woman's words this time.

The second kiss shook Katja out of her surprise, setting her ablaze with anger. Though Calder didn't appear to be an active participant, he did nothing to turn the slut away. It was bad enough to be left outside like so much unnecessary baggage. To endure being dishonored by her husband's leman in front of the clan was more than too much.

How could she have thought Calder to be different than any other man she knew? Men might cover their intentions behind the occasional pretty word or a few kind deeds, but she possessed the ability to see that they all allowed their baser needs to lead them. In less than two days her husband proved to be no different.

Spinning on a heel, she started off toward the door again. A small hand intercepted her, threading around her arm. A girl a few years younger than she, with dark brown hair and deep blue eyes, gazed at her.

"Please dinnae let my stupid brother upset ye. Lorna likes to make a scene, pretending to be more than she is. I'm Torri, yer new sister."

Katja instantly saw the resemblance to Calder. She brushed her skirts in an effort to rid them of the dust of travel, taking a moment to cool her ire. A wizened old woman with white hair approached, a welcoming smile on her face. Piercing blue eyes assessed her up and down in a slow movement. Another set of MacGerry blue eyes.

"Ye be my fool grandson's bonny new wife. I'm Beitris. Ye must be tired and hungry from yer travels. Come. I'll call for a bath whilst ye eat."

Katja took a deep breath. She couldn't very well hop back on Skündi and ride to Ruadhcreag. With no other option, Katja allowed each woman an arm as they climbed the stairs. Stopping at a door on the fourth floor, they entered a large chamber devoid of decoration. A small table and chairs, large bed and two trunks concluded the meager furnishings. A small door at one end of the room and a hearth with a well-worn claymore hanging over it were the only other notables—clearly a man's room. She spotted her things on the bed.

"Whose room is this?" Katja asked, knowing the likely answer.

"'Tis the laird's chambers, now yers, Lady . . .." Beitris waited for her to supply a name, her brow at a questioning angle.

A wave of embarrassment washed over her for speaking so abruptly. "Please forgive me, madam. My name is Katja, and this is Freki." She curtsied to the elderly woman who nodded approval.

"Please, is there no other room? I cannae stay here. The laird is a stranger to me, and based on what I witnessed below, I dinnae feel comfortable sleeping here."

Beitris tilted her head slightly, an odd smile playing about her lips. "As ye wish."

Katja grabbed her saddlebag and they retreated one floor to a modest room. With a bed half the size of the laird's and two smaller chairs set in front of the hearth, it would suit her needs. Only hers.

* * *

Calder knew from the moment Lorna surprised him, she meant to stir trouble. The unexpected welcome and overwhelming praise from the clan robbed him of his wits long enough to temporarily forget about his bride. They praised him as a hero, but in truth Katja deserved their gratitude.

The flash of anger lit his new wife like a beacon on the shoreline when Lorna kissed him. 'Twas one more thing to make amends for, one more thing to repair if they would have a marriage in truth rather than in name only.

Grasping the troublemaking wench by the shoulders, he shoved her roughly away from him. "Lorna, ye insulted my wife, yer mistress." He allowed his words to vent the suppressed frustration of the past two days. Every person hushed into silence at his castigation, all eyes centered on him. "Dinnae be surprised if she has ye placed in the pillory or whipped for such a presumptuous act. Whatever her judgment, be aware I'll support it. Ye will cease yer familiarity with me and use only my title—if ye speak to me at all."

Calder had never chastised someone so thoroughly, so publicly before, but her insult demanded it. With the mess he'd made of things already, he didn't require anyone else's help to make matters worse. He needed to make known his expectations on how his people would treat his wife. He'd deal with any disrespect swiftly and harshly.

Lorna's eyes flared angrily then narrowed, her features pinching with defiance. Glancing around the room, it was clear everyone awaited her response. She gave a shallow curtsy and wheeled about, heading toward the kitchen.

The celebration continued, though noticeably subdued. Calder dragged a hand through his hair, feeling the weight of the past two days pressing down. Luckily, Torri and his grandmam had intercepted Katja and escorted her upstairs. They would take care of her needs and see her settled in. He knew she'd have no desire to talk to him at the moment. She'd need time for her ire to ebb. Though curious about her skills with a blade, he didn't want to test those abilities on his own flesh.

Someone pressed a tall mug into his hand. "Here laddie, something to wash away the dirt from the trail."

Calder caught a familiar gleam in his uncle's eyes—the glitter of I-told-ye-so. He accepted the ale and moved to his place at the high board, Finn and Robbie at his side.

Calder blew out a breath. "Go ahead and say it." He drank deeply to brace himself against the teasing scold begging to be set loose.

"Say what? That I warned ye? That yer leman is a devious bitch? That ye are runnin' out of ways to offend yer wee bride after only two days? Nae, that'd be too cruel. 'Twould be like kicking a defenseless puppy." He chuckled within the mug now at his lips, the echo making his laughter more irritating.

Calder shook his head when Robbie joined in.

"She's a bonny thing, I'll give ye that. Mayhap she chose the wrong brother." Robbie slapped him on the back, laughing along with Finn.

Calder took another long drink before releasing a sigh of exasperation. "Give me a raid and I know how to plan it without getting caught. Give me a sword and enemy, and I'll find a way to win. Give me an angry female, and I'm as lost as a ship in the mists."

"Nae doubt Beitris and Torri are up there now soothing her ruffled feathers and tellin' tales of yer greatness." Finn gave a hoot of laughter before refilling both their mugs.

Calder grunted, his face in his hands. "Nae doubt. If ye see a wee blonde head riding west, ye'll know my bonny wife chose her blackguard of a father over her thrice-cursed husband."

Chapter Seven

Robbie clapped Calder on the shoulder. "So, now ye are a rich man, brother, what are yer plans?"

Glad for the interruption from his dismal thoughts, Calder allowed a crooked smile to appear before answering. "Sinclair says the two *davochs* have thirty crofts in good condition, already planted and ready for winter."

Finn rubbed an ear. "Aye, 'tis true. We've raided the area often enough to know they're well cared for. Land canna work itself though. We need twice as many hands as we have to tend it properly."

"I thought to contact MacCairn about a manrent bond. Their holding is mostly on a bog, and they keep breeding lads. We need more men, whilst they have a shortage of women and decent land. Our young widows need husbands to see to them and their bairns. Mayhap an agreement can be made that benefits us all."

Finn nodded. "I like yer thinkin', laird. 'Tis a good plan. Who is the MacCairn now?"

"Broc MacCairn is laird. His father died a few months ago when he and his men ran across raiders outside of Hacraig. I havenae spoken to him recently, but know him as a fair and honest man."

Finn dipped his head, stroking the grey stubble along his jaw. "The raiders are becomin' too bold. Ye'd think the king's man would be involved by now."

"They've been verra clever. They havenae attacked any of the king's people or property. No one knows where they are, but with as many scouting parties that have gone hunting, they're well-hidden. I suspect the deep glens southwest of Hacraig near the loch."

"What'll ye do aboot Lorna?" There was no mistaking the teasing in Finn's question. Calder winced at his uncle's change of topic.

"I'll insist she's among the first taken to wife by a MacCairn. She can cook and clean, and likes bed play. She'll make a decent wife if a man can hold her interest. The sooner she's out of the keep, the better."

"Dinnae forget the MacFies," Robbie chimed in.

"Aye. Ten families and five single men have agreed to join us, and should arrive within the next few days. The five agreed to live in the keep as men-at-arms until they take wives. We'll more than double our numbers and holdings within a fortnight, with enough coin and supplies to make a fresh start come spring. While it addresses our immediate problem, 'tis not the same as our own kin."

"Dinnae let yer mind second-guess these decisions, lad. Ye've done what ye had to do for our survival. Those who canna see the wisdom of it will either come around or not. Ye will be able to seek yer rest at night knowing ye've done all ye can."

"Da would be proud of what ye've accomplished in such a short time, brother." Robbie's response was low, sincere.

Calder smiled and clapped an arm about Robbie's shoulders. In spite of their constant teasing, Robbie seemed to think he could do no wrong. He and Torri were all he had left now. Except for his wife.

His wife.

He'd put off going to her the past two hours. It was time to seek her out and explain himself. Not that he could think of a reasonable explanation for leaving her outside, only to be insulted by his leman when she joined them. He could only hope she would give him a chance to apologize before drawing a blade. He'd prefer to die with a clear conscience.

* * *

A bath and meal sounded like a perfect way to quiet her inner storm. As Katja entered the room, Torri immediately made herself at home, flopping belly-down onto the bed. Beitris spoke to a woman who hurried away, quickly returning with a tray of bread, cheese, and cider.

"What happened to yer eye?" Torri asked with all the subtlety of youth.

Katja quirked her lips into something between a smile and grimace as she recalled the encounter with the ogre she called father. If the Fates smiled upon her, 'twould be the last time she ever laid eyes on the wretched man.

"I said something to my sire that displeased him."

Torri's eyes grew large. "And he struck ye for it? My da always said a man shouldnae strike a woman. Must have been an awful thing ye said."

This time her mouth committed to a smile. "Yer da was right. My sire isnae a good man." She quickly changed the subject. "How many years have ye, Torri?"

Torri bounced up from her prone position and padded over to the chairs where Katja and Beitris sat.

"Ten and three. And ye?" She untied the leather lace holding Katja's braid in place, combing her fingers through the thick blonde tresses.

"I've ten and eight seasons as of last month." She reached for a chunk of bread, then leaned her head back, enjoying the soothing touch. With three older brothers, she always longed for a sister. As she chewed, Katja took in Beitris' wrinkled face. Her hands lay folded on her lap, her fingers gnarled and swollen. The sulfur-colored band spiraling around her spoke of her pain. Though her body appeared wizened, her eyes reflected intelligence and kindness.

Beitris caught Katja staring at her hands and hid them within the folds of her skirts.

"Do they pain ye much?" Katja's voice softened.

Beitris shifted in the chair. "Mostly at the end of the day and before a storm."

"I'm sorry." Her heart lurched with compassion for the older woman so much like her grandmam.

Beitris made a shooing motion. "Pain reminds me I'm still on the right side of the sod." She winked as her face brightened. "Now tell me the tale of how ye came to be my newest granddaughter."

Katja took a deep breath and related all she knew, leaving out the consummation to protect Torri's innocent ears. When she mentioned her sire's previous attempts at wedding her, the lass scrunched her face.

Torri folded her arms across her chest, chin jutting upward. "When I'm of age, my brother willnae make me marry a man auld enough to be my grandda."

Katja and Beitris shared a mirthful glance. "I am sure your brothers will entertain your every wish, Torri," Katja ventured. *As would mine, had the earl not been such a terror.*

Servants interrupted, carrying a wooden tub and buckets of water. Katja's breathing hitched. She knew bathing in castles wasn't a solitary affair. At Ruadhcreag, everyone left her alone, even when washing. No one treated her with hostility except her sire, but his displeasure toward her meant most avoided contact with her as if she didn't exist. Having people in the room while she bathed brought a sense of discomfort. When it became clear Torri and Beitris intended to aid her, she quashed her awkwardness and quickly disrobed.

Both women's eyes widened when she removed the dirk from her left forearm, the one strapped to her calf, the one at her belt, and finally the one at her nape. *If four blades shock them, 'tis a good thing I dinnae have on trews and boots, doubling the number.* She quirked a smile, shrugged her shoulders and stepped into the warm water of her bath.

Torri's hands gathered her hair and wet it. "Lean back and I'll help. Ye have such beautiful hair, milady. 'Tis like threads of sunshine."

"I thought we're sisters?" Katja chided softly.

"Aye."

"If so, ye should call me Katja."

The pleasure of Torri's fingers massaging her scalp and the relaxing aroma of the scented soap eased the tension coiled tightly within her shoulders. She hadn't realized how taut her muscles had become over the strain of the past two days. With a sigh, she relaxed and let go the worries plaguing her. Finally, the water cooled and she stepped from the tub.

"Does yer dog always stay with ye?" Torri asked, giving Freki a sidelong glance.

Katja nodded and smiled. "He does."

"I'm not sure my brother will allow him to sleep above the hall. The rest of the dogs stay below stairs." Torri wrapped the soap in its linen cloth and set it aside.

"Freki is well-mannered. He sleeps where I sleep." If Calder pressed the issue, she would sleep below stairs as well. Based on what transpired in the hall, she doubted he cared where she slept. She pushed back the flicker of anger threatening to undo the good her bath had accomplished.

Gooseflesh rose along her skin. Even with a blazing fire in the hearth, the chamber remained chilled. The poor condition of the shutters allowed in the crisp autumn air. Torri handed her a drying cloth then a warm wool dressing robe. Beitris studied her, a comforting smile on her face. Katja's cheeks heated at the scrutiny.

"Everyone is talking about how yer dowry will save us. That we'll have plenty of gold, sheep, and grain. Is this true?" Torri looked at her expectantly.

"Torri! That's not a polite question to ask." Beitris raised an eyebrow, giving her granddaughter a glare of disapproval.

Katja carefully controlled the scowl on her face. "'Tis no matter. My tocher includes many acres of fertile land with crofts, as well as a goodly amount of gold. I dinnae know about grain and sheep. Your brother and my sire are privy to that part of the agreement, not I."

The reminder of being nothing more than an unwanted wife with a small fortune rankled. She sent a silent prayer of thanks to her deceased grandda. Without his generosity and foresight, who knew where she'd be today?

"Come, Torri, let us leave Katja to her rest." Beitris motioned for her granddaughter to follow her. "The bell for supper will ring right before dark," she told Katja. "We'll wait for ye at the bottom of the stairs."

Katja nodded, offering the best smile she could muster at the thought of approaching the people who'd witnessed Lorna's earlier disrespect.

Beitris patted her hand. "Not to worry lass. All will be well. We've needed a lady round here for a long time. I'm too old for the task, and Torri is too young and headstrong. Remember, men are daft creatures and often do stupid things. 'Tis in their nature. Dinnae be too hard on the lad when he comes beggin' for forgiveness." Her cackle drifted over her shoulder as she and Torri left the room.

Katja dropped the bar across the door and settled to rest on the bed beneath thin, worn blankets. Freki snuggled beside her. Beg her forgiveness? No man ever asked for her forgiveness. No, that wasn't true. Calder did ask her pardon for his role in their shameful wedding. The painful memory sent a shiver up her spine.

He'd also apologized for not being able to provide the comfort she was used to. She snorted at that idea, perking Freki's ears. Though not a grand structure, Fairetur could be a fine home. From what she'd seen thus far, it merely needed a few repairs—and a woman's touch.

Would she forgive him if he indeed asked, as Beitris suggested? One heavy sigh later, she realized aye, she would. It wasn't in her nature to hold a grudge. However, forgiveness didn't equal trust. The situation provided a perfect excuse to keep her distance from the man who melted her defenses with a smile or the slightest touch.

She couldn't afford to be vulnerable with any man. She would not wind up like her mother, emotionally attached to a husband who only sought her out when he wished to mount her, not appearing to care if she lived or died. It was too dangerous. Though, if she pushed her husband away, he likely would seek comfort from that bulbous-bosomed bitch.

"I dinnae care, Freki. He can tup the wench until their eyes cross." Her voice broke, bending her declaration on a sharp breath.

Freki swiped his tongue across her cheek.

A squeezing pain centered in her chest as she imagined Calder lying with the red-haired harlot. She wiped away an errant tear. Wrapping her arms about her middle, she refused to acknowledge her feelings on the matter. She would tend the keep and nurture relationships with her new sister and grandmam. She and Freki had new lands to hunt and explore with no tormentor telling her what she could or couldn't do, nor telling her she was unworthy. It would be a better life than she had before—even if some viewed her as the enemy.

* * *

Calder stared at the top of the stairs and exhaled deeply. He climbed the flights daily to and from his chambers. So why this time did the climb appear more daunting than a trek up Ben Morven? In the snow.

Because a well-armed lass up there likely wants to carve off a few of yer tender bits.

Taking a steadying breath, he grabbed the rope railing attached to the wall. Worn slick from decades of use, the knots in the thick hemp gave him a firm, familiar grip. Saints only knew everything else had changed considerably in his life this past fortnight. He thought of Finn's words and for the moment borrowed his uncle's confidence.

Calder knocked quietly at his chamber door. No answer. He put an ear to the heavy oak but heard nothing within. Taking a deep breath, he opened the door, only to find his room empty except for her sword and bow lying on his bed. Curious, he picked up the sword.

The hilt held a number of interlocking metal tines formed to protect the hand. He swung the blade back and forth, checking the balance. The lightweight design surprised him. The center groove running the length of the double-edged blade dove deeper into the steel than any he'd seen, taking away much of the weight. While a wee bit narrower and shorter than his own sword, it was a formidable weapon, nevertheless. Calder marveled at the craftsmanship made especially for a smaller person—for Katja.

Placing the weapon back in its scabbard, he resumed his hunt for his wife. With her sword and bow in his possession, when he caught up with her, she would only have her dirks. Somehow that knowledge did very little to comfort him. As he approached the staircase again, he heard the voices of his sister and grandmam. He caught up with them on the second floor.

"Where have ye placed my wife? I saw her things in our chamber, but it dinnae look as if she's been there."

"Lady MacGerry requested her own chamber. We put her in one of the guest chambers on the third floor." A hint of merriment threaded Beitris's reply.

Torri placed a hand over her mouth and giggled as the pair of troublemakers hurried down the stairs.

Calder scrubbed his face with one hand. Her own chamber? Aye, his bride was still angry with him. He walked back to the third floor and tested the first door. Empty. The second proved the same. He stood at the last door, the room next to Torri's and tried again to come up with an explanation. Boar's bollocks! Even he didn't believe the poor excuses that came to mind. No, he'd been honest with her from the start. He would continue as he'd begun. No matter how difficult, he vowed to always tell her the truth.

He struck the door tentatively with his knuckles. "Katja."

A muted growl answered. Well, at least he'd found her. Thinking only about avoiding a well-placed dagger, he'd forgotten about her wee *Cù Sìth*.

Calder squared his shoulders. He was the MacGerry, and she his wife. He would pledge he'd have no other but her. He'd see to her welcome tonight, assuring her position within the clan. They would then move on together. It was as simple as that.

He knocked again, this time harder. "Katja."

This time silence.

Taking a deep breath to stifle his frustration, he tried again. "Katja."

"Aye." The voice sounded soft, distant.

"Open the door so we can talk." He bit back the words that tumbled harsher than he'd intended.

"I was asleep," came the reply. "Can it not wait till after supper?"

Calder shoved a hand through his hair. She'd probably not slept well last night on the ground after such a vexing day. She no doubt needed rest. And it gave him a reprieve for a couple more hours. "Aye, seek yer rest. We'll talk tonight." He waited for a response but heard only silence.

He headed down the stairs to the study and penned a missive to MacCairn, asking his reply to a manrent agreement. Once finished, he found enough time before supper to check on how the croft repairs progressed.

* * *

Katja awoke to the sound of a bell ringing. She sat up, confused for a moment, and glanced around a strange room, Freki next to her. Remembrance flashed through her mind. She was in her new home.

Supper would be served soon. She'd decided earlier not to avoid going down this evening. It was important to show her new clan a couple of insults would not discourage her. She'd endured much worse on a regular basis at Ruadhcreag. The strength of her Viking heritage stiffened her spine.

Beitris and Torri awaited her at the bottom of the stairs, and Katja found a bit more courage in their company.

Katja halted at the entrance to the hall and turned to Freki. *Fresta.* She lowered her palm toward the floor.

Freki dropped to a prone position, pleading in his eyes.

"Dinnae worry, *bolli*. I'll bring ye some table scraps." She patted his massive head and continued toward the crowd settling on benches in front of the trestle tables. Though used to seeing many people in her old home, it surprised her to see so few men here. The older men and young lads well exceeded those of fighting age. The startling picture before her explained their dire need for an end to the feud more than any words ever could.

As she, Torri and Beitris entered the hall, voices died away. A man hopped down from the dais at the head of the room and made his way confidently toward them, a grin spread across his face. Katja immediately recognized a younger version of Calder. Though not as tall as her husband, he carried a bit more muscle. Coming to a halt before them, he bowed gracefully.

"I'm Robbie, Calder and Torri's brother—now yer brother by marriage."

Robbie's infectious smile drew a brief one from her in return. "'Tis a pleasure to meet ye, Robbie, I'm Katja . . . Sinclair." Heat crept into her cheeks and she found herself enjoying his attention. What was it about the MacGerry brothers? They could charm the bark off a tree.

He grasped her hand and brushed a light kiss over her knuckles. Her smile vanished and she dropped her gaze. She could not recall a man ever doing such a thing. When she glanced at him again, his eyes sparkled with a mischievous gleam, bringing to mind his Uncle Finn.

Robbie offered his arm. She hesitantly placed her hand upon it, allowing him to escort her to the high table where the laird sat, deep in discussion with the older man who'd played the pipes during their arrival.

As Katja reached the high table, Calder rose and took her hand from Robbie. Knowing his smile to be as entangling as any spider's web, she set her gaze on the wall behind him before dropping into a deep curtsy.

"My laird."

Calder's grip on her hand tightened. He hesitated, silent, perhaps waiting for her to make eye contact. She refused, keeping her gaze on a spot across the room just to the left of his shoulder. With a brief sigh, he turned them both toward the people present.

"This is my wife, Katja Sinclair, now Lady MacGerry. She willingly left home and kin to wed her father's enemy for the sake of peace. She is yer new mistress and I ask ye to treat her with the same respect ye did the last Lady MacGerry, my mother. No one chooses the clan they are born into, and all know daughters have naught to do with the actions of men." He looked around the room and raised his cup.

A few voices murmured obediently, "Lady MacGerry!"

The tepid response did not surprise Katja. If anything, the number of men who raised their mugs or touched their bonnets was unexpected. However, she predicted the animosity swirling around many gathered at the tables. The hatred in the room surrounded her like a living being. She fixed her attention on the meal, ignoring the harsh colors churning about her. The clan's mixed reactions didn't seem to go unnoticed by Calder. Once they were seated, he leaned toward her.

"They will adjust. 'Twill take time for some. Once they see ye are a good lass and have their welfare in mind, they'll come 'round."

She gave a curt nod, keeping her gaze forward. Calder broke off a piece of dark, grainy bread for her and filled her cup. The bowl of pottage before her appeared simple but hearty. With each bite, he seemed to deliberately brush her arm or shoulder, or touch her thigh with his. The masculine scent and heat radiating from his body made her hunger for something besides food. His consideration and proximity tempted her to revel in the closeness he offered. She could not. She would remain strong and keep her heart safe.

"Now ye have secured yer bride, what duties do ye tend to next, brother?" Robbie winked at her from his seat on Calder's right.

Relief poured over her once Calder's attention turned to his brother. The distraction allowed her time to rein in her scrambled emotions. She summoned the memory of the earlier insult, savoring it, using it to feed her anger and harden her resolve.

"We have two more crofts to make ready for the MacFies who will arrive over the next few days. And what does my baby brother do on the morrow? Surely ye've had yer fill of thatching whilst we were gone?" Calder's teasing tone reached her ears.

"Cook is out of meat. I thought to go hunting. Can ye spare someone to accompany me?"

"Nae. We need all the hands we have to complete the work before the snows hit. If the larder wasnae bare I would press ye into service, meager thatching skills and all."

Distracted by the man next to her, Katja noticed for the first time no meat graced the board, including the table where she sat. In fact, the food served at the lower and high tables was the same fare. The kitchen staff at her old home had always prepared choice meats and delicacies for her sire and any guests he'd invited. Those below the salt ate well, but their tables lacked the extravagant morsels and treats prepared for the earl.

"I'll go with ye, Robbie. Freki and I would like to know yer lands and help with the hunt," Katja offered, eager to do something to benefit her new clan.

Calder's head whipped around, disapproval etched on his face.

Robbie headed him off. "'Tis a grand idea. Ye had time with Katja on the way back from the earl's, Calder. Grandmam and Torri were with her all afternoon. Spending the morning hunting would be a pleasant way to get to know my new sister."

Katja stared at her new brother by marriage, wondering if the grin he wore pained him. His face split so wide, if he didn't desist, she feared an injury. By the expression on her husband's face, he might very well do the injuring.

Chapter Eight

Calder had sensed Katja's presence the moment she entered the hall. He'd noticed Robbie's vigil, but thought he watched for the serving lass he'd been bedding the past fortnight. When Robbie purposely made his way across the room, Calder knew he was up to no good. Startled, he watched the corners of Katja's lips turn upward. Rarely had a smile graced her lips since they'd met, and damned if his younger brother hadn't coaxed one from her this eve. Her glowing blush as the young MacGerry played the courtier caused Calder to ball his fists and consider knocking the grin off his brother's face.

To worsen matters, his mischief-making grandmam shot him a knowing smirk at his poorly-veiled reaction. He scowled in response. Why couldn't Beitris be less sharp of wit and a touch more dour like a respectable *cailleach*?

He chuckled to himself as Katja sat as far away as possible on the bench, avoiding physical and eye contact with him. If she thought he would allow her the same cold distance he witnessed in the earl's keep, she'd soon find otherwise. The MacGerry clan might be small and poor, but they never lacked in affection and laughter. He winced to remember Christer's words about her living in scorn and isolation.

He purposely touched her as they sat together, each time gauging her reaction. It was clear such attentions unsettled her, making her blush and flinch. Though she didn't know what to make of his casual touches, he recalled she'd enjoyed their lovemaking until he'd rushed things, then ruined the moment with suspicion. If he could draw such passion from her their first time together, they had much to look forward to when winter shortened the days and lengthened the nights.

Absorbed in the carnal direction his thoughts carried him, he missed the devilry Robbie instigated when he mentioned hunting. He'd related what Sinclair's man had told him about her ability to hunt to both Robbie and Finn. Now Robbie used the knowledge to willingly goad him by jumping on her offer to go hunting. If he said *nae*, 'twould label him tyrant for no good reason. If he said *aye*, it gave Robbie opportunity to create more mischief.

"The truth is, we do need the meat if the larder lies empty. Since we have peace with the Sinclair, there should be no danger if ye dinnae travel too far. I confess I'm eager to see if my new bride can hunt as well as is rumored." He waited for the reaction he knew to be forthcoming.

She grabbed the bait.

Straightening in her chair and tipping her chin upward, she turned to Robbie. "I will meet ye at the stables before dawn. I suggest ye bring an extra horse to carry all the game we will fetch."

Those within earshot chuckled at her boast. Calder gave her thigh a gentle squeeze beneath the table, causing her to jump. She finally met his gaze. He didn't like the hurt lurking in her eyes. Guilt raked him anew, knowing he'd authored this latest injury. He'd pledged not to cause her pain, to protect and care for her. Finn was right. In two short days, he'd created enough damage to last a lifetime.

When Katja rose from the table, he followed suit, offering his arm. "Allow me to show ye about the keep."

She hesitated a moment, then settled a hand on his arm. The grimace and feathery touch shouted she would rather be anywhere but with him.

"I thought to show ye the laird's solar first." They walked to the chamber on the wall directly behind the high table. Opening the door, he waited for her to enter the dark room. Embers lingered in the hearth from an earlier fire, the pungent aroma of smoldering peat filling the air.

Calder grabbed a taper and touched it to the glowing coals. He then lit a lantern sitting on the worn wooden desk, the light chasing the darkness into the corners. When he turned, his bonny wife stood, feet shoulder-width apart, arms crossed in front of her chest, her expression forged of iron. She needed only a flaming sword to appear as a Valkyrie of legend.

Saint's blood, she's magnificent!

"'Twas unthinking of me to leave ye on yer horse today. I dinnae have a good excuse. I got carried away by the revelry and forgot about the reason why we celebrate. 'Tis ye they should have been cheering, not me."

Her features softened. A breath later, her iron mask snapped back into place.

"Ye're the one who came back with a bride and large tocher. Ye're the hero who saved the MacGerrys from starvation. Ye're the one who ended the feud. I'm the soiled wife ye dinnae want. Now that ye've had me, ye can go back to yer whore whilst I tend to yer home. My only request is ye dinnae shame me in front of the clan with her again."

Each word hurled at him carried a measure of desolation he'd never heard before. He sensed her stoic façade lay as fragile as an early layer of ice on a loch. One misstep would send him plunging into the frozen depths of her heartache. The pain she so valiantly fought to hide poured off her like a cold winter rain. He clearly underestimated the severity of wounding caused by years of her father's rancor and his own unthinking behavior.

Calder leaned against the desk to steady himself, lowering himself to her height. "Ye arenae an unwanted bride. I told ye the day we wed I am greatly pleased to have ye, with or without yer tocher. I'll admit I made a poor decision to assume ye werenae a virgin when I found ye without a maidenhead. Ye yerself were surprised by that particular discovery." He tilted his head, awaiting a response.

Katja's chin notched up fractionally but she remained mute.

"'Tis true Lorna was my leman, but I pledged my troth to *ye*," he continued. "I'll have no other in my bed from here on. I rebuked her in front of the clan for her insult, and only await yer word on her punishment. I suggest the pillory, but can round up a lash or rod if ye want her beaten."

Katja's nostrils flared and her arms dropped to her sides, fisting as they lowered. "I dinnae want her punished. I want her gone from the keep!"

Calder swore he would hold his temper even if she railed at him. Mirroring her fierce expression, he spoke in a slow, calm voice belying the anger threatening to surface. Anger at Lorna for forcing this argument, and a wee bit at Katja for disagreeing. "No one will disrespect ye in such a manner without penalty. I will have her removed at the first opportunity. Ye choose the method, but she will be disciplined."

Katja inhaled a deep breath, loosened her fists, and paced the room twice before coming to a halt. "Ye willnae take it kindly if I tell ye how to discipline the men, aye?"

Calder arched a brow. "Aye."

"I'm the mistress of the keep now?"

"Aye."

"The staff are my responsibility unless ye find me lacking in the job. Lorna is my charge as long as she remains. If ye rescue me now, how will they act once ye turn yer back? I will go along as planned and work amongst them to gain their regard. If Lorna or anyone else disregards me, I will deal with them as I see fit, as ye would yer men, agreed?"

Calder closed his eyes and forced down his rising ire. She was right. His interference ran the risk of undermining her authority, something he couldn't do. "I'll agree—for now. Be certain I'll be asking about what transpires. If she makes a habit of insulting ye, I'll step in. I swore to protect ye. I keep my word."

Katja relaxed ever so slightly, lowering her weight back to her heels, still bearing the countenance of a warrior queen. Her gray eyes sparked.

"I can handle that bovine bawd. However, if she insults me again, ye might not recognize her the next time ye see her."

Calder choked back laughter. Was his wife merely angry at Lorna's insult, or did he also detect a wee bit of jealousy?

"Handle her as ye see fit, short of maiming or killing her. Would ye like to continue the tour?" He offered his arm and a smile, believing the breach between them no longer loomed as a gaping chasm.

She exhaled and placed her hand on his offered arm as if she still didn't trust him. He frowned at her reticence. It was then it hit him.

It was not simply *him*. She dinnae trust *men*.

Other than two of her brothers and Ranald, every time he'd seen her around men she appeared uneasy. From her embarrassment when he and his men stood as she entered her father's hall, to the way Robbie caught her off guard with his gallant attentions before supper, the few times he'd seen her, she'd always seemed ill at ease around men.

Considering how her father mistreated her, it was no mystery.

Now he, as her husband, would get to pay for her bastard father's sins. With as much as his clan gained from their union, offering patience whilst he earned her trust seemed a small price to pay.

Their tour ended on the fourth floor. Pushing open the door with an ornately carved lintel, Calder held the lantern aloft so she could see inside. A large semicircular room beckoned with large padded chairs and table in the center. This room contained the finest furnishings in all of Fairetur. They spoke of a more prosperous time, before the feud. Calder noticed Katja's gaze slowly take in the details and her lips curved upward ever so slightly.

"'Tis verra fine. What is this room?"

"'Tis the Lady's solar. 'Tis yer room, wife."

She turned to him, her expression softening further. A flash of disbelief appeared in her eyes before she walked to the padded window seat.

"The windows face south giving ye as much light and warmth as the day offers. My sister and grandmam use it from time to time, but mostly it sits empty."

As she made a slow circuit around the room, her hand touched every item within. The chairs, tables, large trunks, loom—nothing escaped her delicate perusal.

"I've never had a chamber like this before. 'Tis lovely. Thank ye."

Calder's face eased into a warm acceptance of her gratitude. It came as no surprise to hear she didn't have a place of comfort after seeing the meager space she lived in before. He escorted her to the bedchamber she occupied on the third floor. Standing by the door, she averted her gaze, her unease clear.

"I've never had an unwilling lass and I willnae start with my wife. Yer rightful place is in my bed, in my arms, Katja. I understand ye need time to adjust—though I dinnae like it. If ye leave me waiting over-long, I'll be forced to make a midnight raid one floor away and steal me a bonny Sinclair lass."

He tried for a light, teasing tone, but his hunger for her betrayed him. Before she could turn away, he swooped down and claimed a kiss. She shrank back, stiff against his lips, clearly still rattled by the day's events. But Calder followed her with his mouth, not binding her to him in any other way. As he deepened their kiss, his desire ignited her hunger, and her hands snaked around his neck, holding him to her. He encircled her shoulders with one arm while his other cupped the soft flesh of her bottom, pressing her against the erection begging to be quenched within her warmth.

To his surprise, she returned his hungry kisses with fervor. Without breaking contact, he pushed the door open and pulled her inside, kicking the door closed behind them. His mouth then left hers to nibble and kiss the tender flesh of her neck. With every gentle bite he extracted a moan or sigh. Each passionate sound she made stoked his lust hotter and higher. He lightly kissed her abused cheek and eye.

Removing his arm from about her shoulders, he cupped her breasts, teasing the delicious nipples hidden beneath the woolen gown. The smell of lavender and the scent intensely hers, teased his nose.

Her hands tugged impatiently at his shirt and belt, a sound of frustration as she struggled with his clothes. He smiled and raised his arms, allowing her to remove his leine and toss it aside. Satisfaction grew knowing he'd inspired a passion in her as ravenous as his own. Her fingertips touched his bare chest and he almost heard the sizzle from the heat of her hands on his skin.

They both startled as Freki's wet nose nuzzled her hand then his, making certain all was well. Katja's hand left Calder's chest long enough to assure the beast her husband's embrace was welcome.

Freki appeased, Katja returned her attention to her husband, mirroring Calder's actions, nipping and kissing at his neck, her breath rapid and shallow. Groaning at her ardent response, he moved his hand from her bottom and plucked the laces of her gown. Loosening her garment, he shoved it aside, their fevered touches growing more frantic. He lifted the hem of her chemise and placed his hand upon the satiny skin of her leg.

"Oh, Calder." Her voice a husky whisper.

"Aye, love."

His hand crept up her thigh, stroking and teasing, unfastening the sheath at her calf. Her knees buckled once, threatening to give way. Sweeping her into his arms, he carried her to a chair in front of the hearth. The cherried embers cast an alluring glow, enhancing the rosy flush tinting her ivory skin. As he set her down, he removed her chemise, leaving her gloriously bare before him.

A certainty beyond understanding settled within him that he would never desire another as he did this woman. He smiled at her gasp of shock as his fingers found their goal. Gently, he resumed his stroking, delighting as she relaxed, giving him her trust.

"Calder, what are ye doing?" Her lips formed a delicate *O*.

"I am proving my worth as yer husband, my noble Viking." He nuzzled her neck, drifting lower, tickling her belly with his short beard.

"You mustn't—"

A moan cut off the rest of her response as Calder stroked the nub nestled between her folds. The scent of her arousal filled his senses, spurring him on. Katja's breaths shortened, a thin cry spilled from her lips.

Calder leaned back to admire his handiwork. His beautiful Katja lay draped over the chair like a replete feline. Gathering her in his arms, he placed her on the rug in front of the hearth. He lay beside her, slowly stroking from her breasts to the top of her thighs. Her eyes flickered open, and her hand settled over his heart, tangling with the hair on his chest.

"Mmm. No doubt the kirk would call that sin."

He smiled at the sleepy quality of her voice. "No doubt, if we bothered to ask. However, what happens between a husband and wife in their bedchamber isnae the kirk's business." He leaned down, pressing the softest of kisses on her lips. She immediately opened her mouth, taking control in a lazy fashion. With a sinuous move, she rubbed her chest and hips against his, deepening their kiss.

"Ride me Katja," He whispered in her ear.

A smile rested on her lips as she considered his request. Placing her hands on his chest, her light touch pushed him to his back on the furs. She rose above him and straddled his hips, sinking gradually until she sheathed him fully.

Placing both hands on his chest, she moved against him, her hair cascading over his torso. What started as an unhurried pace climbed to a furious rhythm. He forced himself to hold out for her, biting his lip against the storm threatening to be unleashed. Wide-eyed, she convulsed around him.

He exploded, the most powerful release he'd ever known. Depleted, he slumped against the rug, Katja atop his chest, her body quivering. He wrapped his arms around her, intending to never let go.

Sweet Mary, she almost killed me!

His fierce Viking, his passionate lover, his wounded wife, all three bound together in a form that set him aflame with one glance. He sent up a silent prayer of thanks for the complicated woman enfolded within his arms. As he listened to their labored breathing and the pounding of their hearts, he pondered how long he could hold her before she regretted their actions and withdrew.

He caressed her from her shoulder to the curve of her hip in a continuous path, hoping his lingering attentions demonstrated his interests in her went well beyond simply slaking his lust. Her breathing slowed to normal and she grew still. He wondered if her serene state was due to him still buried inside her, his gentle touches, or the firm grip he had about her with his other arm. Perhaps all three. He couldn't bear to leave her body, lose her warmth, or stop touching the velvet of her skin.

Calder whispered in her hair. "I dinnae want to let ye go."

"I must rise early for the hunt," was her sleepy reply.

"Aye, and I have crofts to repair."

Eventually, Calder rolled Katja to his side, stood and picked her up. Carrying her to the bed, he pulled the coverings back and settled her on the sheets. He collected her chemise and she swiftly put it on, covering her nakedness. He tucked the blankets around her and placed a gentle kiss on her lips.

"Sleep well, milady."

She nodded, a number of emotions he couldn't read flashing across her face. Calder banked the fire, dressed and departed, deeply sated but unsatisfied.

Chapter Nine

Katja awoke later than she intended the next morning. The first traces of dawn spilled through the cracks in the worn wooden shutters—those same shutters letting in the curst cold air occupying her room. Gathering her courage, she rose from the comfort of the bed and the large beast keeping her warm. Slipping on trews, tunic, boots and her leather jerkin, she washed her face, gathered her weapons, and headed down the stairs, Freki at her heels.

Stepping outside, she spotted Robbie with their horses already saddled, along with a third as requested. A waterskin and small bag hung from her saddle. Early morning rays slipped from behind the trees and she blinked, nearly missing the apple Robbie tossed her way. She bit into the fruit and the sweet juice trickled down her chin.

She saluted Robbie with the half-eaten apple. "My thanks. Forgive my lateness."

"Not to worry, dear sister. Calder warned me ye might sleep in a wee bit this morn." The teasing tone of his voice matched the twinkle in his eye.

A flush of heat crept up her neck. Turning away in a flurry of embarrassment, she mounted Skündi, motioning Freki alongside, and waited for Robbie's instructions.

Robbie swung aboard his own horse. "I thought we might seek out a red deer or two. Grouse are plentiful this time of year. If we have enough time, we might stop by the river and see if we cannae coax a few salmon out of the water."

"Coax them out of the water?"

"Beguile, entice, bewitch them. If that doesnae work, we will use this weir." Robbie winked and pointed to a contraption of long stakes and woven netting lashed to the back of his horse.

"Ye're a rogue, Robbie MacGerry." Teasing from a man who was not her brother left her flustered. She sighed. *I'd best get used to it. It seems to be their favorite pastime.*

Robbie reminded her of her brother Patrik. Though Robbie was older than she, he was even more at ease and playful than her younger brother. It was another reminder of how little mirth existed behind the walls of Ruadhcreag.

* * *

Several hours later, Robbie's voice jarred her from deep thought. "Katja, are ye listening?"

She pulled herself abruptly back to the present, noting an expression of concern on Robbie's face. "Sorry. My attention was on finding more game."

A raised eyebrow and sly smile told her he didn't believe a word.

"I think we did well enough for one day, with just the two of us and yon wee beastie."

Glancing over her shoulder at their packhorse, she agreed they did very well indeed. With a deer across the back of each horse, four braces of hares, several grouse, a score of salmon and trout, she silently gave thanks they lived up to her boast at supper the night before. Katja found it admirable they'd accomplished so much, considering how distracted she'd been.

All day, her mind rolled over the words and actions of the previous night. She'd berated herself more times than she could count for falling so easily into Calder's arms. Her skin heated and her breasts tingled once again as she thought about the liberties she allowed him.

Allowed him? I all but begged him.

Waking to reach for him twice in her sleep last night, Katja knew she was no better than the shameless slut he kept around to meet his needs. A simple kiss from him fevered her unlike anything she'd encountered. After he broke through her meager resistance, he could have done unspeakable things to her and she would have welcomed it. Heat rolled through her belly. He *did* do unspeakable things, and she enjoyed them far too much. What's worse, her treasonous body yearned for more.

"He's a fine man and will make ye a good husband and father to yer bairns."

Robbie's rumbling voice shook her loose from her self-flagellation. She hadn't noticed he'd drawn closer.

"I know." She'd understood this the first time they joined. However, he was still a man, and she knew better than many, men allowed their coarse instincts to rule them. She hated herself because it seemed she carried her mother's curse of falling too easily for a man who could not care as deeply.

"Must be a big change becoming married and taking up residence in the heart of enemy territory."

Katja recognized Robbie's playful tone. "Aye." She cut him a quick glance, then kneed Skündi to a faster pace.

As they topped the next hill, the village came into view.

"I say we ride past the croft where Calder works to show off our bounty. 'Twill put him in his place after last night's comments about yer skills." Robbie clearly could not miss the opportunity to provoke his older brother.

"Nae. We dinnae have enough sun left for such foolishness," Katja insisted. "The deer need to be skinned and dressed whilst daylight remains."

Robbie's shoulders rose in an exaggerated sigh, though the mirth on his face betrayed his feigned disappointment.

They entered the kitchen through the back door, putting the surprised workers into a flurry of motion with their haul. Making a quick trip to her room, Katja changed into one of the sturdy woolen kirtles she wore when working. Returning to the kitchen, she grabbed a knife and set upon gutting and deboning the fish. The kitchen staff watched her in astonishment. At Katja's silent questioning stare, the workers busied themselves with their tasks.

With quick motions that bespoke years of experience, she cleaned and tossed the fish into a bucket of brine. While others worked on the grouse and deer, she moved to skin and dress the hares, careful of the hides, knowing the pelts would provide welcome warmth and softness for the bairns once the weather turned.

"Do ye have a smoking bothy?" Katja glanced at the woman introduced to her as Cook. A short, stout woman of indeterminate age, she kept the rest of the women occupied in a kind but firm manner.

"Aye. Just beyond the well, milady."

"Please have someone start the fire. These fish should be ready to hang once the coals are ready."

Cook dipped her head, an expression of satisfaction upon her face. "Yes, milady. Do ye think the laird would enjoy a black pudding?" She looked at Katja expectantly.

"Aye, I do. Let's salt and smoke all but one deer. Roast the stag tonight, and what's not eaten can be used for stew over the next few days."

A grin graced Cook's face. "'Tis a fine plan, milady. And 'tis good to have a mistress again. The laird's mother was a fine lady, but she dinnae know her way about a kitchen like ye do."

Twin layers of yellow and lavender wove together around the older woman, bearing the happy truth of her words, and Katja recognized her first true ally apart from the immediate family she'd married into. Tears formed in the back of her eyes and a burning sensation crept up her throat. Simple appreciation should not move her so, but it did. She nodded, ducked her head ,and continued to prepare the game in front of her.

Hours later, Katja surveyed the evening meal preparation with satisfaction. She'd intentionally ignored red-haired Lorna all afternoon, allowing Cook to direct her tasks. Truly, as long as Calder's relationship with her remained in the past, it didn't bother her, though she did wonder why her husband seemed to find her desirable after having the fulsome woman in his bed.

Her efforts to avoid Calder's former leman did not prove fruitful. Carrying a large platter of roasted venison to the great hall, Lorna bumped into Katja, spilling some of the hot grease onto her arm. Katja hissed with pain.

Lorna ducked her head. "Pardon, milady. The tray is heavy."

Though her words carried an air of innocence, muddy red and dark green auras of anger and resentment told otherwise. Katja nodded and walked to the other side of the kitchen where a bucket of fresh water sat. After cleaning her gown and arm as best she could, she applied a burn salve to the site and awaited the woman's return.

Lorna entered the kitchen, brushing carelessly past Katja. Snatching the end of the woman's braid, Katja wrapped it in her hand twice and jerked Lorna around until they stood face to face.

"I dinnae care if ye rutted my husband blind before I came here," Katja growled. "However, ye will have nothing to do with him from here on. And if ye so much as touch me again, I will beat ye myself until yer own mother willnae know ye."

Releasing the braid, Katja pushed the larger woman away.

Lorna's startled expression twisted to rage, her hands clenched at her sides. "Calder will tire of ye soon enough if the bruise on yer face is any sign. Ye are naught but skin and bones. He will seek me again once he gets an heir on ye and no longer needs to soil himself with a Sinclair *siursach*!"

Katja curled her fist and stepped into a punch the way Ranald had taught her, connecting with the side of Lorna's jaw and sending the hateful hag to the floor in a graceless heap. Cook took a step and nudged the inert body with a booted foot.

"Dinnae fash, milady," she said. "I will have this one scrubbing privies, feeding hogs, and cleaning chimneys until she learns respect."

Cook scanned the shocked faces of the other women, hands firmly planted on her broad hips. "If I hear another word against our mistress, ye can expect the same treatment, except I'll be usin' a rod instead of me fist."

She gave Katja a nod then barked her orders to the staff. "Get back to work. The meal willnae serve itself."

Katja shook out the pain in her hand, a surge of confidence overshadowing the memory of her sire's wrath should she dare stand up for herself.

Mother of God that hurt! But it felt so good.

With no time to change clothes before the meal, she wore the kirtle stained from the afternoon's work and Lorna's attack. Perhaps arriving to supper wearing evidence of the day's labor would show the MacGerrys their new mistress wasn't one who demanded pampering or avoided hard work.

The men rose to their feet as she entered the hall. Katja came to an abrupt halt, her new-found confidence fleeing in the face of all the attention. Calder took her hand and settled her into the seat beside him.

"Robbie gave us an account of the hunt today. It seems Ranald dinnae exaggerate yer abilities."

Katja allowed her lips to creep upward ever so slightly at his praise. She glanced at Robbie who winked at her, a grin on his face.

"She's as accurate with that bow of hers as any I've seen. The only advantage in my favor was distance. I killed a doe, but 'twas Katja who felled the mighty stag lying before ye, with a wee bit of assistance from her four-legged hunter. She staggered him with a neck shot, and the beastie did the rest. I swear I've never seen a hart go down so hard. Freki caught most of the hares, too."

Everyone in the room stared at her. The compliments and scrutiny made her throat close, while something akin to fear shivered up her spine. She couldn't catch her breath and winced at the stabbing pain in her chest. An overwhelming urge to flee the hall seized her.

Calder pressed a cup of wine into her hand. "Drink this," he murmured.

She took a long drink and concentrated on steadying her breath, eyes down, avoiding the stares of those around her. A moment later, whatever had gripped her faded.

She glanced up to see Calder's assessing look, his lips carved into a scowl. For some reason, it entered her head that a frown didn't belong on such a handsome face, and foolishly wished she knew how to make him smile.

"Are ye ill?" Concern deepened the pitch of his voice.

Katja drew another deep breath, clearing away the remainder of her panic. "Nae, whatever it was has passed."

She continued to watch him from beneath her lashes. Though easing a bit, the remnants of a frown marred his features as he placed food on her plate and motioned for a servant to refill her cup.

Another drink and calming breath seemed to pacify him.

"I know ye are still settling, but Finn and I need to meet with a small clan just north of yer dower lands before winter sets in. We'll be offering a manrent bond to the MacCairn clan. Thanks to ye, we have the land and supplies for this. Now we need the people."

She nodded agreement. "Did I hear another group will join us?"

"Aye. The MacFies. They're a poor clan who recently lost their laird to fever. The man had no known heir. Their clan's holding is small and there's a question of where the leadership will fall. Some decided to move on, and a few have ties here through marriage. As ye have seen, we dinnae have enough men to tend the fields and keep up with work around the castle."

Not wanting to insult the condition of his home, she said nothing in response.

"A wagon with supplies from yer father should arrive in the next few days," Calder continued. "The rest of yer possessions will be in the wagon."

Katja thought of the rest of her clothing and the handful of books she owned. Other than two pieces of jewelry her mother brought into her marriage, she possessed nothing else. Even those now belonged to her husband.

"Robbie and Beitris will look after ye. Let them know if ye need anything. We should only be away a few days."

He leaned close until his leg touched hers and whispered into her ear. "I'd hoped to spend more time proving my worth as yer husband. With winter creeping on, I'll soon have plenty of time to show ye all the ways we can bring each other pleasure."

The images of last night's love play rose in her mind, threatening to steal her wits. Katja's breathing hitched and warmth pooled low in her belly. Before she gave in to the desire to throw her arms around him and demand he take her upstairs and show her what he meant, she leapt from her seat.

"I'll see to it Cook has plenty of food and drink ready for yer journey, husband."

Without giving him an opportunity to respond, she darted to the kitchen as though to outrun the red aura of lust she knew arced about her—if she only stopped a moment to *see*.

* * *

Calder spent the next morning in the saddle, musing over what had happened to Katja the night before. Her hasty retreat under the guise of arranging supplies for their departure was easy enough to see through. As though caught in the grip of an unseen phantom, she'd bolted for the kitchen. He'd seen a similar look of fear on the faces of untried lads on the eve of their first battle.

"What's put a scowl on yer face this morn, Laird? 'Tis not our meetin' with the MacCairn." Finn spoke quietly enough the other two men with them couldn't hear his question.

Calder grunted his response.

Undaunted, Finn dug in. "A man with a face like that is fashed aboot a lass."

Calder shot him a look of frustration. "What else, Uncle?"

"Ach, I noticed yer bride seemed a wee bit nervous last night. D'ye know why?"

"Nae. 'Tis part of the problem. She turned pale as a specter and stopped breathing for a moment. I wondered if she'd seen a *bean sith*."

"She seemed well enough until the people's attention turned to her."

Calder startled at the observation. "Ye think that is the problem?"

"I do. She's usually calm till a few pairs of eyes light her way. I'm thinkin' she isnae used to the notice."

Calder let the information settle. It fit with the rest of what he knew, her distrust of men, her discomfort over casual touch. Now he could add distress due to attention from a crowd. Distress? Hell, what he'd witnessed was nothing short of terror. He'd almost smelled the fear rolling off her. She'd run a holding more than twice the size of Fairetur. Would she not have been around greater numbers than his hall could boast?

He recalled how she appeared unremarked in her father's hall when they arrived, and her reaction to the MacGerrys' show of respect. It was obvious she wasn't accustomed to such attention. He rubbed the rough cross around his neck and wondered how the devil he could aid her in this. As the clan's new mistress, she'd be the object of constant observation and gossip.

Not for the first time since becoming laird, he wished he could seek his father's advice. The mysteries his wife presented made it doubly true. Other than seeing to her care and protection, he didn't know the first thing about keeping a wife. Well, other than the time they spent in the bedchamber. For all he knew, she could be carrying his bairn. *Saints blood*! He'd not yet gotten used to the idea of being a husband. The thought of becoming a da scared him witless.

"Easy, Armunn," He murmured, relaxing his posture. He'd unknowingly tightened the reins, causing his horse to dance at his rough handling. The beast settled and Calder turned to his uncle.

"How did ye handle Aunt Noreen when she did something to nettle ye?"

Finn frowned and tugged an ear. "My Noreen was a sensible lass. Anytime she dinnae like somethin' I did or said, she'd let me know swiftly. There was no lettin' things lie aboot to fester. However, she was raised in a loving home by good, God-fearin' folk. There's no tellin' what yer wife endured all these years."

Calder swore under his breath. "If the bruise adorning her face is any clue, she had a tormentor rather than a father."

Silence hung thick as the patches of fog covering the low ground.

Finn shifted in his saddle. "Recall the mare auld Angus found wandrin' on his land?"

"Aye."

"She'd suffered somethin' terrible from abuse and starvation. D'ye remember how we turned her 'round?'

"Da asked me to feed her by hand everyday whilst I offered soft words and strokes. After a bit, he introduced others to her care, but made sure I spent a few minutes with her each day."

"She soon settled behind the plow like she was born to it. I'm of a mind yer bride needs the same care old Belle did."

"Ye think simply seeing to her needs, offering kind words and gentle touches will be enough? I believe a woman is a wee bit more complicated than a plough horse, Uncle." Somehow the saying sounded easier than the doing.

"Aye, unless ye have a better plan." Finn chuckled, drawing the attention of the other two men.

Not wanting to make a fool of himself in front of the men, Calder spurred his horse on, ignoring Finn's shout of laughter.

***

Katja met Beitris and Torri in the great hall for the morning meal. Serving women brought bowls of oat porridge and a pitcher of cider. The smells of steaming oats and autumn mingled in the hall. They eagerly tucked in. Katja frowned at the bitter taste of her porridge and wished for honey to mask what seemed to be perhaps a bit of moldy oats. She mentally added a thorough cleansing of the larder to her list of things to accomplish soon.

"What are yer plans today, Katja?" Beitris inquired.

Katja glanced up, distracted from her meal. "I'm to meet Robbie in the laird's solar this morn. He's to show me the results of this year's harvest and how Fairetur is run."

Katja placed a hand over her stomach as it gave a queasy gurgle. Something wasn't right. She waited for what little she'd swallowed to settle before eating more. Unfortunately, her morning porridge had no intention of abiding peacefully.

"What's amiss?" Torri placed a hand on Katja's arm, her brow furrowed.

Katja rose from the table, one hand covering her mouth and bolted for the door. Barely making it outside, she turned a corner where she was partially concealed, bent over and heaved, emptying the contents of her stomach. An intense burning sensation spread as her body purged itself of whatever she'd consumed. Freki nudged her shoulder and whimpered.

After another bout of retching and a few coughs, the sickness passed, leaving behind only a fiery tingle dancing along her skin.

"I'm fine, laddie." Her words were meant to comfort them both, though she wasn't sure it was the truth. It was no ordinary sickness producing the lingering sensations. Luckily, the cramping receded before Torri's voice grew near.

"Katja. Are ye well?" The girl's voice carried a note of distress.

Katja wiped the sweat from her face. "I think I will be. Do you feel ill?" She prayed whoever poisoned her food didn't target all three of them.

Torri gazed at her a moment, shaking her head before understanding dawned. "Someone tainted yer food!" she exclaimed, placing a hand over her mouth, eyes wide with dismay.

"Beitris." Katja cried softly, scarcely able to find her voice at the thought of the Torri's grandmam also a victim.

Torri's look of dismay turned to one of panic. She and Katja raced into the hall to find the older woman inspecting Katja's bowl, an intense expression on her wrinkled face. Beitris waved them over.

"Someone put wolfsbane in yer porridge, milady." Her voice was low enough only the three of them heard. Immediately, their eyes turned toward the kitchen where a flash of dark hair disappeared through the door.

"Did ye empty yer gullet?" Beitris asked anxiously.

Katja nodded, fair certain no poison lingered, but she needed to be careful how she proceeded. Fatigue seeped into her, urging her to seek her bed.

"Aye, there is naught left. However, I dinnae feel well. I need to lie down a wee while."

Beitris reached for Katja's forehead. The old woman's hand felt remarkably cool and she frowned as she touched Katja's heated skin. "I'll mix a purgative then have Cook meet us in yer chamber. She needs to know what happened and say who has been in her kitchen this morn. Until we discover who did this foul deed, we'll see all yer food is tasted before 'tis served."

Katja rose from the table. "Please tell Robbie what happened. I will apologize later for missing our appointment."

"Let me see ye upstairs." Torri put an arm around Katja and escorted her up the stairs to her door. Even though only fatigued, Katja allowed the girl to coddle her, reminded of Morag's nurturing manner.

"Go and speak to Robbie. He'll want to know of this morn's events." Leaning against her door, Katja patted the girl's shoulder reassuringly.

Torri narrowed her gaze. "Will ye be well if I leave?"

"Aye. I promise to crawl into bed and wait for ye to return."

Nodding, Torri slipped down the stairs, purpose in her step.

Katja entered her small chamber and placed a brick of peat on the dying embers. Stoking the coals, she slipped out of her gown and slid beneath the coverlet, placing a dirk under her pillow. Freki joined her on the musty old mattress. Someone had taken advantage of her husband's absence to poison her. The thought should frighten her into wakeful vigilance. However, her body had other ideas. Closing her leaden eyelids, she gave in to sleep.

When she woke, Beitris sat in a chair next to the bed, her white head bent over a partially embroidered square of cloth, eyes closed, jaw slack. Katja smiled, remembering her own *amma*. She'd watched over Katja whenever she fell ill, and often dozed while doing so. Beitris's quick acceptance of her into the family melted her heart. She'd already found more warmth here in two days than she had the past several years in her own home.

A foul smell wafted in the air and Katja wrinkled her nose. She spied a mug on the small table next to the older woman, its contents the likely source of the odd odor in the room.

"Ye are awake, then?" Beitris stirred and appraised her with blue eyes which seemed to miss very little.

"How long did I sleep?"

Beitris clucked her tongue. "D'ye mean, how long did *we* sleep?" She rose and opened a wooden shutter. "By the looks of the sun, mayhap a couple of hours, nae more. How d'ye fare?"

Apprehension skittered along Katja's spine. "Much better. Still a bit weak and tired, but better. It seems the wolfsbane dinnae have time to work its evil."

Beitris's brow wrinkled further. "Aye. Ye purged the poison before it could take root and do real damage. Yer body must have recognized it right off. 'Tis lucky, that." She reached for the mug. "I'll feel better once ye've sipped this. 'Twill cleanse any remaining poison from ye."

Katja accepted the mug with reluctance. Swirling the contents renewed the odor filling the chamber. Katja scrunched her nose, placed the mug to her lips and tipped the pottery cup, sending the foul brew down her throat with a grimace.

Beitris cackled. "Aye, 'tis a nasty brew, but most good ones are. This one will have ye runnin' to the privy the next few hours. 'Tis a small price to pay."

"My thanks." Katja's response was only half-hearted, causing another chortle from her self-appointed nurse.

A gentle knock sounded as Torri opened the door and stepped inside the room. Concern wrinkled her brow as she hurried to Katja's side.

"Are ye better, then?" Worried eyes searched Katja's face.

Katja smiled, nodded, then rose from the bed, allowing Torri to help her dress. Another knock a few minutes later prompted the girl to open the door. Robbie stood in the doorway, his face hard, arms crossed over his chest. His assessing look, more intense than his grandmother's, missed nothing.

"If ye dinnae wish to go over the books this morn, all ye had to do was say so. Nae need to go to such lengths to avoid me." A wary smile flickered across his face, though Katja recognized he hid behind the scold, softening the seriousness of the matter.

Robbie stepped inside the room, closing the door behind him. "Torri interrupted my morning, spinning some fanciful tale. I'd hear it from the two of ye, if ye please."

Katja quickly recounted the morning's events.

Robbie's eyes narrowed on Beitris. "Yer certain 'twas wolfsbane?"

"Aye. There's nae mistakin' the taste."

Robbie's expression hardened. "Saint's bones! We've a murderer on our hands." Jerking open the door, he stepped into the hall and gave a sharp order to a man standing outside.

"Lady MacGerry, as clan *tanist*, ye are my responsibility in the laird's absence. Please take yer rest and recover from this foul ordeal and trust me to meet with Cook. I will find the fiend responsible for trying to relieve my dear brother of the best thing ever to happen to his blighted life. We can resume our discussion of the sorry state of our holdings when yer feelin' better. I've posted a guard outside yer door. No one comes in without permission and should ye feel up to joining us later, he will keep an eye on you should the craven vermin try again."

She nodded at Robbie and again experienced the oddly sweet sensation of having a champion. She shifted her gaze over the puzzling conflict of yellow joy she associated with Robbie's lively personality and streaks of purple, a certain sign of guilt. How could he be both? Was he happy the attempt on her life failed? Or shamed to have not found success?

Chapter Ten

As Beitris predicted, Katja spent the rest of the afternoon and early evening dashing to the privy, as the old woman's draught did a thorough job of clearing out her bowels. By the time the cursed remedy ran its course, she was too tired to go down for supper, nor did she wish anything to pass her lips for fear of it not lingering. Instead she sipped watered wine until sleep claimed her.

"At least yer color has returned." Robbie gave Katja an approving nod the next morning as he opened the holding's books on the worn desk in the laird's solar. Pale lavender of truth tinted the edges of his normal yellow aura, reassuring her.

"Cook says she has no idea who put poison in yer porridge. With as many as have been in and out of the kitchen, almost anyone could have accomplished the task. Anyone but Lorna. Cook assures me the woman dinnae step a foot in the kitchen, as she cleaned privies all day. The old dragon has taken this attack on our new mistress personally and assures me nothing will be served to ye that doesnae pass her lips first."

Katja thought to protest, but Robbie's stern expression halted any objections. She simply curtsied her thanks and acceptance, and turned her attention to the ledger books spread before them. The numbers scrawled on the pages took a bit to understand. Whoever made the most recent entries possessed a heavy hand with a quill.

"As ye see, our stores willnae last us through till the early harvests." Robbie raised a brow at Katja.

She understood his implied message. "Aye. My husband had no other choice but to agree to the earl's terms."

"Calder told me the details of yer marriage contract. I know my brother. He'd have never agreed to the sudden events if many lives werenae at risk."

Katja dropped her gaze. "I know. My sire used clan MacGerry's dire situation to force Calder into aiding him in a last humiliation of me." Her voice barely rose above a whisper.

Robbie tilted his head, his look intense. "Why would yer da do such thing? Calder dinnae say. He only said he wished to get ye away from Ruadhcreag as quickly as he could."

Katja avoided a direct answer with a shake of her head, hoping neither Calder nor Robbie would push for the reasons her sire displayed hatred toward her. "One thing is certain. Ye desperately need the gold my tocher provides. If Calder's trip is successful, the spring planting should greatly improve."

"Aye. The question is, how many of us will survive to see the end of winter?"

Katja met Robbie's gaze and realized living well-fed under the thumb of a tyrant seemed a better fate to some than starving to death surrounded by love.

* * *

True to his word, the earl sent two wagons full of supplies, along with a fair number of sheep. Barrels of foodstuffs and sacks of grain dwarfed Katja's small chest of belongings. Christer led the men who accompanied the rest of her tocher—a welcome surprise.

Her brother released her from a crushing embrace and tilted his head to take her measure, his glaze lingering momentarily on her bruised eye. "How do ye fare, sister?"

"'Tis been only four days. How different could I be?" She kept her voice steady, not willing to give much of her recent experiences away.

Christer grinned. "Ach, yer a new bride and mistress of the clan we feuded with for nigh on a hundred years. What could possibly be amiss?"

His humor pulled a reluctant smile from her. She shoved aside thoughts of her humiliation during their wedding and Lorna's public insults, along with the memory of her poisoned porridge. Her marriage with Calder helped forge a fragile peace between their clans. She'd not be responsible for seeing the alliance broken.

"I'm well, in truth. Some MacGerrys have been quite welcoming. My husband says the rest will come 'round with time." She stood her ground, refusing to wilt beneath her brother's piercing gaze.

"Yer eye 'tis a lovely shade of green and purple, though mayhap not yer best look. I wish ye had heeded my advice with Father." He shook his head and sighed. "I suspect ye are safe here, but ye will send word if things turn sour?" His tone sounded more like a command than question.

Katja tipped her chin. "Peace after three generations of bloodshed is worth whatever biting words or harsh looks I might encounter."

Christer shook his head. "I still dinnae like it. Yer laird and husband isnae here to give an account."

"As I told ye, my husband is away meeting with another clan to arrange for more hands to work the fields. Winter shows signs of early arrival, with only so many days before the snows halt any work outside."

"Aye, the manrent agreement. Yer brother by marriage mentioned it." Christer nodded toward Robbie who assisted in unloading the last of the supplies.

Robbie approached them, his arm extended to Christer. "Yer

sure ye willnae stay the night and depart on the morrow? Ye and yer men are welcome."

"Thank ye for the offer, but the earl was quite clear he dinnae want to test our new accord by our entering the keep or eating from the goods provided. I promise to take advantage of MacGerry hospitality once the snows melt."

The sight of Sinclair and MacGerry men warily working together firmed Katja's determination to make her marriage work.

The unloading was quickly accomplished and the Sinclair men prepared to leave. Her parting with Christer contained none of the sting of the last. She now knew her place, and though not all accepted her, Katja held the regard of the laird and his family. It would be enough.

Seeing the empty wagons amble down the road toward Ruadhcreag and her few possessions taken into the keep put a stamp of finality on her circumstances.

"Come, sister, let us see the supplies into the keep then ye can log yer first entries into the books." Robbie's call snapped her out of her thoughts.

She added each precious item to the still too-short list of provisions in Fairetur's ledgers. Robbie turned the sheep and cattle over to a couple of old men and a handful of lads who, along with four dogs, introduced the new additions to the rest of their meager herd.

Supper was festive, occasioned by the arrival of much needed food and sheep. Katja was pleased to note the swirls of angry red auras, while still present, were fewer this eve. A surprising number of nods of respect and smiles were aimed her way. Though well short of Calder's prediction of a queue to kiss her hand, fewer angry glares were a welcome sign.

Calder had sent word they would remain another day or two

with the MacCairn. Resigned to sleeping with only Freki the next two nights, she and the dog climbed the stairs to the third floor. In truth, she missed Calder. She considered the notion of moving into his room. He was her husband now and she had resolved to make a good wife. With a smile, she recalled his claim she belonged in his bed.

With a stirring of happiness in her chest, Katja opened the door to her chamber. Freki growled low, his hackles raised in warning. He stalked toward the bed, a rumbling threat resonating in his chest. He bumped the foot of her mattress with his snout and something moved under the coverings. Snatching her sword from the corner of the room, she unsheathed the blade and used the tip to pull away the bedclothes, one layer at a time.

She flung the last of the sheets onto the floor, revealing twin adders coiled on her bed, their heads raised in a deadly pose. They hissed their displeasure, their thick brown bodies entwined, a black serrated pattern across the ridge of their backs. With a flick of her wrist, Katja beheaded the first before Freki could lunge.

"*Halda*!" Freki froze at her command, though he growled menacingly at the remaining viper. With another snap of her wrist, she sliced the second snake in half, shuddering in revulsion as it writhed on the bed. She used the blade to fling them across the room in front of the hearth where they continued their death throes.

A tremor echoed through her as she considered what this meant. First, poison in her food, then venomous snakes in her bed. Regardless of what Calder thought, at least one in the clan considered the Sinclair's daughter a poor choice of wife for their laird. This villain apparently viewed her death as payment for her sire's sins against the MacGerry.

Even with the serpents dead, Katja was unable to climb into her bed where the twain had coiled. Instead, she sat in the chair by the fire, blankets pulled tight about her. She watched the adders with morbid curiosity as life ebbed from their wriggling bodies. Loathing shuddered through her at the sight, though she couldn't turn away. Robbie must be informed, but she knew he would set a guard on her and see her chamber watched. It was one thing to be loathed by her father, but it was another to have someone want her dead badly enough to make such brazen attempts.

What next? If the miscreant was bold enough to enact attempts on her life in the hall or her chamber, where could she be safe? She longed for Calder's return—but would his presence stop whoever was behind these attacks? Freki lay on the floor in front of the hearth, ears perked, eyes fixed on the door, as if he understood she remained in danger.

Katja woke with a start to a knock at her chamber door. Lines of morning sun streaked the floor. Freki growled softly.

"Easy, laddie." She placed a hand on Freki's head, comforting them both.

"Katja, are ye awake?"

Torri's voice carried through the wooden panel. Katja rose, covered the snakes, and unbarred the door. "Good morrow, Torri. I trust ye slept well."

The girl smiled and nodded, then frowned as she took in the state of the bed and the blankets draped over the chair by the hearth.

"What has happened?"

"'Tis best if ye fetched Robbie. I'd prefer to tell the tale only once if ye dinnae mind."

Torri's gaze swept the room again. "Aye, I will be right back. Robbie is in the hall breaking his fast."

Katja waited until Torri's dark head disappeared down the steps, then closed the door, settling the bar in place.

Footsteps in the corridor and Robbie's familiar voice prompted her to open the door. His gaze scanned the room then snapped to her.

"Good morn, Katja. My wee sister says ye have another tale for me. Looking at yer chamber, it should be a right entertaining one." His lighthearted words clashed with his hardened glare.

Katja drew away the hearth rug to reveal the cloven snakes.

Robbie's eyes widened then narrowed once more, a muttered curse describing an act she didn't think physically possible hissing past his teeth. Torri's fingernails dug into Katja's arm.

Squatting on his haunches, Robbie examined this latest threat. "I take it from the state of yer bed, ye found them beneath the coverings."

Katja nodded.

Robbie's jaw tightened as he stared at the lifeless bodies. He turned his gaze back to her. "Ye know I must place a guard on ye, aye? My brother will skin me alive should anything happen to ye whilst he is away. And I dare say yer brothers would soon be at our doorstep seeking revenge."

Katja ignored the mention of her brothers and not her sire. It was God's own truth her sire would not shed a tear over her death. As much as she hated the idea of a guard, she knew it was useless to argue.

Following Robbie's suggestion she spend time around those she knew, she spent the day in the kitchen making cider and vinegar from remnants of the fall apple crop. Freki lay on the floor by the back door, gnawing a leg bone from yester eve's stag.

In spite of the cool late autumn day, heat from the boiling cauldrons made the kitchen oppressively hot. Young Dugan had been assigned by Robbie to guard her this day, but instead, he watched one of the kitchen lasses. Both appeared to be nearing marrying age, mayhap ten and seven summers, and flirted with their eyes and smiles all morning. Katja thought it sweet, but Cook scolded Shea for not keeping up with her work.

Katja filled a tankard with barley water and walked to the door. "I need a wee breath of fresh air. Dugan, I will stay right outside the door and will yell if I need ye."

The lanky lad tore his infatuated gaze from the lovely young kitchen maid long enough to acknowledge Katja's words with a nod. She slipped outside, hiding her smile.

The breeze outside lifted the kerchief she wore, drying the sweat off her neck and face. Freki followed, his teeth clicking against the bone he carried. He plopped down, capturing the bone with his paws and continued to lick the end. She walked a bit, hands on her hips, stretching her lower back, which was tight and sore from bending over all day.

"Milady, milady!"

A man Katja didn't recognize rounded the corner and strode her way with a purpose. Freki rose to his feet and growled. The man slackened his stride, eyes fixed on the dog.

"*Fresta.*"

Freki halted obediently and sat, muscles taut, waiting for her command.

"Do I know ye?" Katja asked.

The man stopped several feet away, his hands spread in submission, his eyes darting between her and her companion. The aura of brown and dark blue surrounding him alerted her he was afraid to speak to her of the errand he'd been given.

The man shifted uneasily, eyes shifting from her face to the side and back. "Nae, milady. I be from the MacCairn clan. I was with the group ridin' back with yer husband when his mount threw 'im."

Katja's hand flew to her throat as she fought sudden fear.

"How badly is he hurt?"

"'Tis a nasty gash on his head. We fear he's dyin', milady. The laird asked fer ye. I was sent to fetch ye quick."

"Sweet Mother Mary! Let me run and tell his brother." She took a step toward the kitchen door.

The man reached as though to stop her, halted by a low growl from Freki. "Milady, we dinnae have time. The laird may pass afore we get there if we dinnae hurry."

Panic sliced through Katja at the urgency in the man's voice and the thought of Calder dying and her arriving too late. She crossed herself with a swiftly muttered prayer, then picked up her skirts and ran to the stables just as Titus walked Skündi out, saddled and ready to go, her bow and quiver of arrows slung across the horse's withers.

"MacCairn jes told me aboot the laird. Wee Jamie and me will be prayin' for a miracle."

Katja nodded absently to the stable master, too frightened to be distracted by speech. Hands and legs trembling, she mounted Skündi while MacCairn climbed aboard a sturdy pony. Freki pacing tirelessly at their heels, they followed a trail north and west for a few leagues before veering off the path. Topping a ridge, they made for a small vale on the other side. At the lea near a burn a mile or so further, MacCairn pulled up.

Katja looked about, puzzled. "I dinnae understand, where is my husband?"

Two men emerged from a small patch of woods, a crossbow in one's hands, a snarl of hatred on the face of the other. "Concluding his business with the MacCairn, I'd wager."

"Auld Liam?" Katja asked, cold disbelief clenching her insides.

Liam nudged his pony closer. "Aye, ye evil bitch. Ye wouldnae die from poison nor vipers, so I had to find a way to get ye from beneath Robbie's nose."

Her gorge rose, burning her throat, dismayed to realize he was the one who wished her dead. A hate-filled mix of dark red and grey swirled mist-like around Liam. The intensity of it nearly stole her breath.

With an effort, she found her voice. "Why do ye hate me so? Would ye hold me accountable for the sins of my sire?" Glancing about, she realized how remote their location, and how alone she was. It would be days before anyone found her remains. Freki whined anxiously and Katja quailed, knowing Liam's scheming meant her beloved dog's death, too.

Liam's eyes glittered. "Hate ye? Ye're a Sinclair, 'tis bad enough. The fact yer the daughter of the Sinclair laird makes ye the get of the devil hisself!"

Freki's whine roughened into a low growl. Auld Liam glanced at the beast, tugging on his pony's reins, pulling him back a step. "Kill her and that cursed beast," he barked at the man with the crossbow. "Then bury the bodies."

"Wot aboot a wee bit of fun afore?" the other man asked, his gaze crawling admiringly over Katja.

"I dinnae care. Sully yerselves with the wench if ye wish. Only be certain no one finds her when yer finished."

Auld Liam pointed his pony toward the ridge and trotted toward the MacGerry keep.

The two men leered at Katja. "Come now, darlin'. Let Rab have 'is way wi' ye easy-like, and I promise ye a swift end." The man beside her, now calling himself Rab, reached for her horse's reins. With a swiftness born of panic and the determination to thwart their plans, Katja drew the dagger hidden in her sleeve and slashed the man across the forearm. He jerked his arm to his chest, the sudden movement causing his pony to dance with agitation.

"Ye *buidseach*!" he spat. "Ye will bleed fer that!"

Katja's blood boiled. "Freki, *ganga at*!" She pointed at Auld

Liam who had turned toward the commotion.

With the sleek move of a predator on the hunt, Freki charged after Liam, hitting his full speed in two strides. The third man swung about, firing his crossbow at the wolfhound. He missed by a wide margin, the bolt buried in the hard ground several feet away.
Leaning low, Liam kicked his pony, urging him into a run. Covering the ground in great strides, Freki easily caught them with a massive leap, knocking the devil off his pony. Liam hit the ground hard, bringing up an arm to keep the dog at bay. He cried out as Freki's jaws clamped down on his arm.

"*Hirda!*"

Responding to Katja's command, Freki released Liam and stood atop him, snarling a warning. Drawing her attention back to the man at her side, Katja slipped the dagger from its sheath at her nape and hurled it at Rab, hitting him in the throat. He fell from his horse, writhing in agony, hands gripping futilely at the gaping wound in his neck. The other man dismounted his lunging pony and struggled to reload his crossbow. Katja snatched her bow from its sling and an arrow from her quiver. Standing in the stirrups, she nocked and drew back the arrow, training the tip on the scoundrel.

"Cease! Throw your weapon to the ground!"

The man ignored her command. He placed the end of the crossbow on the ground, stood in the weapon's stirrup, pulled back the string, and reached for a bolt. Without further warning, she let fly her arrow as the man raised his arbalest. Her shot pierced his chest, staggering him backward to the ground with a thud. Katja dismounted, nocked another arrow, and stalked to where the man lay, his hand clutching the feathered end of her ash shaft. His shallow breathing and slowing movements foretold his end. She picked up his crossbow and hurled it toward the burn. When she turned back, the man's body jerked once as he drew a last stuttering breath.

With both henchmen dead, Katja turned her attention to Auld Liam. Freki stood watch over him, though it seemed unnecessary, as Liam had yet to rise from his fall.

She motioned Freki away. "*Kvala.*"

Freki stepped over Liam and took his place at her side as she strode to where her tormentor lay, his eyes focused on the heavy grey clouds filling the sky. The sound of hoof beats caught her ear, and she again nocked an arrow, ready for whoever charged over the ridge. Robbie, followed by Dugan and two men whose faces she recognized, topped the hill and made their way to where she stood. Katja dropped her bow and knelt beside the old man. Robbie dismounted and joined her.

"What happened here?" Robbie demanded.

Katja bristled at his tone. "Auld Liam lured me away with a tale Calder had fallen from his horse and lay dying. He waited with another to murder and bury me where I couldnae be found."

Robbie grasped Liam's leine in both fists and shook him. "Why, auld man?"

Liam blinked twice. "Because she's Sinclair's spawn. I dinnae bury kith and kin the last three score years to see this Sinclair bitch placed as lady over my clan." Liam's words slurred as he spoke, his voice fading.

Robbie's fingers curled into Liam's shirt, lifting his torso from the ground, drawing the villain close. "I'll see ye hang for this," he swore.

Liam coughed once, a wracking sound. "Sorry to disappoint ye, laddie, but her *Cù Sìth* did the job for ye." His voice cracked.

Robbie rolled Liam to the side, exposing the back of his head. His grey hair matted against his skull, thick with blood. The sharp edge of a half-buried rock glistened red. Blood soaked the earth beneath him and his eyes glazed with imminent death. Liam's lips moved, but Katja heard no sound. He repeated the phrase, this time loud enough for her to hear.

"*Arte et marte.*"

"Odd, those should be his last words," Robbie said as he eased Liam back to the earth and closed his eyes with a slow sweep of his hand.

"What do they mean?" Katja asked.

"*By skill and valor.* 'Tis the MacGerry motto. How he found valor in this hateful deed, he can explain to his maker." He rose, wiping his palms slowly across his plaide. "Dugan, you and the lads see to his body. Wrap him in his plaide and lash him to his pony. We'll see him buried on MacGerry land."

"What about the other two?" Dugan asked.

Robbie spared the pair a glance. "I dinnae know them. Leave the miscreants for the carrion crows. Their sins this day dinnae make them deserving of a Christian burial."

The young men nodded and set to their work. Katja stared at the bodies stilled by death's embrace.

Three men slain, all by my hand.

Katja bent over and retched as the grisly reality of what had occurred settled upon her. Robbie's hands steadied her while her stomach discarded its contents, though not her guilt.

"Coo, now. 'Tis not yer fault. Ye are a brave lass for winning the day. Take a breath and tell me the whole of the tale."

Dugan handed her a skin of ale. She nodded her thanks, then rinsed the taste of bile before taking a long draught. Freki nuzzled her hand and lay beside her with a huff. Her voice shaky, Katja disclosed the events of the past hour, her hand winnowing Freki's ruff for comfort.

"How did ye find us?" she asked.

"Titus sent Jamie after me, then gave us yer direction," Robbie replied. "'Twasnae hard to follow yer trail, particularly after ye left the path." He settled a gentle hand on her shoulder. "Come. I'm not letting ye out of my sight until Calder returns. We'll take supper in the laird's solar as I consider the nasty business of rooting out Liam's accomplices."

Heartsore and weary, Katja pulled a piece of dried meat from her saddlebag and fed it to her guardian. "Where would I be without you, my braw laddie?" she crooned.

Freki all but inhaled the treat. He nosed his mistress, giving her hand an affectionate lick. Still shaky from the aftermath of battle, she mounted Skündi and fell in with the MacGerrys for the trip home, Freki trotting unconcernedly at her side.

Dugan avoided eye contact, and a purple mist swirled around him, indicating guilt or shame. She assumed he blamed himself for letting her fall into Auld Liam's hands. She did not fault him. Men as determined as Liam always found a way to get what they wanted.

Though she'd felt safe at Fairetur her first few days, she did no longer. Even with Robbie and Freki guarding her, she feared it impossible to overcome threescore years of hatred. How long until someone tried their hand again at murder? How many times until someone succeeded?

Chapter Eleven

Supper passed in strained silence. Though Beitris and Torri knew something terrible had happened, resulting in Auld Liam's death, neither questioned her over the meal. The venison stew was only a day old, but to Katja, it had lost its savor and she picked at her food. Events of the afternoon rolled over and over in her mind. The scent and sight of blood remained imprinted on her memory. More than once, Katja searched her hands and kirtle for blood. She caught Robbie watching her and it startled her to see the light green of pity about him faded, giving way to a washed out blue of confusion. After a moment, she dismissed the change, unable to dwell on the puzzle. He likely mulled the events of the past few days and debated how best to expose Liam's accomplices.

Katja turned to the serving lass clearing away the remains of the meal. "Please let Cook know I'd like to bathe before retiring for the night." The girl curtsied, light blue auras of fear and confusion surrounding her. Katja couldn't blame her. Gossip traveled quickly in a small keep. No telling what tales circulated about Liam's demise.

She didn't know what Robbie had told Dugan and the other two, only he'd instructed them to spread some version of the day's events in an effort to flush the others involved.

A light knock on the door sounded, then the kitchen lass' head appeared around the panel.

"Yer bath awaits, milady." Her eyes remained fixed on the floor boards.

"My thanks." Katja rose, as did everyone at the table. The

continued courtesy confused her.

"I'll see ye to yer chamber," Robbie stated, his voice firm.

"Torri and I will see to yer bath. None will dare cause mischief with us aboot." Beitris rose slowly, the sharpness of her gaze belying her apparent feebleness.

Her throat prickled at her new family's demonstrated support, and she ducked her head for fear of giving away how powerfully their acts of kindness moved her.

* * *

The shuffle of boots on the stairs in the middle of the night woke Katja from a light slumber. By Freki's calm reaction, he recognized the sounds and deemed them no threat. Once awake enough to recognize Finn's muffled laughter, she realized her husband had finally arrived. She drew a simple kirtle over her head, deciding to forego footwear. Raising the bar at the door, she peered into the shadowed corridor. She noted Robbie no longer stood guard at her door and had likely followed the men another level up to Calder's chamber. Not wishing to awaken Beitris and Torri in the next chamber, she padded noiselessly into the passage and up the stairs.

Male voices grew louder and anticipation of seeing her husband after more than a sennight grew, lightening her heart. She chided herself for such weak female emotions. Was she so far gone that the mere thought of a glimpse of her husband sent her heart flying? Pausing on the landing, she admitted, aye, she was. Her lips twisted ruefully and Katja shook her head before continuing down the hall. Calder's chamber door stood ajar, light spilling into the corridor.

"Do ye think 'tis wise to set yer leman up in a croft on yer wife's dower lands?" Finn's unmistakable voice posed the question.

Katja snatched her hand from the latch as though it had bitten her and stepped away from the door, her ears tuned to Calder's answer.

"My wife said she wanted Lorna gone from the keep. I'm fulfilling her wishes."

Perfidious bastard! Thoughts of Calder keeping his whore close at hand stole her breath. Her palm pressed against the sudden pain in her chest and she slipped further into the shadowed passage.

"Ye dinnae plan to consult Katja?"

Katja snorted. At least Robbie questioned her husband's odious plan.

"Ye also?" Calder's retort rumbled low. "I've had enough of this auld man prodding and poking, telling me what I should and shouldnae do. Dinnae ye start, as well."

"We need to speak of Katja." Insistence filled Robbie's words.

"I can see to my own wife." Calder's sharp words brooked no argument.

"Ye dinnae understand." Robbie's voice rose with frustration.

"Nae, not tonight. I'm bone-weary and 'tis past lauds. I'll see ye in the hall in a few hours."

Feet shuffled on the wooden floor and Katja descended the stairs with silent alacrity. She closed the door of her chamber before Finn and Robbie made the landing on her level. Leaning against the portal, hugging her middle against the pain of betrayal, tears flowed freely as self-pity gripped her. Pain unlike any she'd known raked across her heart. Her mother's sweet face came to mind, and with it understanding as Katja grasped the depth of suffering once a woman gave her heart away. She had believed her husband to be true to his word. It wounded her beyond words to face the reality of his betrayal.

Get a hold of yerself. He's a man like any other. Ye're lying to yerself if ye think a few pretty words and gentle touches make him any different.

She wiped her eyes as anger emerged from self-pity. Her spine stiffened, desire to depart this wretched place blooming fiercely. How foolish to think having Beitris and Torri's regard would suffice. Even the fear of knowing some in the clan wished her dead did not compare to the pain of discovering her husband kept his hateful whore. She recalled his words from only a few days earlier.

I pledged my troth to ye. I'll have no other in my bed from here on.

The trust she'd allowed to grow collapsed in ruins. Now that he'd gained the peace and coin and land he needed from their union, all that remained was for her to bear his heir. Heat settled in her chest. She'd sacrificed enough. She would not become her mother. And if she stayed at Fairetur even one more day, anger might cause her to do something to her deceitful husband or his shameful strumpet. Though justified in her own eyes, she doubted anyone else would see it thus.

I dinnae belong here.

The truth of this revelation echoed through her and settled into her bones. She could not remain, nor could she return to her sire's home. Katja shuddered at the idea of living under *that* degenerate's thumb again. He'd made it clear he never wanted to lay eyes upon her again—a feeling she heartily reciprocated.

Katja considered her plight. An urge had grown in her during the past few months to escape her father's abuse. She had considered fleeing to her mother's family on more than one occasion throughout the years. But the travel was long and fraught with danger. Was it worth the risk?

I willnae be a faithless man's possession.

Daybreak hastened, little more than an hour away. The gates

would soon be raised for those repairing crofts and tending flocks. The MacFies were due to arrive soon, so the keep would be busy for a late autumn day. She could be away before anyone noticed her missing.

Changing quickly into riding clothes, Katja packed only what she needed and slipped from her room, Freki a shadow at her side. She paused outside Beitris' and Torri's door. Ignoring the tug at her heart, she clenched her fists and jaw, pivoted on her heel and glided silently down the stairs to the kitchen. Busy with the morning meal, Cook merely nodded when Katja took a round of bread, cheese and dried meat from a tray on the long serving table. The happy yellow aura swirling about Cook inspired a bittersweet smile in Katja's heart. Without a word, she and Freki stepped through the door into the keep.

"Yer up early, milady." Jamie yawned and rubbed the sleep from his eyes, straw still stuck to his clothing, proving where he'd slept the night. Katja strode into the stables.

"Aye. I thought to ride to the loch this morn." It was easy to smile at the lad as she remembered he was one of the few who had truly welcomed her. She fluttered a hand in a shooing motion. "Go back to yer bed. I can tack my horse."

Jamie grinned and shook his head. "Nae, milady. Titus would have me head if'n I dinnae do it fer ye. Besides, I'm already up."

The lad made short work of readying Skündi while Katja secured her weapons and saddlebag. Jamie bravely patted Freki's massive head, earning a wet swipe of the dog's tongue for his boldness. The spoiled beast leaned his head into the lad's hand until Jamie scratched his favorite spot behind the ears. Freki heaved a contented sigh and bumped the lad with his meaty shoulder.

"I think he likes me, milady." Jamie's enthusiasm drew a smile from Katja.

"Aye, he does at that."

"That first day, I feared he'd eat me."

Katja smiled indulgently, her eyes burning with emotion. She drew a deep breath and pushed the strong feelings down. Grasping the reins as firmly as her wayward determination, she mounted the waiting horse.

Jamie yawned as he waved farewell. With Freki at her heels, Katja walked Skündi to the main gate. Falling in with some lads and two old men headed for the crofts, Katja plodded alongside, nodding and smiling when anyone made eye contact. Once through the gate, she turned west and spurred Skündi to a canter to perpetuate her story of heading toward Loch Beaggorm. The pain of leaving clenched at her heart, and she pressed a palm to her chest to ease the sting.

I willnae stay where I amnae wanted. I willnae live my mother's life.

The words tightened her resolve, but tears filled her eyes and she let Skündi find his own path.

Once over the hill and out of sight of the keep and village, she turned southward into a small burn and backtracked east toward the road to Hacraig. The water washed away Skündi's hoof prints as quickly as he made them. After they'd traveled well past Fairetur, she directed him northward until they came across the eastern road. It was almost a two-day ride to Thurso and the coast by her reckoning. She'd seen it on the map and heard her sire and brothers talk enough of ships arriving and leaving with goods from the seaport to know its location.

Her only uncertainty was how difficult it might be to obtain passage to Lerwick on the Shetlands. Aunt Runa and Uncle Lund would welcome her with open arms. Her uncle would be pleased to see what had become of the awkward bundle of fur he'd given her a few years back.

Katja shuddered and pulled her cloak close about her. After an overcast morn, the day beamed mostly clear with a gentle but cold north wind that hurried her on her way and formed an icy resolve around her heart.

* * *

Calder rose, feeling refreshed and hopeful. Negotiations with the MacCairn were complete, and he now had the lads needed to tend Katja's dower lands. At the thought of his wife, he smiled, looking forward to seeing her this morn. After a quick wash, he dressed and made his way down the stairs to break his fast.

He entered the hall, quickly noticing the strained looks his grandmother sent his way. Torri appeared distressed, his brother openly angry, and his uncle's gaze riveted grimly on the bowl of porridge before him. Katja was nowhere to be seen. As he took his seat, a serving lass placed a bowl of porridge and a mug of cider on the table.

"Why the sour faces this morn? Where's my lovely bride? 'Tis not like her to sleep late." Calder stirred in a dab of honey with the cooked oats and dried apples.

"I'll happily answer yer questions—in private." Robbie sat, arms crossed, a scowl marking his features—a look identical to the one he wore last night.

"Is aught amiss?" Calder put down his spoon and regarded his brother.

Robbie rose and walked to the solar, opening the door expectantly. Calder cradled his bowl in one hand, his cider in the other, and followed, a frisson of unease slithering down his spine. Beitris and Torri entered ahead of him.

Finn rose, his joints popping as he straightened his back, and took a hobbled step toward the solar. "Wait fer an auld man. I've a feelin' I dinnae want to miss this."

Once everyone found a seat, Robbie began the story with the poisoned porridge. Torri and Beitris added details as the tale went along. Calder listened, stricken, his porridge forgotten as he listened to the story of betrayal and attempted murder of his wife. His jaw tightened until his teeth cracked.

"Saint's blood!" he exploded. "And did ye find who Liam worked with at the keep?"

Robbie shook his head. "Nay. The only thing I do know is it wasnae Lorna. She was accounted for each day, and dinnae serve in the kitchen nor above stairs on those days."

"She may not have done the deed, but I'll wager she had a hand in this evil," Calder fumed, wondering why he didn't take his uncle's advice earlier regarding his former leman.

"I truly believe Lorna is innocent," Robbie protested. "I pressed her hard, threatening the noose if she dinnae speak the truth. She was genuinely afraid and dinnae appear to have any knowledge of what Auld Liam was about. If anything, Liam kept her in the dark to give him a dupe should he need one."

"Where is Katja now?" Calder demanded.

"I asked about, and she left at daybreak to ride to the loch, according to Titus." Robbie's scowl deepened, as if he didn't believe the story.

"Why would Katja leave the safety of the keep?" Bewilderment rattled his brain. "Bring Titus to me. I'd have it from the man, himself." Calder smacked the table with an opened hand, bounded from his chair and toward the door.

"It werenae Titus, but young Jamie who tacked Katja's horse and spoke with her. I questioned him twice to make sure. Tully was on watch at the gate, and he confirmed Jamie's story. Yer wife turned west once she came to the road."

Calder scrubbed his face, struggling to understand why she left. "It doesnae make sense for her to leave the keep alone. Fleeing to avoid future difficulties doesnae make sense, either. And 'tis not like her to act the coward."

"Coward?" Robbie snorted. "Nae. Ye dinnae see the two men Liam set on her. One had a nasty gash on his arm, likely from trying to grab her, and both had her arrows buried deep in their chests. She set her beast upon Liam, and had just approached him when we rode over the ridge. The lass has steel in her spine."

"Aye, I believe it," Calder replied. "However, what I dinnae believe is that she has ridden off for a day at the loch." His heart lurched. "It seems between my poor treatment of her and Liam's devilry, my bonny bride has decided to wash her hands of Clan MacGerry."

Chapter Twelve

Skündi's strong gait allowed him to cover ground for hours without tiring. Katja was thankful for such a fine horse, though she knew her sire only provided her with a quality mount because anything less would reflect poorly on the earl. Freki trotted alongside. After two brief stops for water at the burn cascading near the road and to allow Skündi to graze the dying grass, they arrived in Hacraig before daylight abdicated its rule.

Katja drew deeper into the hood of her cloak and, under the cover of gloaming, passed through town unnoticed, stopping at a small inn on the northern edge. A portly man appeared in the doorway, his soiled apron identifying him as the innkeeper. He took in her appearance with a frown.

"Good eve, m'lady. The Pig and Plough isnae elegant, but if yer in need of a room and a hot meal, ye've come to the right place."

"Good eve to ye, sir. Aye, I wish lodging and food for the three of us."

The innkeeper eyed her yet again, then shifted his attention to Freki. Katja faltered. She hadn't considered the likelihood of public houses not allowing her companion entrance.

"I dinnae allow dogs in me inn, and I dinnae wish trouble from an angry husband or father. The common room will soon fill with lads who drink deeply and delight in causing devilry. A woman alone dressed as a man is trouble if ever I've seen it. Four pennies will earn ye a small servant's room round back on the ground floor fer the night. I'll see yer sup is brought to yer room. 'Twill keep ye out of sight and trouble till morn. Yer horse will get a good rubbin' and his fill of oats. No disrespect, but 'tis the best I can offer."

Katja nodded. "Aye, good sir, I dinnae wish trouble. A room around back seems a wise choice. Include a second meal and allow my dog entrance, and I'll double yer price to a groat. Dinnae fash. My wee laddie's manners are fit for good King Jamie's court."

The innkeeper rubbed his beard as he considered her offer. The colors of mistrust swirled about him. "No offense, m'lady, but I'll see the color of yer coin first."

Katja withdrew one of several silver groats embossed with King David's likeness and handed it to the man. Her grandmam had secretly given her a silver coin each Michaelmas since her mam died and bade her hide them in the hem of her cloak. Katja sent a silent blessing to the woman whose foresight made this journey to her family possible.

The man inspected the coin, turning it over once then twice and nodded. A stable lad waiting at a distance was motioned over.

"Ori will see to yer horse. I'll take ye to yer room and have me wife bring ye two bowls of stew. 'Tain't much, but 'tis hot and fillin'. I ask ye to stay in yer chamber 'til sunrise. Ori will have yer horse tacked and ready to ride on the morrow."

The unspoken message that she was only welcome for the one night—and grudgingly at that—was clear.

The room he offered was tiny but clean. A shabby table and three-footed stool the only furnishings. A straw pallet occupied the largest portion of the space. Katja placed her weapons and saddlebag in the corner on the pallet and hung her cloak on a wooden peg. Though there wasn't a fireplace, the room was warm. The bricked wall and noise told her the kitchen was on the other side and responsible for the heat.

A few minutes later, a knock at the door announced an older woman, a sturdy look about her, carrying a tray containing two steaming bowls, a pitcher and a mug.

"Evening, milady. Here is yer sup. I hope my husband wasnae too rough with ye. He's easy to rile when strangers are aboot. Dinnae fash about yer dog. He's welcome as long as he minds his manners, though the Good Lord knows yon beastie likely behaves better than the rascals we serve this time of eve." Her jovial voice matched her bubbling manner.

The kindly woman approached Freki with a bowl of stew. "'Tis fer yer laddie, aye?"

Katja hesitated a moment before acknowledging the gleam in the woman's eyes. "Yes, ma'am, 'tis."

The innkeeper's wife nodded and squatted before the enormous dog. Freki's nose quivered as he scented the air, his eyes hopeful. She placed the bowl on the floor in front of him and patted his massive head. "He's nothing but an overgrown bairn, he is." She cackled and stroked his wiry fur twice more. Freki ignored her touch as he quickly consumed the stew.

The woman rose, her bones creaking loudly. "Bang on the wall if ye need anything. I'll have water fer ye to wash with in the morn and fresh bannocks to break yer fast."

"My thanks for yer hospitality," Katja murmured.

The older woman smiled, waved a hand, and shut the door softly behind her.

"Here now! Careful with that tray of ale, missy. 'Tis coming out of yer pay if ye spill so much as a drop."

The innkeeper's voice resonated through the thin walls of the structure. Katja shuddered, his demanding tone reminding her of her sire. She smiled as she realized the likelihood of ever hearing his voice again was remote. But her smile faded as a hollowness she'd ignored all day settled over her. Had she done the right thing by leaving? Should she have confronted him, asked—nae, demanded an explanation?

My husband placed his whore in a croft on my dower lands!

Emotions churned her belly as she searched for a comfortable position on the straw pallet. Freki sighed deeply as she tossed and turned. Katja sought to calm her mind, thinking through how she would gain ship's passage to Lerwick on the morrow as a lone woman with a horse and rather large dog. Recalling her less than hearty welcome at the inn, Katja surmised her reception would be no better on the docks of Thurso. She prayed the silver she carried would make the difference there as it had this eve.

A light knock on the door roused her a few hours later. Freki's wagging tail told Katja the innkeeper's wife had returned.

"Good morn, milady. Here is the water and food I promised ye."

A serving girl set a pan of water on the wobbly table. Wisps of steam rose and faded from its surface. Another girl placed a small tray of bannocks with a mug of goat's milk next to the pan. Katja worried it would tumble to the floor, but the spindly, mismatched legs found their balance.

"And something for yer laddie." The older woman tossed a piece of dried meat to Freki. He snatched it out of the air with a loud snap of his jaws. Three more pieces followed, and with each snapping catch, the woman cackled with delight. Katja downed a bannock and the milk, a smile on her face as Freki entertained the older woman.

"I believe ye'd have him spoiled if we stayed another day." Katja couldn't help but smile.

"Och, I'll take my leave. Ye have somewhere to be, and I've a husband and guests to finish cooking for. Ori should already have yer horse fed and saddled." She wiped her hands on her apron and opened the door as Katja quickly gathered her belongings.

"How much further to Thurso?" Katja asked.

The woman nodded toward the road. "Mayhap two hours on that fine horse of yers. Godspeed, milady."

"Thank ye for yer hospitality, ma'am," Katja replied.

As the matron predicted, the stable lad had Skündi tacked and ready to go. Katja placed the remainder of the linen-wrapped bannocks in her saddlebag and mounted. She turned to wave to the woman, but the inn's door had closed behind her. The stable lad tipped his cap to her and strode toward the barn.

The little village of Hacraig began to rouse from slumber. The rusty trumpeting sounds of a cock marked the beginning of a new day. Katja was grateful the ride to Thurso would be a short one. If she followed the road along the river, she'd reach her destination, as the River Thurso emptied into the sea.

After an hour of travel, they came across a drover's bothy and byre off the side of the trail next to the river. From the dust in the distance and fresh manure on the path, herdsmen and cattle had just passed this way. Likely, they were headed for market, an hour or two away.

Katja dismounted and led Skündi to the burn to drink, uninterested in catching up to the cattle and the men driving them. The river had widened, its banks less steep, making it easier to approach. Freki bounded through the stream, snapping at the water. Katja squatted to fill her waterskin and took a long drink. A branch snapped behind her.

"Look what we has here, lads. A prime bit of horseflesh and woman."

Two men approached. The closest man's belly extended over his belt, as repulsive as the rest of his unkempt appearance. The second man was thinner, stood a bit taller, but appeared just as filthy. He hefted a bollocks dagger longer than her forearm. An aura of bright red encircled them both, reflecting their lustful thoughts. Neither carried himself as a warrior, and Katja hoped they were simply thieves. Though the one with the long knife appeared deadly enough.

She glanced quickly at Freki, his ears pinned back, the sound of the rushing water drowning out the rumbled warning lifting his lips. Katja was certain the men could not see him yet, angled as he was below the bank, still in the water. With a subtle wave of her flattened hand, she commanded Freki to stay.

"I dinnae want trouble." Katja met their gazes steadily.

The thin man wielding the bollocks dagger grinned and stepped closer, his crooked teeth gapped and yellow. "Then dinnae give us any when we toss yer skirts and ye'll survive this day with nothing more than a few bruises and a sore quim."

Katja gritted her teeth in anger. Did every man see her as goods to be sold, traded or used for their pleasure? She considered her options, her focus on the man with the long knife. With her sword in its sheath strapped to her horse, she'd have only her daggers with which to defend herself.

In a single fluid motion, she rose, drawing the blade at her nape. Planting one foot forward, she hurled the knife toward the thin man, aiming for his inner thigh. With nothing more than homespun clothing defending his body, her unexpected move found its mark.

"Ye skinny whore!" the man roared, stumbling as he gripped the knife. He yanked the blade from his thigh, and his trews blossomed red. Katja had aimed for the large artery in his leg, and it seemed she'd at least nicked it.

She instantly drew the daggers strapped to her forearms, sending the first flying toward the stout man, targeting the soft flesh of his belly. Without hesitating, she flung the second dagger at the thin man, attempting another hit where her first dagger had struck.

Her throw at the heavier man landed poorly and bounced off his shoulder. He charged her with a roar. Her second dagger found a home on target in the first man's leg.

"Freki! *Ganga at*!"

Released from the command to stay, Freki bounded up the bank and launched himself at the man closing the gap between them. The wolfhound's speed and bulk knocked the fat man to the ground. Freki struck for his throat, but the villain blocked his attack with a protective arm. Sinking his fangs into the meat of the man's arm, Freki shook him, tearing muscle and sinew as the man screamed his fear and pain.

Katja turned her attention to the armed thief who had removed the second dagger from his leg. His trews, now darkened with his lifeblood, told the story. Katja squatted and drew both boot knives, heaving first one then the other toward the man's gut. He blocked the second throw with his dirk, but her first buried itself deeply a few inches below his belt.

The screams from his companion stopped short. Katja drew the two daggers at her belt and strode toward the thin man, her anger flaming. He wrested her blade from his middle, adding it to the pile at his feet.

His breathing grew shallow and he staggered. "Ye've killed me, ye little bitch," he spat, disbelief flooding his words. "Ye've killed us both."

"I told ye I dinnae wish trouble. Ye brought this upon yerselves."

"Who are ye?" he demanded.

"The last person ye shall see on this earth," Katja replied evenly.

She feinted to the right, hoping to create an opening, all too aware he was not far enough gone to be easy prey, knowing his long arms gave him the advantage of reach. Either too smart to fall for her ploy or too fatigued from blood loss to react, he stood dumbly, weaving on his feet. At her second feint, he swung his dirk wildly, right to left, missing her by a fair margin. As she'd suspected, he was no warrior.

Katja followed the path of the blade, stepping toward the man's chest as she buried the first knife in the meaty part of the arm stretched toward her, sending him reeling backward. She drove her second dagger into the notch at the base of his throat above the breast bone, shoving it deep.

His last words were lost in a gurgle of blood as he dropped to his knees. Losing his argument with death, he crumpled in a heap at Katja's feet. She waited for the nausea to come as it had the last time she'd killed. Today, she felt nothing. No anger. No fear. No guilt. Her heart an empty void. She stared into the brute's lifeless eyes, then gathered her blades, adding his to her collection. A quick search produced a few coppers and five silver pennies between the two dead men.

The thought of leaving the bodies next to the burn didn't settle well, so she grasped first one man then the other by the boots and dragged the corpses into the undergrowth, managing to avoid glancing at their faces. After this day was over, she never wanted to think of them again. She strode back to the burn, Freki at her side, and washed away the blood. After giving her weapons a good cleaning, she returned them to their sheaths.

The bollocks dagger might have been impressive from a distance, but close inspection showed it to be of low quality. Both men had carried a large knife for eating and other chores. She placed them in her saddlebag to sell later. Steel was valuable—even poor steel. The thieves' ponies placidly grazed nearby, and neither protested when she gathered their reins and tied them together. Their sale, along with the blades and coins she'd collected, would add to her own, giving her enough to live on for a time.

Freki's low growl stopped her breath. Hot from his earlier fight with the lout, he streaked from Katja's side into the dappled shade of the trees. Stunned, and knowing he would not attack someone he knew, she let him go.

Shouts of anger stirred her from her daze and she raced after Freki, snatching her sword from Skündi's saddle as she passed. Enraged snarls rose over the shouts. Somewhat disoriented in the shadows after the bright light by the river, Katja skidded to a halt, staring at the writhing forms of wolfhound and man on the ground only a few feet away.

The man struck a glancing blow to Freki's shoulder. He stumbled to the side but returned to the fight without a whimper. Katja grabbed his collar and dragged him back, dodging a blade that whipped through the air on level with her hand. She struck it away with her sword and it clanged to the side.

"Freki! *Halda.*"

The man at her feet stared at her through a tangle of dark hair, the left side of his face a mangled rope of old scars spattered with blood from fresh wounds to his arm. He slid backward to a half-seated position against a tree, his movements reminding her of a cornered wolf. An injured, angry, wolf.

"Were the two men who attacked me yer companions?" Katja demanded, her fingers twisting in Freki's collar.

"Worthless louts," he spat. "Bested by a woman."

Katja raised an eyebrow and a sword, tempting him to reassess his own situation.

He snarled. "They arenae friends of mine."

"Then be gone from here, and learn from their mistake."

With a last glare at Katja and her dog, the man tucked his

injured arm against his side and vanished into the forest. She hoped it was the last she saw of him.

Moving to the river, Katja drank deep from the bubbling water, dazed and a bit breathless at what she'd done. Freki stood in the river and lapped thirstily, the current parting around his legs. Skündi nibbled at the grass at the river's edge, snorting from time to time as though to clear his nostrils of the stench of fresh blood.

Katja wished she could erase her actions as easily. She eyed the bodies of the men who'd thought to take her, who'd given their lives to extract what they wished from hers, to discard her when they'd finished.

It dinnae have to come to this. But, from the moment the first man had stared at her, open lust on his face, death was the only end possible. Submitting to their demands would not be an option, and she'd prepared herself for her own death. Though she'd quailed at the thought of what would happen to Freki and Skündi.

Taking a deep breath, she wiped her hands on her cloak and caught Skündi's reins. Still edgy from the battle and scent of blood, the horse flung his head up and backed away.

"*Halda*, Skündi," she soothed, running a hand down the horse's sleek neck. Freki splashed up the bank and pushed between Katja and Skündi. The horse lowered his head, nuzzling the dog. Apparently reassured by the presence of his long-time friend, the beast calmed and Katja led him to the small copse of trees where the dead men's ponies huddled together. One mare squealed and nipped at Skündi, her ears flattened against her skull. He tossed his head and bowed his neck, giving her a shove with his chest.

"*Korrnorr*!" Katja hissed. "I dinnae need ye to alert the world to our presence. 'Tis already gotten me into this much trouble." The horses quieted and she tied them together. She packed the dead men's daggers into a bag hanging from the saddle of one of the shaggy ponies, placing the coins in various places on herself and in Skündi's tack to avoid losing the entire bunch in a theft.

The sun hung heavy overhead and she regretted the loss of time on the road as much as the reason for the delay. Realizing it was only a matter of time before someone else came along the road, she mounted her horse, leading the others to the edge of the dirt trail, hoping to arrive in Thurso before encountering other travelers.

She hurried them along the road, her eyes scanning the terrain from beneath the low peak of her hood, alert for danger. Freki paced at her side, tongue lolling from his jaws, showing no sign of injury. The ground flattened, sloping gradually down to the sea. Travelers rode past with open curiosity for the animals she led. Giving none so much as a nod, Katja made her way into town.

She followed the ring of a hammer on steel, but stopped when she realized she'd mistaken the sounds of a smithy for the noises of ship building. Not daring to approach a man for help, she asked a woman exiting a tavern for directions to the smith's yard. Ignoring the woman's assessing stare at her clothing, Katja reined the horses around and retraced her steps, arriving quickly at her destination.

"I have ponies to sell," she stated as the blacksmith looked up from his work. A misty haze of sulphur brightened around the man as he straightened, a hand braced on his lower back. It quickly resolved into the gray of avarice, but his eyes were on the horses, not her. He was eager to bargain.

"Whose ponies are these?" he asked, his voice gruff. "They are worthless nags."

"I will concede to the fact their bloodline is much inferior to that of my horse, but I willnae take less than fair coin for them. As to their ownership, they are mine."

His eyes narrowed. "I've seen the bay mare before. She's a right terror. And she belongs to Gair Orrock." Chin jutted belligerently, he challenged Katja's statement.

"Describe him," she demanded.

"Older man, black hair, brown eyes. The left side of his face is scarred from a fire." The smith crossed his beefy arms over his chest. "He hates anything Sinclair."

Katja's heart faltered. "I met such a man and two others an hour or less outside town. He now has more respect for women traveling alone, but will live to tell the tale of the fanged beast who ripped the flesh from his arm and rearranged the scars on his face."

The blacksmith's gaze dropped to the dog at her side. Freki panted lightly, his eyes trained on the man speaking to his mistress. After a moment, the man turned his attention back to Katja.

"What of the others?"

"They will not be telling such tales."

This time the smithy's gaze snapped to the bag bristling with weapons.

"I wish to sell the horses and the weapons. I have my own, and need the coin."

The man scowled. "I will give ye fair coin, but not for the mare. Gair willnae offer silver for his beast when he comes for her."

Katja faltered to know the manner of the man Freki had sent fleeing for his life. It was true she'd likely made as dark an enemy as she would ever find, but she planned to be away from Thurso on the next ship bound to Lerwick. With luck, this Gair Orrock would spend several days nursing his wounds before he returned to town.

After a short negotiation, she and the blacksmith came to terms and she rode toward the center of town. Now that she'd put a bit of time and distance between herself and the louts who'd accosted her earlier, she found she was exceedingly hungry. Purchasing a slab of cheese and bread for herself and a pouch of dried meat for Freki, she continued to the harbor to ask about booking passage to Stromness, the first leg of her voyage to Lerwick.

Darkness blanketed the little town as Katja left the harbor. Her ears rang from the curses and lewd suggestions she'd received from the men at the shipyard. Half of them dismissed her as nothing more than trouble and a curse for even touching their ships—the others offered her a place aboard at a descriptive price that curdled the food in her stomach and burned her ears even now. To make matters worse, the few whose attention sharpened at the mention of coin refused to allow Freki on board.

She ruffled the dog's ears. "I dinnae know what to do, Freki. I willnae leave ye behind, and ye are a bit too large to smuggle aboard."

The dog whined and thumped his tail on the ground. Katja sank onto her heels next to him, drawing comfort from his sturdy body and the deep friendship. Since she'd received the wee lad as a scrap of bony fur from her Uncle Lund, the dog had scarcely left her side—and then not willingly.

She dug another scrap of meat from her pouch and Freki accepted the offering, chewing the tough, dried fibers a moment before swallowing. Katja settled back against the rough wall of the building she'd found shelter behind and closed her eyes, her mind spinning with the problems laid before her.

A warning rumbled low in Freki's chest and Katja jerked instantly awake. Her fingers tightened on the dog's ruff, but his growl did not abate. She glanced about in the gloom with bare movements of her head, sliding her free hand to the dagger sheathed at her boot.

Freki lunged forward with a roar, tearing free of Katja's grasp. Skündi lurched a step away, startled. Katja sprang to a half-crouch, dagger clenched in one fist, fingers spread wide in her open hand. A muffled cry reached her ears.

"Help!"
"Freki! *Halda*!"

Chapter Thirteen

The dog drew back, head lowered, hackles up, eyes fixed on the small body on the ground before him. The lad eased his arm away from his head, his tattered sleeve not unlike the coat he wore so Katja couldn't tell if the damage had been done by Freki or not.

"Get up," she said.

The lad shot her a terrified look. "He'll eat me!"

"Only on my command." She raised her brows. "Will ye obey me?"

With a slow nod that gradually increased in vigor, the lad climbed cautiously to his feet. Katja noticed his other sleeve just as tattered as the first, and the halves to his threadbare coat were fastened together with a rope tied about the lad's skinny waist.

"What's yer name, lad?" she asked, struggling to keep her voice stern, battling the part of her that longed to hug him close, feed him, and demand he bathe more than once a year.

He rubbed a grimy finger along the side of his nose, a wary look in his eyes.

"I'm called Donnan," he said, his words twisted as though he loathed parting with his name.

Katja inspected him, from the top of his sable, matted hair to his bare feet so dark with filth, she'd thought him shod at first. His black eyes sparked with a hint of defiance.

"Empty yer pockets," she commanded. He drew back.

"Ye cannae force me to!" he sputtered. "'Tis my things, not yers!"

Without breaking her gaze, she motioned at Freki. He took a

menacing step forward, lips curling to expose white fangs.

"Freki is named for one of Odin's wolves. He is the descendant of wolves of the northlands, fierce enough to take down a marauding beast without a second thought." She tilted one brow. "Shall he convince ye to yield?"

Donnan stared agape at the enormous wolfhound. For a moment Katja wasn't sure if he was paralyzed with fear or measuring his chances for escape. With a sudden move, the lad quickly stripped his coat from his thin shoulders and handed it to her, a quake in his arm.

Katja accepted the garment gingerly and peered inside the two large outside pockets. A moldy bread crust and a bit of dried meat proved to be the sole contents of one, a pair of jagged black stones in the other. With a frown of disappointment, she withdrew a silver coin from an inside pocket, her fingers encountering three other coins, each wrapped in a scrap of cloth so they would not jingle against each other.

Donnan met her look with a rakish grin. "They are mine, now."

"Ye lifted them." She didn't have to ask. But she did want to hear his response.

He shrugged. "I work when I can. But when I cannae, I do what I must."

"Where do ye work?"

He indicated the docks with a jerk of his chin. "I run errands for the men whilst they unload the boats. A bit of ale, a bite of dinner. I keep what I dinnae spend."

"And when they dinnae have errands for ye?"

"Drunk men are fair game." Defiance lit his face. And melted Katja's heart. The expected aura of gray, indicating greed, did not appear. Dark green of resentment, which she completely understood, twined with a faint line of purple, proving he was ashamed of the life he led.

He can be of use to me, and mayhap I can help him. She rubbed her chin with her fingertips thoughtfully and handed his coat back to him. He thrust his arms into the tattered sleeves and belted it around his waist.

"I will pay ye to help me," Katja announced.

Donnan stilled, his aura melting into the pale blue of confusion. "Will ye turn me in for thieving?" he asked. His eyes darted to Freki who had relaxed and stood at Katja's side, panting lightly.

"I offer ye a chance to change yer life for the better. Will ye consider my proposal?"

His wary gaze searched hers, and Katja calmly gave him time to consider.

"What do I have to do?"

Satisfaction bolted through her and she fought the urge to smile. "I need passage booked on the next ship bound through to Lerwick. For myself, Freki, and the horse."

Donnan whistled low. "They willnae allow a woman aboard. They're bad luck on a ship." His eyes widened. "Honest! I dinnae lie." He took heart at Katja's nod. "I've been aboard lots of ships! Most make a run from here to Stromness, and thence to Lerwick. And 'tis hard to find a ship with space for a horse. They dinnae like dogs much, either. Especially big, ferocious ones."

"Can ye name such a ship as could carry all of us? Including ye?"

"Me?" Donnan asked, clearly startled. "Why me?"

"It doesnae look as if ye have much to look forward to here. My uncle owns a ship building business in Bremirehoull on the Shetland mainland. He can always use diligent, honest lads." She managed not to flinch, hoping Donnan could mend his ways enough to become honest, and her uncle would see the benefit of hiring the scruffy lad.

"It would be a fresh start for ye. Mayhap in a few years ye will have enough skills to hire aboard as a hand if ye wish or make the decision to continue learning to build ships."

Donnan's eyes widened, and the hint of a smile tugged at the corners of his lips. "Aye! I only need a steady job. I willnae have to pick pockets when I have a bit of coin in my own." His voice lifted, the words coming faster. "I could work all day—I'm strong! And I dinnae eat much. And I can sleep anywhere."

He cast a look behind him and Katja spied an upended wooden crate, a blanket draped over it and pulled to one side as though creating a curtained room.

"'Tis yer home?" she asked softly.

Donnan's hands fisted. "'Tis mine," he answered, a wealth of bitterness and despair in his words.

She longed to hug him, tell him his worries were over, but such actions and words were foreign and not easily acted on. She settled for a brisk nod.

"Let's find a ship."

* * *

Calder reined his horse to a halt and dismounted next to the loch. His heart plummeted. Despite the dour predictions of his brother and uncle and his own words of guilt, he'd hoped to find Katja here. He peered into every shadow, every eddy that nudged the bank, each rock large enough to hold his wife. The hoped-for sight of silver-blonde hair and soft gray eyes did not arise.

His gaze turned to scan the ground. The soft earth bore the scars of both horse and deer tracks, and he could think of nothing that would make Katja's horse's prints stand out.

He paced the edge of the loch, but in the end, was forced to admit he was no closer to truly tracking her than he'd been earlier.

Where could she be? She is no experienced traveler. She admitted she'd never left Ruadhcreag before. Would she return there?

Calder shook his head. *Was my treatment of her such that she'd go back to that bastard father of hers?* His stomach clenched at the thought. He'd meant to give her a life of kindness, understanding and love like she'd never known. He'd hazard a guess she'd never faced hatred quite like she'd experienced the last few days. Thus far, his plan had failed spectacularly. He spat on the ground to rid himself of the bitter taste of discouragement.

Mounting his horse, he reined it reluctantly toward the Sinclair border, hoping to find his bonny lass before he reached Ruadhcreag.

Long shadows lay across his path by the time he reached the Sinclair stronghold. He rode into the keep on the heels of a few workers, wooden tools in hand, returning from the fields. Within moments he was surrounded by three Sinclair warriors, bristling with suspicion and well-sharpened arms.

"Hold!"

Calder turned his head at the voice, relieved to find Katja's brother, Christer, striding toward him.

"What has happened?" Christer's face, normally ruddy from the sun and wind, glared, now dead white.

"Yer sister is well," Calder hastened to reassure him—at least within earshot of the Sinclair soldiers. "May we speak in private?"

With a nod, Christer dismissed the men and Calder dismounted, handing his reins to a stable lad with an admonition to feed and water the beast, but to keep the horse ready for when he called.

The two men sought a corner of the keep between two buildings. Others passed them with little interest as the hour for the evening meal was at hand. The aroma of cooking meats drifted on the breeze and Calder's stomach rumbled, but he ignored it.

"Katja is . . . rather, she was fine the last time my grandmam saw her."

Christer frowned, his eyes narrowing. Calder waved his hand in a sue for peace. "I have been verra busy getting the clan settled for the winter. I havenae been an attentive husband." He ducked his head. "Things have been tough for Katja."

Christer ground his teeth and Calder nodded. "She had expectations—hell, *I* had expectations—and she had every right to an easier transition to her new life. But I bungled things, Christer, and she has been missing from Fairetur since early this morning."

Briefly he told Christer what he knew, cringing to hear his wife's troubles spoken from his own mouth. He half-expected to hear the whistle of steel an instant before it cut him down, justice for allowing such near-tragedies to befall her.

"'Tis obvious she isnae here, though I couldnae for the life of me see her living beneath her da's rule again. But I have no idea where she could be." It pained him to admit he knew so little about his wife. "Can ye help me?"

Christer breathed deeply, his agitation apparent. "Ye swear to me the man who instigated this is dead?"

"Aye. And I have Robbie scouring the clan for any accomplices." He spread his hands wide, palms up in supplication. "I have learned a bitter lesson. I willnae neglect her again. Not her comfort, nor her safety, nor her happiness."

Christer leveled a look at him, and Calder felt scalded to his toes.

"Not all of this is yer fault," Christer said. "Our clans have been at war for too long, and there are those on either side who willnae accept the truce with grace. I stand by my earlier opinion that ye will be a good husband to her."

"I must find her and convince her 'tis truth."

"She wouldnae come here," Christer said. "Ye understand why. The only place I can think she might go is to our uncle's house, but it is many miles from here."

"I dinnae care," Calder vowed, heartened to hear Christer's suggestion. "I will go there now. How do I find it?"

The man gave him a withering stare and Calder felt his heart plummet.

"Lund Sjoberg lives in Bremirehoull on the Shetland mainland. Ye must book passage from Thurso across the North Sea to Stromness and from there to Lerwick."

"That's several days' journey from here." Calder stared at Christer, aghast. "Anything could happen to her along the way. She wouldnae consider such a thing."

Christer nodded. "Aye. I believe she has considered it before, though never provoked strongly enough to attempt the journey."

Their gazes locked. Calder sought understanding and mercy, but knew he would receive neither. His lack of understanding had caused too great a rift. "I've sent her to her death."

* * *

Katja pulled the peak of her hood low over her brow and stepped firmly onto the broad plank. The cog ship rolled beneath her feet with the swell of the tide and Skündi shied back, the whites of his eyes glowing with fright.

"*Hannja, bolli*," she murmured, placing her palm gently over the animal's nose. "Take it nice and easy." Giving the horse a moment to settle, she strode confidently forward, hoping Skündi would follow. Freki skulked at Katja's other side, ears tipped forward, scanning the ship intently, favoring the rough men who stared at them with challenge from his dark eyes.

Donnan scurried across the deck. "Here's where yer horse stays." He waved to a small area beneath the forecastle, heavy rope netting hung on three sides to create an enclosed area against the hull of the ship. To Katja's surprise, a bit of fresh-looking hay covered the rough boards, providing a thin cushion atop the planking as well as fodder for the horse.

"Ye did well," she murmured to the lad as she fastened the ropes onto a cleat on the ship's wall, securing Skündi in his temporary stall. Donnan beamed and motioned her forward. "There isnae a berth for ye, as this ship only makes the run from Thurso to Stromness carrying cargo and few passengers, but ye can stay in the captain's cabin if ye wish."

Katja shot him a startled look. "Ye dinnae tell him I am a woman and sought privacy, did ye?"

Donnan scowled. "Nae. I'm no' daft. I told him ye were from an important clan on business in the north. He willnae be using his cabin for the run, and will be happy to accept coin if ye wish to stay there. We should arrive in less than a half-day," he added, trying for an air of casual, superior knowledge.

Katja smiled. "Thank ye, but Freki and I will stay with Skündi during the trip. He has never been aboard a ship at sea before."

"Me, neither!" Donnan admitted before he flushed, remembering he'd given himself the airs of a seasoned deck hand.

"Then we shall encourage each other, aye?"

The screech of wood startled her, putting her on guard. The men had stopped staring and now scurried about the deck, dragging the loading plank on board and setting to their tasks. A swarthy man sidled over to her.

"'Tis a pleasure having ye aboard, milord," he rasped, his voice more suited for shouting over storms than pleasant conversation.

Katja tipped her head forward, adding more shadow to her face.

"Thank ye," she murmured low in her throat to give it a husky quality. She bumped against Donnan. He shot her a glance then cleared his throat in understanding.

"Milord wishes to be left to his thoughts." He leaned close to the ship's captain. "He has a lot on his mind about his business and all."

The burly man gave a nod of his head. "And I have a ship to tend. Tell yer master we will do our best to give him a calm journey."

Katja released a sigh as the man stalked to the other end of the ship, shouting commands as he went. A single square sail in the center of the deck unfurled. Once away from the berth, wind caught the heavy canvas, pushing the boat into the North Sea.

Sea birds wheeled overhead as they docked a few hours later, screeching their hunger to the ships docked at Stromness. Workers bent to the task of unloading the ship and setting up for its return to Thurso. Katja and Donnan would need to board a second ship to make the long trip to Lerwick. The day half-spent, Donnan collapsed to the ground beside Katja.

Once again, her gender and the animals she refused to leave behind stalled her plans, and the wait to learn of Donnan's success in finding berth on a ship destined for Lerwick seemed over-long. Katja eyed the lad with poorly concealed exasperation when he finally returned. "Well?"

"The skunners thought I'd palmed the coin!" Donnan exclaimed, indignant.

Katja tilted her head.

"Aye, but I'm honest, now," he protested. He snatched a small stone from the street and flung it to the ground, a release for his resentment. "I found a captain willing to take us to Lerwick, but it cost me the last of the coin." His eyes rounded, and Katja caught the slight intake of breath of a child awaiting punishment.

"Ye did well, Donnan. 'Twas a difficult task, and ye persevered until ye made it work. The extra coin willnae beggar us." She gave him an encouraging grin and was rewarded with his bright smile and a return of his brash confidence.

"'Tis a larger ship and I can wait to eat when we reach yer uncle's shipyard. He'll feed us, aye?"

Katja laughed. "I can feed us before we sail. Dinnae fash." She fished in one of her pockets and retrieved two bits of silver. "Here. Bring us back a feast. Dinnae forget Freki."

Donnan's face lit with delight and he carefully placed one bit in each pocket, supporting her belief of not putting all her coin in one place. "I'll be back!"

He took to his heels, skidding to a halt at Katja's call. He looked at her expectantly.

"Be sure to get something sweet, too," she told him. With an emphatic nod, the lad was gone.

"Do ye think I, a mere woman, can barter a measure of oats for Skündi whist we await young Donnan's return?" Katja mused aloud as she ruffled Freki's ears. Skündi snorted and shook his head as if he understood and approved her new quest. Katja led the animals down the cobblestone street that divided the town in a rather serpentine manner. Narrow lanes branched in all directions.

"I hope we dinnae become lost," she murmured, tightening her grip on the horse's reins. A quick question to a passing merchant, bolts of cloth stacked on his shoulders, gave her the direction to a nearby stable.

The stable master was too busy to remark on a woman alone, and waved a nearby lad to fetch a bin of oats and another of water for her tired horse. Skündi quickly devoured his feed and Katja let him drink his fill before they returned to the area near the docks where Donnan waited.

* * *

Calder spurred his horse faster, trying to outrun his guilt and the images of Katja alone on the road to Thurso. He risked much traveling alone, though he had no MacGerry men to spare, and had chosen to travel without an armed guard to slow him down. A woman alone—even with a furry monster at her side—was not likely to make the trip unmolested.

Darkness fell around him. He'd refused Christer's offer of hospitality for the night, though Calder understood he would only have access to the men's barracks, out of the earl's sight and knowledge. Aside from Calder's unwillingness to spend time anywhere near Katja's father, the urgency to find her was too great, and Christer had seemed relieved when Calder had left without lingering even for refreshment, though he'd had the stable lad add a waterskin and a bag of oat cakes to the saddle as he brought Calder's horse to him.

Damn, damn, damn! Could his problems possibly get any worse? He would leave managing the holdings to Robbie and Finn. His uncle understood the process of preparing for winter, and his brother was young and tireless. Calder dismissed the issues the new land and holders brought and focused on his bride.

Christer's words haunted him.

"She's ne'er been our father's favorite. Even as a sweet, comely child, he dinnae bother disguising his disgust. Our *amma* protected Katja after our ma died. But once *she* passed and Katja took over her responsibilities, he rarely wasted an opportunity to discredit her."

He'd paused, staring at the pebbled ground as if it held the answer to an ancient riddle. "Do ye believe in the *sight*?"

The question had stilled Calder's heart with the murmur of *witchcraft*. He shrugged.

Christer nodded. "An ability to see things others cannae— whether a person is telling the truth, or if they are nervous over something. Katja calls it an aura. Different colors tell her different things." He sighed. "The Sinclair women often have this gift. Or it would be a gift except my da used the knowledge it brought to cheat and control the men he had dealings with. He wanted to use Katja in such a way, but *Amma* swore the lass dinnae inherit the sight. The earl cursed my ma for her Viking blood. Said it tainted the Sinclair heritage."

Calder hadn't understood Christer's words entirely. Still didn't, though they perhaps told him why the earl hated Katja. The man was a tyrant, unable to love what did not bring him power and prestige. His sons were strong, stern, and he'd been able to mold them into warriors of some renown. He'd married Elke Reginulfsdottir for her link to her brother by marriage's ship building trade and the sailing contacts which benefitted his clan. And because her beauty made him the envy of many men, though he was quick to disregard her when her expectations of him did not match his whims.

Calder's chest tightened. Poor Katja. His beautiful, strong, smart wife had had little chance for a normal childhood. And he'd had little experience in courtship and the ways to let a woman know she was cherished. So far in her short life, Katja had been rejected by her father and neglected by her husband.

His hands fisted on the reins. The clouds thickened overhead, obscuring the moon, but the path to Fairetur was familiar even in the dark. Thunder rumbled through the woodlands and rain pelted down. Icy rivulets coursed past the neck of his cloak, snaking frigid paths down his back. Winter was only a single storm away.

Chapter Fourteen

"We have passage on The Gull, but we must hurry!" Donnan's hands flew as he waved Katja toward the docks. He crammed a bannock into his mouth, crumbs sputtering lightly as he continued.

"The captain is leaving now," he said, swallowing as he gathered a waterskin and bedroll from Katja. "There's a winter storm brewing and he willnae wait on us. He wants to be in Lerwick for ship repairs before the passage is closed for the winter." He grabbed Katja's hand, dragging her forward. "Come on!"

Freki whined and Donnan loosened his grip. "I'm not hurting her," he snorted at the big dog. "But we cannae be laggards today."

"I'm coming, Donnan," Katja replied, hiding her grin at the lad's assurance, such a contrast to the hesitant, defensive child she'd befriended only a couple of days earlier. And the new clothes she'd bid him purchase lent him a jaunty air, though it had taken her remark that his presence reflected poorly on her before he'd agreed to spend the precious coin.

Donnan scampered ahead, tossing instructions and a 'hurry up' look over his shoulder. "Pull yer hood over yer eyes, and take longer strides. Ye walk like a lady. And, give me Skündi's reins. Ye wouldnae walk yer own horse, aye?"

Katja pulled her cloak firmly about her, denying the icy breeze access inside. Cold stung her cheeks, and her eyes watered as the wind picked up. No one spared them a second glance as they crossed the plank onto the ship. Hoarse commands, snatched across the deck by the wind, fought to be heard above the creak of strained ropes and pullies and the groan of wet, burdened planks. The deck shifted beneath Katja's feet like a living thing, and Skündi skittered nervously, the thud of his hooves adding to the din.

"*Korrnorr*," she crooned softly, placing a palm on the horse's sweated neck. Freki leaned against Skündi's legs and the beast quieted.

A wiry man sidled up to them. "Tie the horse there," he instructed, pointing to a large, rusted ring bolted onto the side of the single cabin on the deck. "If ye've left anything behind, ye will have to send for it later. We leave now."

The boarding plank shrieked as a lad scarcely older than Donnan dragged it aboard. Skündi flung his head in the air, taking mincing steps away from the sound.

"*Kvala*," Donnan said with a firm tug on the reins, surprising Katja and settling Skündi with the single Norse word. He shrugged one shoulder at her questioning look, and she set the information aside for later when they were out of earshot of the deckhands.

"Cap'n will be about," the man added. "If ye have a need, ask for me. Name's Knut." He tilted his head. "The crossing'll be rough. Keep yer horse and dog out of our way." With a nod to emphasize his words, Knut strode away, his balance unaffected by the ship's roll.

"There's no stall?" Katja questioned Donnan, her voice low.

"'Tis no concern of the captain's if the horse washes overboard. He was the only one leaving for Lerwick who would consider taking him aboard. Him and the dog." Donnan gave Freki a pointed look.

Katja realized the truth of his words. "Thank ye for yer help. I am glad we will miss the storm."

Donnan gave her a gap-toothed grin. "Miss it? We're going to be in the middle of it!"

* * *

179

Katja stared at the door. A dagger placed in the upper hinge kept the heavy panel from closing completely, allowing biting, salt-laden air to circulate in the room. She'd closed the door at first, anxious to retreat from the bone-chilling storm. But she quickly discovered the cabin too small, the odors of unkempt seaman and last week's food an unsavory trade for the frigid but clean air beyond the walls.

Skündi and Freki huddled in the doorway, taking up precious space and adding their own wet-fur odors to the malodorous mélange. Combined with the pitch and yaw of the battered vessel, the cloying smells roiled her stomach, and Katja swallowed cautiously against the dinner she'd eaten hours earlier. But she couldn't remove either animal from the cramped cabin, and the captain and Knut had been too busy to notice.

"Do ye think we'll sink?" Donnan's pallid face shone in the dark, weakly reflecting the blue glow of the moon as black clouds scuttled across its surface.

Katja attempted to gather sympathy for the lad, nestled in the corner of the room, his arms tightly wrapped about his middle. She found it difficult to speak, her head empty of thought as a cold bead of sweat slid between her breasts.

"I dinnae think I'd mind," she murmured, her distress getting the better of her. Freki whined and shoved his head deeper into her lap. She clutched his ears and tried to steady her racing heart. The irregular beat made her dizzy and each toss of the ship threatened to overbalance her precarious grip on reality.

She caught a glimpse of Donnan's startled eyes, round with dismay, and bit her lip. "I thought ye were excited to race the storm." She teased him gently, forcing a smile to her lips.

Donnan squirmed, ducking his head as he bolstered his courage.

"I *was* excited," he offered, a faint grin lighting his face. "It wasnae as fun to catch it as I thought it'd be."

Katja laughed softly. "Aye. I dinnae believe I have my sea legs yet."

"I'll do better next time," Donnan avowed.

"Dinnae fash," Katja replied. "I believe I saw a green face or two among the sailors before we came in here. Mayhap the captain dinnae expect such a storm."

The two sat silently as the winds screamed outside, the ship moaning a descant as it tossed back and forth in the heaving waves. Skündi's hooves clattered on the pitching boards as he struggled to maintain his balance. There was nothing Katja could do. Morning would find them approaching either Lerwick—or the bottom of the sea.

* * *

Calder reined his tired horse through the gates at Fairetur, the sentry acknowledging him with a brief salute. Dawn crested the mountain, touching the grey stones with silver and rose. He dismounted, leaving Armunn in a stable lad's sleepy care, and trudged wearily into the hall.

Tables already in place, a few heads looked up from steaming mugs. Torri leapt from the bench with an anguished cry as she flung herself into Calder's arms.

"Where is she? Where is my sister?"

Calder cupped the back of her head against his palm and drew her to his chest. Dropping a kiss on her curls, he gently set her to his side and stumbled to the table. A space for him appeared on the bench between Beitris and Robbie as they each shifted apart. Across from them, Finn's dark eyes mirrored his worry.

Accepting a mug of watery ale from a serving lass, Calder waited until she strolled out of earshot before he lifted his gaze to the concerned family around him.

"She wasnae at Ruadhcreag." He wrapped his cold fingers around the heated mug, longing for a way to warm the bleakness inside him. A buzz of voices sprang up around him. He lifted one hand for silence, wondering when his limb had become so heavy.

"I spoke with one of her brothers. He thinks she may have journeyed to her mother's sister's house."

Sighs of relief floated about. Tense shoulders sagged. Voices dropped to a calmer register.

"Where does she live?" Torri asked, her bright tone shadowed with worry.

"Lerwick."

Confusion and surprise darted him like well-aimed dirks. Calder shook his head. With expectant gazes, the family quieted.

"I must give Armunn time to recover whilst I put together provisions for the trip."

"There will be no crossings to Lerwick this time of year, lad," Finn declared. "Yer bride will have to remain in Thurso until ye fetch her."

"I dinnae find the prospect of her staying unprotected in Thurso any comfort, Uncle," Calder warned, hating the growing darkness inside him.

"Why would she have traveled so far, Calder?" Torri asked. "Why was her da such a bad man?"

Calder patted his sister's hand. "He wasnae nice to her when she lived there, and he dinnae wish her to return. 'Tis difficult to explain to ye, lass, but the Earl of Sinclair resented his daughter for many reasons. He wanted her dowry and lands for himself, but her grandda made sure he could never take them from her. And he wanted to use her to further his avarice, but she wasnae willing to assist him."

And that was as much as Calder was prepared to reveal of the issue of Katja's *sight*. That his wife could possibly *see* things about him he would rather keep private was not something he was ready to discuss. Though Christer was not certain she was blessed with the power, it made sense as Calder reflected on Katja's wariness around himself and others. Eerie it may be, but his wife saw more of those around her than mere body movements and facial expressions.

Calder wondered what colors the auras were for anger and love. And when he found Katja, which one would she believe?

* * *

Haggard faces stared at the rose-gold streaks of dawn breaking through the dark clouds in a burst of light. The storm had passed scarcely an hour ago, subduing the waves to a more comforting roll, bequeathing a well-earned sense of ease on all who labored to bring the ship into safe-harbor.

Bedraggled but firmer on their feet, Katja and Donnan leaned over the rail. Excitement thrummed in her breast as the shoreline approached.

Lerwick! She breathed deeply, the crisp, salty air filling her with a sense of expectation. Ships' masts silhouetted dark against the pale blue sky like trees stripped of their branches. Drifted snow softened the harsh lines, gold and pink in the early sun. Men moved about on the docks and ships, gulls left their perches to inspect the new vessels coming into harbor, their voices shrill in the clear morning air.

"We made it," Donnan crowed. His hands gripped the rail tightly, but his face was awash with joy, his stance on the rolling boards firm.

Katja eyed him indulgently. "Think ye'll make a sailor, young Donnan?"

His look turned pensive. "I'm verra glad to see land," he admitted. "But I think I would like to be a sailor someday."

"Ye can be whatever ye wish, lad," she said. "Work hard, remain honest, and men will honor ye."

Donnan nodded vigorously. "Are ye certain yer uncle will take me as an apprentice?"

"I believe I can convince him to give ye a try," she teased.

The ship docked in its appointed berth less than an hour later. Donnan had been loath to leave the rail, fascinated with the activity around him. Katja led Skündi and Freki from their meager shelter, determined to be among the first to unload. Freki leaned against her legs, and Skündi shook himself like an enormous dog, but offered no objection to the slow roll of the deck.

Katja gave a short nod to Knut as the loading plank clattered to the dock. She would have liked to thank him for the skills that kept them on the topside of the waves the night before, but wariness of giving away her identity as a woman kept her silent. He waved them away, and Katja led her small group ahead of the struggling sailors, their brawny arms laden with cargo.

The dock had become a busier place in the time it had taken them to arrive. The boards were slippery with half-melted ice and snow, and jostling bodies made the journey away from the ship hazardous. Katja at last halted at a prosperous-looking stall where a burly man counted coins into a bag.

"We are looking for Lund Sjoberg," she coached Donnan in a low voice. The lad repeated her statement and received a jerk of the man's head in answer. Donnan flipped a copper coin into the air and the man caught it deftly, tucking it into the bag with a delicate *tink* as it joined its new mates.

Katja searched the men in the area indicated, her gaze flicking from face to face, hoping to find her uncle quickly.

There! The white-blond head wasn't that remarkable in a port whose ancestry boasted almost pure Norse bloodlines, but his broad shoulders and commanding presence filled her with a sense of familiarity and her knees nearly buckled in relief.

"Uncle Lund!" she cried, forgetting to lower the pitch of her voice. The man twisted about, his gaze speeding over her without pause. Then—he halted for the length of a breath, and faced her. He stared, his narrow gaze widening as he recognized the truth.

"Katja?" He stepped toward her and, at her nod, spread his arms wide.

She shoved Skündi's reins into Donnan's hands and fled into her uncle's embrace where all the acceptance and love she'd ever wanted awaited her. He swept her off her feet and whirled her about, either oblivious or uncaring of the stares of those around him. Freki joined in the fray, leaping about and barking, tail wagging madly.

"Get by, ye hairy misbegotten son of a wolf," Lund exclaimed, elbowing the big dog aside. "*Halda!*"

Freki dropped to the ground at the command, his tail swishing excitedly across the boards.

Lund grinned and set Katja back on the ground. "Ye've taught him one command at least." He tilted his head. "What brings ye to this port in such weather, lass?" He huffed at her, and Katja held back her laughter at his sudden change in attitude, relief at being almost at journey's end and among family making her giddy.

"I've come to visit ye and Aunt Runa," she replied. Glancing over her shoulder, she indicated Donnan. "And I've brought a guest."

Lund scowled, his gaze taking in the lad's rumpled appearance.

"What manner of whelp have ye attached yerself to, Katja?"

"He is the only reason I am here and not stranded in Thurso, Uncle. He found a place aboard a ship where they dinnae ask about my gender or my dog."

"And that's another thing," Lund rumbled, fisting his hands on his hips.

Katja tapped his forearm lightly. "Could we discuss this at the house, Uncle? Please?"

"*Hannja!*" His bellow brought a young lad skittering to his side. "Run ahead to my house and inform my wife we have guests."

The lad nodded and ran off in a flash.

Lund inclined his head to Katja and extended his arm. "Milady," he murmured, his tone even. "May I assist ye onto yer horse?"

Katja beamed at him. "Thank ye, Uncle. Donnan can ride with me."

She caught the lad's skeptical look and gave him a reassuring smile. Though unnecessary, she allowed her uncle to give her a boost onto Skündi's back, and Donnan scrambled up behind her. He fidgeted for a moment, then grabbed either side of her cloak in his fists, and Katja urged Skündi after her uncle's rangy gelding.

They soon left the bustle of the docks and busy streets of town for a small, low house only a short journey beyond.

A single, commanding bark rent the air. "*Kvala,*" her uncle murmured as he dismounted. A dog even larger than Freki appeared at his side, eying the newcomers warily. He made no further sound, but curled a lip as Freki stalked a pace forward.

"*Kvala,*" Katja rejoined to settle Freki, and the two dogs faced each other, hackles raised.

"He's grown almost to his sire's size," Lund commented as he lifted Katja from her horse. She opened her mouth to protest his help as unnecessary, but his desire to assist was genuine and she accepted his hug as he wrapped an arm about her waist and escorted her up the walk to the house.

* * *

Sundown arrived early, with the hint of snow on its breath. Calder hunkered beneath his plaide and urged his horse to greater speed.

"Pick up yer feet, Armunn," he admonished his steed. "We willnae make Thurso this night, but I'd prefer to reach Hacraig and find an inn with hot food and sturdy walls before we halt."

Armunn obliged by breaking into a slow, ground-eating lope. They paused beside a small burn, stones and nearby limbs frosted with rime in the misty air. Mud sucked at Armunn's hooves as he waded fetlock-deep into the water for a drink.

"Easy, lad," Calder admonished. "Too much of this icy water'll curdle yer stomach." He swung into the saddle, wincing at the muscles in his legs protesting the long ride.

A warm glow of light through cracked, shuttered windows welcomed Calder to the Pig and Plough long after darkness descended. The door opened, spilling raucous laughter and a drunken lout onto the cold ground. Another man stumbled after him, pivoting precariously to deliver a garbled protest to his mates inside.

Calder drew Armunn to a halt. "I dinnae know if I hope Katja traveled through here, or not." Of all the things she could be facing, all the possibilities he'd tortured himself with throughout the long day, beholding the deplorable behavior of drunken men was enough to eat into the very marrow of his bones.

A stable lad shouted at him from the doorway of a sturdy building on the edge of the small yard.

"Will ye be needin' a place for yer horse this night?" He wiped his mouth with his sleeve and Calder caught the whiff of roasted meat on the air. His stomach rumbled.

"Aye. A stall, a bit of hay, and information if ye have it." Calder slid from the saddle and led Armunn to the barn.

The lad's eyebrows lifted at the small coin Calder offered. "What sort o' information do ye seek? My master . . ."

"Willnae know we spoke," Calder assured him.

With a grin, the lad tucked the bit of silver away.

"I wish only to know if a young woman has passed this way. She is likely alone except for her horse and dog."

The lad bobbed his head. "Och, aye! Two or three nights back. She lingered the night, then left."

Calder's chest squeezed tight, his heart pounded. "How did she fare? Was anything amiss?"

The lad shook his head. "Nay. The innkeeper gave her a small room and bade her remain overnight. His wife took her meals to her."

His relief was dizzying, and Calder could not suppress his grin. "Thank ye. I will leave Armunn in yer care and return for him in the morning."

Clucking encouragement, the stable lad led the horse to his stall and began removing his tack. Calder hesitated in the doorway, fist propped on the portal as he considered the news.

It was certainly a comfort to know Katja had made it safely this far. Though it was troubling to learn she traveled openly as a lass, and the dog certainly identified her without question. He needed to find either the innkeeper or his wife. He had more questions and needed the answers.

He crossed the yard, head ducked against the knife-like wind, thankful he'd reached the inn and wouldn't be sleeping in the open this wintery night. He thought briefly of the hazardous crossing from Thurso to Stromness, of the ice already forming on the branches and stones. Of the weight of ice on a rigged ship in the gale-tossed ocean.

Unable to shake his disturbing thoughts, Calder grasped the latch and entered the boisterous inn.

Chapter Fifteen

The room glowed a cheery gold from the robust candles and the enormous fireplace set into the far wall, making it feel overheated. The door closed on Calder's heels, cutting off the bitter wind, and he inhaled a lungful of smoke, heat, and the ripe aroma of under-washed bodies that all but choked him. Blinking against the light from a hearth large enough to have no difficulty containing the large boar roasting over the low flames, Calder made his way to an empty chair.

"What can I get for ye?"

He glanced up at the throaty purr of a female voice, past the full bosom jiggling at eye level, to the lass hovering next to him. She cocked an eyebrow and gave her torso a slight waggle, increasing the bounce of her breasts above the neckline of her gown.

"A mug and a platter," he replied, refusing to stare at her generous offer.

With a toss of her head, the serving lass hurried away. Calder took a moment to inspect the room. A few heads had turned in his direction as he'd entered, but no one appeared to pay him any attention now. Voices rumbled, benches clattered against the stone floor, and laughter sparked here and there across the room.

An arm reached past him and set a platter of steaming meats, a chunk of bread and a wedge of cheese before him. Calder glanced at the wrinkled hand, following the attached arm to the smile on the older woman's face.

"Are ye the innkeeper's wife?" he asked.

She gave him a dubious glance. "Aye."

"I would like to ask ye a couple of questions later, if ye wouldnae mind," he replied, giving her what he hoped was a winsome smile.

"Are ye certain ye dinnae wish to speak with the lass, there?" she countered with a jerk of her chin in the direction of the serving wench of the inspiring endowments.

Calder's neck heated. "Nay. I believe my wife wouldnae care for my interest in another's charms—considerable though they may be."

The woman canted her head at him. "A fresh outlook, to be sure. And one that speaks of a man newly-wed and satisfied." She gave a short nod. "Take yer time over yer dinner. The rowdy bunch will be awa' home shortly if they're to make it before the storm hits."

"Storm?" Calder straightened in his chair.

"Aye. Not to worry, lad. The Pig and Plough has stood through many a winter storm. I imagine 'twill last another. 'Tis early yet in the season." She gathered empty mugs from the other end of Calder's table where three other men had vacated their spots, leaving a pile of wreckage behind in scattered platters, gnawed bones, and a tipped-over mug.

Leaving the innkeeper's wife to go about her business, Calder waited impatiently for the common room to settle for the evening. Games and conversation lingered on the fringes, but soon snoring arose from various piles of plaides and other bedding scattered around the room. A man, wrapped anonymously in a cloak, glared at him from his bench in the corner. Hair on the back of Calder's neck bristled.

Another man stopped to speak with the stranger, gaining his attention. Calder eyed them over the edge of his mug. The stranger disagreed with whatever his companion proposed, for he shoved away from the table, rising to his feet with an abrupt move, one arm tucked tight against his body. He sent an inscrutable look across the way, and Calder's breath hitched as the firelight emphasized the puckered skin and ruination on one side of his face. The dark eyes narrowed beneath bristling black brows, but a moment later, the men were gone, Calder staring after them.

"With the storm's approach, I haven't a spare room to offer ye, but ye are welcome to spread yer plaide here with the others." The innkeeper's wife dropped heavily to the bench across from Calder. "Have a care for yer pocket, though. I cannae swear yer coin will remain if ye arenae careful." She shrugged. "I cannae keep watch all night."

"I thank ye for a moment of yer time," Calder replied. "And I will sleep with one eye open."

The woman snorted her short laughter and took a sip from her mug.

"Ye were right earlier—about being recently wed. My wife and I have been married only a few weeks. I have been too busy with clan business to spend the time with her a lass needs when she is newly away from family and friends."

"Lost yer wife, have ye?" she asked shrewdly.

Air whooshed from Calder's lungs. His stomach dropped. "Aye. I know where she's headed. I'd like to know how far I am behind her."

"Describe her," the woman invited.

"Ye get many unaccompanied women at the Pig and Plough?" Calder countered.

She shrugged. "I dinnae care to help a man who cannae take care of a good lass. Mayhap ye are different?"

Calder sighed. "Ye are right. I havenae taken care of her. But I hope to convince her I can change."

"Can ye?"

"I recognize I've neglected her, though readying the clan for winter is important." He glanced at the woman for sympathy, but she merely raised a brow. "I have no wish to haul her home against her will. I do need to see to her safety."

"Does yer wife have a wee dog?"

"Wee? Nay. My wife has a dog bigger than the horse I rode here on."

The woman laughed. "Yer lady wife arrived three nights ago. She remained here unmolested, and departed the next morn. I have no idea where she traveled, save she continued north toward Thurso."

"Aye. She has kin on the islands."

"Then lad, ye may as well return home until spring. With the wind kicking up like a disgruntled bear, there will be no ships willing to make the crossing until the weather clears." She rose tiredly to her feet. "Good luck and Godspeed, lad. If she is already on the islands, she is beyond yer reach."

* * *

A woman appeared in the doorway of the house, wringing her hands in the folds of her apron as she craned her neck, searching the faces of the approaching riders. Katja's heart lurched at the familiar face, so like her mother's she nearly burst into tears.

"Aunt Runa!" With a cry, Katja leapt from Skündi's back and bolted up the walk. Shaking with relief and exhaustion, she curled deep within her aunt's embrace.

Half-laughing, half-crying, Runa at last held Katja at a short arm's length. "Look at ye, Katja! Had I not known better, I would have sworn my own dear sister had returned to me." Her gaze traveled Katja's face. "Ye look exactly like her." She trailed the backs of her fingers down Katja's tear-streaked cheeks.

"Come in, Elkesdottir. You are most welcome here."

With Runa's arm draped around her shoulders, Katja strolled inside the house, leaving Lund and Donnan to care for the horses. Freki ambled at Katja's heels.

Runa motioned for Katja to be seated. She chose a chair in a broad beam of sunlight, delighting in the fall of warmth across her shoulders and back. Runa quickly arranged a pot of hot ale and mugs on the table, pouring Katja a portion before she claimed her seat.

"What brings ye to Lerwick, Katja?" Runa asked.

Katja hesitated, her fingers wrapped around the warm mug, then took a sip. Setting the cup aside, she gazed at her aunt. A pale blue aura of confusion quickly blended into the glowing yellow she remembered of her mother's joyful, generous sister. The colors gave Katja strength.

"I have come to visit, Aunt," she began.

Runa tilted her head, her smile genuine and encouraging.

"Father . . .."

Runa's glow puddled into the muddy red of anger as a frown twitched the corners of her mouth. She gripped her mug tightly, dropping her gaze to the table before bringing it back to Katja.

"Yer father allowed ye to travel here on yer own?" Her voice was brittle.

Katja shook her head. "He doesnae know where I am." She averted her gaze. "Nor does he likely care unless it hinders the contract he made with my new husband."

Runa leaned back in her chair, clearly taken aback. She regarded Katja, then poured another portion into her mug. "Ye've a tale to tell, *Niese*. Ye must tell me everything."

* * *

Sunlight canted in through the window, green and gold through the thick panes. A maid slipped through the room, silent except for the hiss-hiss of her slippered feet on the stone floor. Finishing her task, she departed the kitchen, leaving her mistress and Katja alone once again, except for Freki who gnawed contentedly at a bone in the corner.

"Do ye believe ye did the right thing, *min niese*?" Runa asked.

Katja sighed deeply. Her throat was sore from the hour or more of talking it had taken to tell her aunt her story. Her backside was numb from sitting in the chair so long. And her heart ached with confusion and other emotions she wasn't ready to signify.

"He swore he would honor me—and left me less than a day later for the arms of his leman. He swore to protect me—and I have managed to survive three attempts of murder on my own. And he swore to care for me, yet I discover he has set his leman up in a cottage not far from our home." Her eyes, swollen from earlier tears, itched, and she swiped at them with the back of her hand. Runa silently passed her another slip of finely woven linen edged in delicate lace.

"I believe him innocent of the poisoning and such," Katja sighed, clenching the scrap of cloth so tight no amount of ironing would ever smooth its surface. Her face hardened. "But I willnae stay and wonder each night if he has been with *her* first."

Runa rose from her chair to stand behind Katja, circling her arms about her shoulders and pulling her close. "My poor wee lamb. Yer da has always been a source of trouble for us, and it seems he failed once again—and this time at the task of finding a loving husband for such a beautiful daughter."

Katja sniffed. "He doesnae see me as such."

"He is a fool. Always has been. Though he was charming enough when he decided to woo yer ma." Runa released Katja and swiveled to take the seat next to her, a hand lingering on Katja's arm.

"He arrived in Lerwick with a crony, seeking a shipwright to patch a boat. They had unwisely sailed late in the winter season, wishing to accomplish some trade others were too cautious to attempt in bad weather. He struck a bargain with Lund, and in the time it took to finish the repairs, decided Elke was the woman for him."

"I dinnae understand," Katja said. "He was often cruel to her—said her Norse heritage tainted the Sinclair bloodline."

"Yer da was often a fool." Runa mused. "He was astounded how beautiful she was. How sweet and kind. He couldnae keep his eyes off her silver-blonde hair." She gave Katja a sad smile. "Ye look just like her, Katja. Ye are so verra lovely."

Katja dropped her gaze, confused by the light green aura of pity mingled with the pink of love surrounding her aunt. "Not lovely enough to win my father's heart. Or my husband's," she added in a forlorn whisper.

Runa gave Katja's arm a gentle shake. "Dinnae let their idiocy change the woman ye are. Ye are strong and fearless—the wee lass who let none gainsay her the last time I saw her. The young woman who even now bristles with no less than four blades tucked beneath her sleeve and tunic.

"Stay with us as long as ye wish. Ye have yer uncle and me to stand with ye should either of those two fools dare show their faces here."

"Thank ye, Aunt Runa," Katja replied, not certain what provoked her tears more—her da for his years of abuse, her husband for breaking his promises to her—or the absolute love and fierce protection in her aunt's voice as her pink aura swirled strong. "I will make myself useful."

"Dinnae fash over that, Elkesdottir. Ye are family, and treated as such." She rose, giving Katja a saucy grin. "And family always makes itself useful."

She bustled about the kitchen, inspecting the pots bubbling above the fire on the hearth. Rich aromas wafted through the room as she stirred the stew. Dipping a ladle in the rich broth, she spooned a serving for Katja.

"Here ye are. A nice warm bit of soup to finish taking the edge off the cold and fill up those empty corners in yer belly. The men willnae be in for the noon meal for an hour or more, and I have a feeling ye need nourishment after yer long journey."

Katja sniffed the contents of the bowl, her eyes widening as the scant contents of her stomach rose alarmingly. "Thank ye, but—" She clapped a palm over her mouth against the roil of her belly and fled the room.

* * *

"Where is Katja?" Lund asked as he hung his heavy cloak on the peg beside the door. He gave his wife a peck on her cheek.

"She is resting," Runa replied, tilting her face to his kiss as she placed a platter of bread and a trencher of stew on the table. "Apparently, the storm last night roiled more than the waves." She took a seat next to him. "Her stomach dinnae take kindly to my offer of an early lunch."

Lund slurped a generous spoonful into his mouth, sucking in a breath of air as the hot broth hit his tongue. He swallowed and tore a hunk of bread. "Did she tell ye why she is here without chaperone or guard?" he asked, gesturing in the air with his spoon.

Runa took a more ladylike sip of her stew, ignoring the drips from her husband's spoon to the table. "Aye. The fool my sister married wedded my sweet niece to a thoughtless bastard much like himself. She has had enough and I dinnae blame her."

Lund's brows lifted in harmony—high enough to merge into the lock of hair that spilled over his forehead. Runa absently tucked the strands behind an ear, trailing her fingertips down the line of his jaw as her husband's eyes darkened dangerously.

"I'll thrash the bastard within an inch of his life!" he declared.

"Which one?" she murmured, returning to her soup. "Her father has both neglected and abused her since Elke died, and bound her to a gold-hunting scoundrel who openly keeps a mistress." She sipped her broth in silence, then placed a hand gently on Lund's white-knuckled fist.

"Mind the spoon, love. Ye dinnae wish to break another."

Lund shot her a guilty look and relaxed his grip. "They arenae fit to be in the same room with Katja," he growled. "She will stay here," he added with a decisive nod.

"Lund?" Runa's soft voice drew his attention. "There have also been three attempts on her life since she wed. Poisoned porridge, adders in her bed, and an outright attack after being lured away from the keep."

Lund's anger drew the air from the room. The fire on the hearth sputtered. His voice rumbled low, yet cold as ice. "If either dares set foot in Lerwick, I will kill them."

Runa nodded. "I thought ye would see things my way."

* * *

Calder shuddered as he rode away from the Pig and Plough.

Fierce, icy gusts whipped his plaide around him, pelting him with tiny pellets of sleet. Armunn ducked his head and skittered sideways, trying to plant his broad rear into the bitter wind.

"We must reach Thurso," Calder muttered, repeating the litany he clung to like a drowning man to a fraying rope. Thurso lay only a short distance ahead, but the weather made hope of reaching the seaside town with fingers and toes intact doubtful at best.

"I dinnae like the storm brewing any more than ye do, lad," he reassured his horse. "But we cannae leave Katja alone, and I fear for her safety."

Threads of memory from Robbie's tale wound through his mind. His Katja had killed three men—including auld Liam who was a battle-scarred warrior. Calder could scarce credit it, but Robbie had insisted she'd had no help from him.

Christer's face had darkened angrily, but he'd shown no real surprise when Calder had mentioned the facts to him.

"We knew she wasnae favored by our da, and his scorn was mimicked by those around him. She was given scant respect, and my brothers and I feared someone would overstep what few bounds there were. We could do little more than give silent warning to visitors. So, we taught her to defend herself."

No small dagger, or sgian dubh, perhaps slipped in a slender sheath down the front of her bodice. Calder remembered the weapons he'd taken notice of when they'd left Ruadhcreag for Fairetur the day of their wedding.

Two dirks in her belt, three in her boots, and one she slid under the plait at the back of her neck which would have remained hidden had he not seen her place it there. Likely a seventh in a sheath attached to her forearm, plus her sword strapped to the back of her horse, and the curved bow in its leather case. And Freki at her side.

His bonny bride was comfortable with her weapons, and she'd

used them to kill.

Had she hesitated? Cut them down without a second thought? Calder scowled. He wanted a wife who could stand up for herself. But did he want a woman who was a cold-blooded killer?

No. That wasn't his Katja. She was not a person who would harm others without remorse. She'd pleaded with him not to have Lorna beaten, for Pity's sake! Though she'd settled the problem with the wench swiftly, she'd not shed a drop of blood. Well, Lorna did wear a wee bruise on her face a few days, certainly less than she deserved.

Armunn sidled off the trail again, finding respite from the wind behind a ledge next to the riverbank. Calder swore under his breath and reluctantly reined the animal back up the gentle slope. He glanced about, anxious to realize he'd been riding with little care to who he might encounter on the trail. Though most would have sense enough to remain inside as the storm brewed, bandits plagued the roads, and those desperate enough to be abroad in such weather would be dangerous, indeed.

Chapter Sixteen

Evening came early, striding the heels of a reluctant sun.
Thoroughly wet, cold, and exhausted, Calder reined Armunn to a
halt outside the blacksmith's shop not far from the docks of Thurso.
No one appeared to be about—not surprising, as the *dreich* weather
kept most sensible people behind doors. Calder tied Armunn
beneath the overhang of the smithy's roof, and approached the
dwelling across the small, mud-churned yard.

After a few knocks on the wooden panel, the door opened. A
grizzled chin jutted belligerently above a well-muscled chest.

"What is it?"

Calder considered the man at the entry, his shrewd eyes
assessing him, understanding a man out in the weather such as
Calder was, could be in great need—and a source of coin. Calder
slipped a silver penny from his sporran.

"I am looking for a horse," he began. "Its rider is a young
woman, with a very large dog at her side. I only wish to know if she
made it this far safely."

At the mention of the woman and dog, the man's eyes widened
an instant before he resumed his scowl. Calder's pulse quickened.
He has seen her.

"I bought a nag from a woman with a dog as ye describe." His
gaze cut swiftly to the barn and back. "Said she needed the coin."

*Nag? He paid her poorly for Skündi and is covering for his
dishonorable act. What befell Katja that she would part from the
horse?* Calder glowered, fisting his hands at his side as he leaned
forward. "Ye stole from her. Paying less than the horse is worth is

theft."

"I paid her good coin," the smith protested. "Take a look for yerself."

Calder gave a short nod, and the man closed the door behind him and led the way across the yard. They entered the warm haven of the stable, the odors of hay and steaming horseflesh hovering in the low-roofed structure.

The smith halted at a small rail pen tucked under the eaves where three horses milled about, showing mild interest in the men. He waved to a sway-backed pony in the corner, standing nose to tail with a nice-looking bay mare.

"That's the nag I paid for. Good silver for a bag of bones that will fetch little more at market."

"That's not her horse."

The smithy tilted his head, his eyes narrowed shrewdly. "She sold it to me."

Calder shook his head. "I dinnae recognize it." He stared at the decrepit nag, its withers tenting the rough-coated hide sharply over the shoulders, promising a rider a painful seat if not padded adequately. "Can ye tell me anything else?" he asked, gaze trained on the beast Katja had somehow obtained.

"She also sold me these."

Calder jumped at the rattle of metal on wood, snapping his gaze to the pile of weapons on a small table. He approached the cache, studying the dirks and knives.

"I dinnae recognize these, either."

The smith shrugged. "A lass—likely the one ye seek, as there is no mistaking her beastly hound—rode up a couple of days ago, wishing to sell two horses and these pieces of *shite*." He waved his hand over the pieces of dull, rusty steel. "I had no reason to not purchase them."

"The weapons and horse—*horses*? Was there another?"

The smith jerked his chin at the bay mare. "That one. But I dinnae give her coin for it."

Calder shook his head slowly, bewildered. "I dinnae know that one, either."

A voice rumbled behind them. "I do."

* * *

Katja moved the food around on her trencher half-heartedly. The aromas of Runa's excellent cooking had faded, much to Katja's relief, and her stomach no longer roiled in protest, but she still had little appetite.

Uncle Lund had taken himself and Donnan off after a hurried meal, kissing both ladies and warning them not to wait up for him. Winter was upon them and he had chores to complete to ensure the boats in his care remained in good condition during the frigid, storm-tossed months ahead.

Runa slipped onto the bench next to Katja. "Stomach still a bit amiss?"

Katja glanced up, startled, her knife thudding to the table as her fingers sprang apart in surprise. "'Tis better, but I dinnae think I can manage much today." She gave her aunt a wistful smile. "I will do better in the morn."

But she fared no better after a night's rest. Icy sweat coated her brow and her gorge rose each time she lifted her head from the pillow. Runa pressed her flat on the bed, handing her a small chunk of bread.

"Eat slowly. If it stays down, ye may have a small sip of my special tisane."

Katja wanted to protest, but the soothing yeasty scent loosened the knot in her stomach from dizzying protest to interested rumble. She took a tentative bite, then another, relieved when it showed no signs of sparking another round of nausea.

"Here. Try this." With an arched brow to the giant dog tucked along Katja's side who eyed her handling of his mistress with some distrust, Runa gently raised Katja's head enough to allow her to sip the warm brew. With a sigh, Katja swallowed and lowered her head to the pillow and closed her eyes.

"I will leave ye for a bit," Runa said as she rose, leaving the rest of the bread and tea on a small table she pulled beside the bed. "When ye are feeling better, finish this. I believe ye will be on yer feet soon."

"I dinnae feel exactly ill," Katja noted. "I am fine as long as I lay flat."

"Ye arenae feverish," Runa agreed. "We will speak of this more when ye are better."

What an odd thing to say. Why not speak of my illness now? Why wait until I am better?

But Katja drifted off to sleep, fingers twined in Freki's wiry coat before she could pose her questions.

* * *

The morning was half-gone, and Katja was loath to remain abed. Lifting her head gingerly, she was surprised to find both her stomach and head clear and untroubled. Happiness swelled and she tossed the blanket aside, dressing quickly as the cold air touched her skin.

She found Runa in the kitchen, instructing the maid on the midday meal. Katja sent Freki outside for a bit of exercise and paused in the doorway. Runa smiled broadly as Katja entered the room, her gaze searching.

"How do ye fare, Elkesdottir?"

Katja popped a bit of cheese from a platter into her mouth with a grin. "Much better, Aunt. I'm afraid I took a bit of time adjusting to land after the storm we encountered on our way here. And, I meant to ask after Donnan, the lad who accompanied me here. Has Uncle mentioned him?"

"He has given him a position, hopeful of making the lad an apprentice when he is a bit older. He has no sponsor, so Lund wishes to observe him before confirming him as an apprentice." She lifted one brow. "Donnan was here at the morning meal, and asked after ye. I am sorry ye missed him. Lund will likely keep him verra busy until the storms drive them inside."

Happy for the lad she'd befriended, Katja nodded, accepting her uncle's decision on the matter. Though she believed Donnan to be sincere in his gratitude and eager to pursue a career, she knew little of him or his ability to remain faithful to the long years he would remain in Lund's service.

She caught her aunt's faint frown. "What is it?"

"Come to the front room, Katja. Tell me more of yerself. I have missed ye these past years. How many has it been?"

Katja followed her aunt into the cozy room at the front of the house. Though her uncle had an office both at the docks and elsewhere in their home, this room was kept fresh and orderly, a place where visitors—business or social—could relax. She made herself comfortable on a wide, cushioned chair, slipping off her shoes and tucking her feet beneath the skirt of the dress her aunt had loaned her.

"It has been almost five years since Uncle Lund gave me Freki as a wee pup when he came to Ruadhcreag on his short visit." She hesitated, recalling the abject loneliness after he'd left, his offer to allow Katja to accompany him denied. Why had she allowed duty to keep her home?

"And I have not seen ye since before my ma died."

"That is too long for us both," Runa smiled, smoothing over Katja's dismay. "How fare yer brothers? I am certain they are braw and handsome."

Katja smiled to recall the trio. "Bjorn is much older than I, and always seems stern, though I imagine being my father's eldest son isnae easy. Christer and I are closer, though Patrik and I are more of an age. Christer has always tried to protect me from censure from others. And he and the earl's captain taught me to defend myself."

"They are the ones responsible for the pile of weapons in yer room?"

Katja's memory pulled her to the men she'd killed, flooding her with guilt. "Aye." She steadied her breathing, determined to not mention the pair of thieves, dead beneath scrub next to the road to Thurso. Her aunt knew of the attack when she was drawn from Fairetur's keep. But what would she think of a niece who killed so easily? She chanced a look. The yellow aura of happiness beamed from her aunt as expected. Clear blue indicating her relaxed state wavered, creating a fine line of pale green. Did her aunt pity her?

Unexpected despair dragged at her. She wanted her love, not pity . . . desperately needed her love.

"What is it, Katja?" Runa whispered. "What do ye *see*?"

Startled, Katja gaped at her. "What do ye mean?" she whispered, her body cold and hot at the same time as fear threatened.

"When ye look at me. What do ye *see*, Katja?"

Muddied red blended to pink with an edge of the medium green of a natural healer. Katja opened her mouth, closed it, then swallowed. "Ye have a light about ye," she managed.

"Tell me. Does everyone have a light?"

Katja nodded jerkily.

"Then it is true," Runa mused. "Elke wanted me to understand, but at the time, I shuddered at what some would consider witchcraft. And because she called it yer curse. But she died when ye were a wee child, and later there was no one I could ask for fear of what might happen to ye."

"The earl wanted to use it—me—to best those he did business with. It would have enslaved me to him more than simply being a useless daughter. And I would have been responsible for betraying many." Katja's eyes brimmed with tears. "*Amma* bade me never speak of it. But it has taught me much about people. Their auras never lie."

"Do they not?" Runa asked, tilting her head. "What does my aura tell ye?"

Katja considered her aunt. "Yers is always yellow for ye are a joyful person. But now 'tis pink which tells me ye love me." She managed a faint smile. "And the green reminds me ye are a natural healer and perhaps wish to help me." Her smile vanished.

"What else, Katja?"

"There is a muddied red light about ye, but I dinnae know why ye are angry with me."

"Ye are correct about the first. I do love ye, Katja. Ye are the daughter I wish I'd been able to give Lund. And I am a healer and would do anything to help ye." She laid a palm on Katja's arm. "But look at me closely, Katja. Do I appear angry with ye?"

"I have made a mess of things." Katja's voice cracked. "Ye have a right to be angry with me. I have lied and killed. Aunt Runa, I have killed men."

"Katja, *bolli*—darling. The anger ye see isnae directed at ye. It is for the times I wished I could have protected ye, for failing to protect my sister. And it is for the men who presumed too much, who wished to harm or control ye, not allow ye to be the beautiful person ye are. I have no anger for ye."

"But I *see* it! It must be directed at me. How can I see colors meant for others?" Katja's breath caught.

"Do ye ever simply look at people? Really look at them?"

"No. I mean, people dinnae like me and I dinnae wish to . . .." Her voice trailed off as confusion robbed her of words.

"Ye learned to avoid them. Ye kept them at a distance so they wouldnae hurt ye. I understand, Katja. But people are made up of so many thoughts. Most of the time ye can overlook what is said and study what they do. Knowing yer da as ye did and how desperately he wanted yer skill drove ye to trust yer special ability, judging everyone on what ye saw on the surface. And in doing so, ye failed to learn to *see* their hearts."

* * *

A man stepped from the doorway, fading light at his back, his face in shadows. Calder's heart tripled its beat at the sight of the arm tucked tight against the man's side. A beam of wintery sun slipped through a chink in the wall and flashed across his ruined face.

"What do ye know of the woman who sold ye the bay mare?" he asked the smith.

The brawny man dropped his gaze and shuffled his feet on the packed earth of the stable floor. Fear and avoidance crackled from him.

"I dinnae buy the mare. I recognized her as yers." He gave a small shrug. "I knew the mare wasnae hers to sell—and ye may claim her as ye wish. I would have sent for ye when the weather cleared."

The scarred man grunted and swung his attention to Calder. "Ye know the woman?"

"I do," he replied evenly. "Do you?"

Calder and the stranger studied each other. A horse snorted, tapping its hoof in the straw.

"Two days ago, two men left my camp—one foolishly substituting my mare for his that he'd lamed earlier with an ill-fitting shoe. When I caught up to them, they were both dead, and the Sinclair lass set her dog on me." With a small wave of his arm, he indicated his injury. "I was caught off-guard or she and the mongrel would both lie beneath the shrubbery with the fools she killed."

Calder staggered a step back. "Ye know her? Ye know her name? She was attacked?"

The man's bark of bitter laughter was the fouler for the way it twisted the scars on his face. "She is a cold-blooded killer, but her instinct is an honest one. Her da is an evil-hearted bastard who cares nothing for the fate of others."

"Is she injured?" Panicked by the man's words, Calder's imagination ran amuck.

"She brought the horses here," the man reminded him. "Smith—did she appear injured to ye?"

"She looked fine to me—beggin' yer pardon, that is," the smith added with a quick glance to Calder.

"Ye are certain?" Calder brought his thoughts back to focus. "Who are ye and why does it matter if she is a Sinclair?"

The man stalked a step closer, into the dust-laden light. "My name is Gair Orrock. Many good people have suffered terribly at the hands of Sinclair, though I am one of only a few left to mourn them. And I have sworn to wipe the Sinclairs off the face of this earth before I die."

"That sentiment hardly surprises me. But the woman looks

nothing like the Sinclair." Calder stopped short of admitting the earl was Katja's sire.

"Nay, she doesnae. But she is the spittin' image of her ma."

* * *

Katja savored the crisp, cold air on her cheeks. Eyes closed as the brilliant mid-afternoon sun burst into yellow and red through her eyelids, she let the warmth of its glare kiss her face as she leaned against the low wall, the stone firm against her back. Her mind was deliciously blank, a balm after the revelations from her aunt.

Reservations soon crept in. Was it true? Had she relied so long on her *sight*, she'd lost the ability to really *see*? She didn't want to consider it. Shied from the pain and responsibility the thought gave her. But, despite her best efforts, Runa's words floated back to her.

When was the last time ye allowed yerself to trust someone? The last time ye accepted someone as a friend? Without using yer sight? Gave them yer friendship in return?

Morag, her old nurse, and Ranald, her sire's captain, were the only ones other than her brothers she could claim as friend. And they'd done their best to protect her whilst staying out of her father's wrath.

Her brothers. Katja shifted uneasily. They were easy to trust. She'd known them since birth, and they'd proven themselves loyal. Time and again they'd warned her of her da's temper, deflected his blow.

She imagined each of her brothers, eyes still closed. Bjorn. Unlike her golden-haired brothers, he was dark-haired like their da. Could that be why her skin twitched ever so slightly when she thought of him? His aura, the faint silver of physical abundance, certainly reflected his sturdy body, his honed muscles and unparalleled fighting abilities. He was the heir, the next leader of the Sinclairs, and the orange thread of authority weaving through his aura proved it. Was the gray mist tying the two colors together merely a blend? Or was the color indicative of dark thoughts? Or melancholy?

Katja released the tension growing in her chest, opening her eyes to stare into the distance, giving her thoughts free rein to range afield, exhaling a slow breath as the revelation lost its hold.

Her beloved elder brother had as much reason as any of them for resentment, dismay, melancholy—perhaps more. How much had her da pushed him to be stronger, harder—who was the man and who was the earl's puppet?

A sobering thought. They all did his bidding. Except for the truth of her gift, they all conformed to his demands, his lifestyle, and the ever-changing rules that kept him firmly in charge. She'd struggled daily to manage Ruadhcreag as he wished, dreading his scrutiny, though perfection was her only goal. Ever off-balance from the earl's demands for more food—better food—on the tables. Though the command would change to less food—and the scathing admonition against wastefulness—once she'd corrected the previous *oversight*. And on to another change in a never-ending cycle.

He was never satisfied. She knew this. Changing his demands kept her under his control, left her no chance to think or act for herself. Kept her concentrating on her next perceived slight, how imperfect she was, how unable to exist without his guidance. What had she ever dared that would challenge his absolute authority?

Against her da's direct orders, she'd raised and trained Freki, her uncle's gift, teaching him commands in Norn as much to honor her heritage as to frustrate her da. She'd dreamt of breaking free from his control, his scorn, the ever-present disdain that ate daily at her heart. And yet, the only time she'd acted on her dream was to leave the man who'd promised her a better life.

She jerked upright, anger sparking through her maudlin thoughts.

"I am finished with dishonesty! No man will ever treat me as chattel again. Nothing will ever convince me to return to a life where my every utterance is only at the tolerance of a man." Memory of her mother's heart-broken grief flooded her with physical pain. "Nor will I condone a life set aside for another woman."

Startled she'd spoken aloud, she dropped her hand to Freki's bony head. With a whine, he licked her hand, nudging her palm when her petting ceased. Ignoring his demand for reassurance, Katja strode forward, boots making faint tracks in the soft, damp dirt of the path that led to Clickimin Loch. A broch, or *borg* in Norn, ancient as the stones forming the walled fort, drew her attention. Resting on a holm in the middle of the loch, it rose like a crumbling crown over the water.

Freki skulked at her side, clearly unhappy with her mood.

"I willnae do it again, Freki, I'm not strong enough to risk my heart again." Katja declared, sharing her thoughts with him as she always did. The realization sparked tears. "Ye are my best friend, Freki. My only friend." She gulped to realize her aunt was right. There was no shame in having a few, intimate friends. But Katja's few acquaintances had remained at arm's length, reluctant to make friends with the earl's despised daughter—and she'd certainly not encouraged a closer relationship.

Freki nudged her hand again and Katja strangled a laugh. "Yes, Skündi is my friend, too." Sniffing, she wiped her eyes with her sleeve. She twined her fingers in Freki's rough coat, the familiar gesture calming her. With a steadying breath, she released the hound.

"*Utgeng*," she commanded. "Go and stretch yer legs. I will be behind ye."

The dog sent her a searching look, then bounded away, flying effortlessly over the rocky terrain with each graceful stride. Katja followed more slowly, unmindful of her path as the shadows lengthened and the growing cold forced her to pull her cloak close. Her exercise soon warmed her, though, and she ignored the dropping temperatures, hopping from rock to rock as nimble as the ponies grazing nearby.

Choosing a large boulder, she sat atop its rough surface, gazing across the loch, the stones of the *borg* glowing gold beneath the setting sun. Bunching the length of her cloak beneath her to soften her seat, she was content to rest. Breathing deeply, steadily, she recovered easily from her exertions. Freki bounded over the brown grass, nose to the earth as he chased a scent. The ponies ignored him, forming small, tight groups against the cold, paying no heed to the wolf-sized dog in their midst.

A cry caught Katja's ears and she glanced over her shoulder. A small form approached, one arm waving widely. Katja slipped from her rock, and Freki halted his hunt, looping his path toward the intruder.

"Freki, *halda*!" a familiar voice cried. Loyal only to Katja, the dog did not stop, but slowed to a walk, ears perked forward as he considered the lad before him.

Katja laughed, carefree and giddy with the sensation. "He willnae obey ye without my command." She halted before Donnan, hands fisted on her hips as she surveyed his yellow aura of joy, the interlacing blue of balance warming her heart. "Ye've commanded my beasts before. Where did ye learn the Norn words?"

Donnan flipped her an impudent grin. "Ye learn a lot of words, living on the docks at Thurso." His eyes narrowed with mischief.

"Ye want to hear others?"

Katja laughed and aimed a light tap to his head which the lad ducked with ease. "Impertinent imp! My uncle will box yer ears to hear such language from ye."

Donnan's grin widened. "As his newest lad, aye. But not as the lad who found his niece and brought her in before she was covered in snow." He waved an arm at the sky. "Do ye not watch the clouds?"

To Katja's surprise, the sky had darkened, clouds dull gray and heavy. A bitter wind buffeted her cloak, burned her cheeks. In accord, she fell into step with the lad, retracing her steps to the house.

"How have ye been, Donnan? Do ye think ye will remain with my uncle in Lerwick? Has he offered ye a place?"

"Yer uncle is a braw man," Donnan replied fervently, the light of hero-worship in his eyes. "I am to be his fetching lad until I am bigger. He is certain to have a place for me as apprentice then!"

His hands sketched the air in excitement. "And the smell of cut wood, the shape of the ships—Katja, I want to be a shipbuilder!"

"Already smitten after only a day?" she teased, her heart filled to the point of pain with pride and happiness for the lad.

Donnan ducked his head. "I cannae repay ye for yer help." Donnan's voice skittered across a range of emotions, and Katja was kind enough not to bring attention to the unmanly squeak.

"I am glad ye have found yer place," she replied easily, ruffling his hair in an older-sister gesture she couldn't resist. "My uncle is lucky to apprentice ye."

Donnan's grin told her everything she needed to know. *How lucky he is to have found a trade that calls to his heart. So fortunate to have Uncle Lund as a master. How wonderful to know he will be worked hard, but with fairness.*

"How about ye, Katja?" Donnan queried, tilting his gaze to her. "Have ye found what ye traveled here for?"

She knew he merely wished for her to be as happy as he, but her heart lurched oddly. "I am both satisfied and unsettled," she admitted, the words spoken slow as she considered her answer.

"I have all the acceptance and love I'd ever longed for in my family. But I am unsure if that 'tis enough."

Chapter Seventeen

The air in the stable thickened, a choking mixture of dust, old hay, manure—and anger.

"How do ye know the earl's daughter?" Calder clenched his jaw, scarcely able to control the fury riddling his body, streaks of heat and cold racing through him, loosening his muscles, sharpening his reflexes—preparing him for battle.

"I once sailed with the Sinclair." Gair bit the words through stiff lips, his derision clear. "Twenty-six years ago, we sought ship repairs in Lerwick. 'Twas there he met the lass he would marry. Her name was Elke Reginulfsdottir."

Calder's stomach clenched. Katja's elder brother, Bjorn, was twenty-five years of age. The man clearly knew both the earl of Sinclair and his long-dead wife. "Ye arenae wrong," he admitted. "Would it pain ye to learn his wife no longer lives?"

Skin blanched white around the reddened, puckered flesh of his face. The man's eyes flashed. "She was too good for him. 'Tis better she died than endured the everlasting sorrow he would bring her."

"He sired sons and a daughter on her." Calder wavered between wary anger and pity for the man who appeared to have suffered much at the earl's hand. "If the lass is the image of her ma, Elke Reginulfsdottir was a beautiful woman."

Drawing back into the shadows like a feral dog, Gair growled. "Beautiful but fickle as a *roane*. When she discovered the earl could offer her more than I, she followed him readily enough."

Calder ignored the man's comparison of Katja's mother to the enchanting water-faeries whose love for the sea overrode their feelings for their human lovers. And Gair's unfounded bitterness toward Katja sent Calder's anger spiraling once again.

"Ye cannae hold her ma's troubles against her daughter."

"She is her father's spawn," the man spat. He lifted his arm into the fading rays of light. "Well-trained by her bastard father." He leaned into the light once again.

"I have her da to thank for this," Gair snarled, a wave of his hand indicating the puckered scars on his face. "We once had a partnership, an agreement for trade. My clan, seafarers, risked much to further the earl's ambition. But when we failed—though taming the winter-stoked sea was an impossible task for even those so commanded by the great Sinclair—he had his men wipe out those who could bring evidence against his schemes. They killed any who drew against them, and innocents, as well. To ensure their task complete, they burned my home to the ground, leaving a precious few forced into reiving to survive. The Orrock clan is now nothing more than a handful of outlaws, trying to remember we once were honorable men."

He stepped forward menacingly, the stench of his anger roiling about him. "He and his kind should be wiped from the earth. Make no mistake about it. If I chance upon the bastard's daughter—and I will find her—she willnae escape her fate."

Calder's blood froze in his veins and his heart thrummed a thin, erratic beat. He would kill Katja? The one sweet and pure thing in Calder's misguided life? Once again, his thoughtlessness had driven Katja into the hands of a man who would not think twice about killing her. He stared at Gair Orrock, fisting his hands to keep from drawing a weapon.

"Ye willnae speak such of her again. I care not what ye do to her father. And ye would find the sons cut from a different cloth than their sire. But they stand a chance against ye, should ye challenge them. The lass, ye will leave alone."

Gair's derisive laughter barked in the cold air. "Have ye not listened to me? Aside from the fact her bloodline alone marks her for death, do ye not understand the threat of this woman? She cost me two men and the use of this arm. What is such a callous bitch to ye?"

Calder leaned into the man's space, bristling with the desire to thrust his dagger into the man's black heart.

"The *lass*," he snarled, "isnae a callous bitch. The *lass* is my *wife*."

* * *

Sea fog thickened around Calder the next morning as he huddled under the eaves of the inn's roof. Winds that could have cleared away the *haar*, had died down, and dull gray clouds, heavily gravid with snow, hovered just above the rooftops.

Had Katja reached Lerwick safely? A ship, returned from its daily run to Stromness, lay at harbor, barely visible through the thick fog. Its captain had recognized Calder's description of Freki, but swore he'd allow no woman aboard his ship. And his assurance the dog had been accompanied by a lad and his master, left Calder confused and worried. Very worried.

It was difficult to imagine Freki in another's hands. The beast was devoted to Katja, and Calder did not imagine even death would change that. He prayed she did not lie undetected beneath a cairn or a convenient shrub, a monument to his stupidity. Victim of robbery and worse.

Was Katja dressed as a man? A much better option, though how anyone could fail to note her gracious curves beneath a set of trews, he couldn't imagine. He'd not thought to ask how she was attired, as she had apparently traveled openly as a woman. Until Thurso. Until her gender brought her no concessions and closed many doors—including those to the ships where it was commonly known a woman—especially one as comely as Katja, and unchaperoned—could draw a sailor's attention from his duty, thus angering storm sea gods and endangering the ship. Though a naked woman was thought to bring good luck . . ..

Calder shook his head. That particular superstition, of an unclothed woman talisman, he'd not heard as he'd sought word of Katja. It was far more likely she'd disguised herself, used an accomplice to purchase passage, and left Thurso—was it nearly five days ago now? He peered at the leaden sky, stifling a curse for the turn of weather that kept him from pursuing her.

Though if Gair Orrock thought to follow Katja, he'd had no better luck. Calder drew a deep breath. The man was fanatical in his hatred of the Sinclairs. And for that, Calder could scarcely fault him. Though the Sinclair and MacGerry feud was one of long-standing, the Sinclairs had not brought the fight to Fairetur's doors. He quailed to consider the effects of such a battle on his clan—his family—Torri and Beitris. The castle was undoubtedly better-fortified than a manor house, but they would not have held out against the Sinclair forces for long.

Calder kicked away from the building and shuffled inside. Standing in the icy wind served no purpose other than to punish himself for his lack of understanding and tact with his new wife. He'd lived in his brother's shadow too long, unburdened by clan worries, taking his ease with the lasses who loved him for his ease and humor—two characteristics notably lacking since he'd become laird. His days of living as a younger son were past. The days of responsible manhood were upon him. And the prospects of appeasing his understandably distraught wife were not good.

* * *

A *snell* wind howled in from the sea, carrying the icy bite of winter to Katja's very bones. She ducked inside the house, thinking better of striding the wind-swept walkway to the stable to check on Skündi. Uncle Lund had reminded her the stable was sturdy and pleasantly warm with the bodies of so many animals close together. But she was restless, unused to so little activity, unaccustomed to the relative quiet of the single-family house. Though she'd promised her aunt she'd make herself useful, the maids left her little enough to do. And her mornings were becoming increasingly difficult.

She paused in the hallway and passed a hand tentatively over her stomach, a different chill skittering through her insides. Nausea when she woke no longer left her wondering if she was only a few symptoms away from succumbing to a fever. Nor did she fear her porridge had been tainted.

Afternoons found her relatively hungry, filching tidbits from the kitchen as she worked to prepare the evening meal. And no number of watchful glances from Aunt Runa deterred her appetite. Katja was powerless over the new hunger gnawing at her.

Voices murmured from the kitchen but she desired a few moments more of solitude. Even the maids now exchanged glances when she entered the room, something she was all-too familiar with, but disquieting nonetheless. Knowing the front room to be empty, Katja pulled a comfortable chair near the hearth and sank into its cushions.

Her stomach rumbled, as empty as a leaky kettle. But she was not ready to begin her afternoon chores. Nestled in the warmth of a soft blanket in a chair before the fire gave her a sense of well-being. Of contentment. Of sleepiness.

Could she be carrying Calder's child? A wave of homesickness washed over her. But she couldn't imagine how that would change her life with Calder. Once she bore an heir, she was of no interest to him, and he'd made it clear he was content to slake his lusts with his leman. There was certainly no guarantee this child would be a lad. A daughter, though precious to Katja, would be of no use to Calder.

She could simply refuse to tell Calder of the child. He could adopt his heir as far as she was concerned. And if he applied himself, it was quite likely the licentious Lorna would soon bear him a child. Katja's heart twisted inside her. More than the attempts on her life, the knowledge he set his mistress up in a cottage, keeping her close at hand, had hurt her immeasurably more. She pushed aside the memory of her mother's grief-ravaged face as she'd gazed longingly at her da. Never would Katja allow herself to become so haunted, so bereft.

But in her heart, she knew she carried Calder's child. A precious gift he surely would not turn aside, no matter if a lad or a lass. Longing for a family tugged at her heart. Could she convince Calder to set Lorna aside? Could she trust him if he agreed?

* * *

The winter storm broke in a burst of clear sunshine. Three days of gale-force winds had brought winter to the islands, cold, unforgiving, and ominous. Bundled safely in the Sjoberg home, Katja's restlessness had slowly settled. And so had her belly.

Free from paralyzing nausea for the first morning in almost a week, Katja flung the door wide in an excess of youthful good health and stepped into the sunlight. Freki raced past her into the snow, plowing through great drifts, flinging sparkling white dust into the air. Katja laughed at his exuberance, feeling at peace with the world.

"'Tis a beautiful morn!" she exclaimed as Runa scolded her from the doorway.

Her aunt sighed. "Enjoy the *glene*, Elkesdottir. We have too few clear skies ahead until this winter is over." She narrowed her gaze. "Are ye well this morn?"

Katja laughed again, this time for the realization she did indeed feel well. "Aye. I imagine I will best Donnan's eating prowess this day."

Runa smiled. "The lad will need to work hard to offset his feed," she agreed, with a shake of her head for the growing lad. "I believe he has grown taller in the few days ye have been here."

Katja dropped one shoulder, not quite willing to fully face her aunt. "And I shall grow apace with him," she stated, her words soft with wonder—and anticipation for Runa's reaction.

"'Tis about time ye realized yer condition," Runa replied. She pulled her plaide about her as she stepped onto the path with Katja. Placing an arm about the girl's shoulders, she hugged her, her cheek against Katja's head.

"I am willing to listen to yer thoughts, Katja. What is happening, what this means for yer life. Ye have only to ask."

Overwhelmed by her aunt's calm acceptance and offer of help—not criticism—Katja nodded jerkily, swallowing hard against grateful tears.

"I dinnae know what to do," she admitted.

"Ye must look to yer heart, lass. The bairn has a da who would likely wish to know of his child. There are many difficulties between ye. What does yer heart tell ye?"

Something inside Katja twisted violently to remember the weeks past. "It is silent, Aunt. Calder promised me caring and protection. I risked my life on his vow. And risked it again to come here when he broke his promise. I willnae risk the life of my child."

"I wouldnae ask ye to bring harm to the bairn. I would protect ye both fiercely from him should it come to that."

Katja's breath hitched. "What if some things are my fault? What if Calder is not the only one who brought problems to our marriage?"

"How so, Katja?"

They strolled slowly down the frozen path, sunlight beaming gently on their heads as the brisk air pinked their cheeks.

"I have thought much on what ye said, these past days," Katja began. "I dinnae know how to make friends or how to be truly close to someone. I desire a marriage completely different from the one my parents had. But I dinnae know how to do this. I believe only what my *sight* tells me. How do I learn to trust these other things? The way someone moves his head, hands—the way they walk and talk. How do I know when a person has changed?"

Runa halted, drawing Katja to face her. "Remember the anger ye saw in me? I still feel that in my heart. But look closely at my face. What do my eyes tell ye?"

Katja tilted her head, staring at her aunt's frank, open gaze. Her eyes rounded—truthful, kind. A slight upward tilt to her lips— humor, compelling.

"They tell me ye wish to help me. That ye care what happens to me."

"I will always care what happens to ye, Katja. I am so sorry ye grew up knowing only derision and fear. My sister and I had little contact after she wed, and the last time she visited, she was withdrawn and terribly sad and wouldnae tell me her heart. I thought there would be other chances to help her, but she died not long after."

Tears built behind Katja's eyes, but she was captivated by the sudden intensity of her aunt's gaze. Her eyes blazed and the grip of her hands tightened.

"Dinnae let that happen, Katja. Always speak to me. I will protect yer confidences as fiercely as yon beastie protects *ye*. No matter what has happened, no matter what anyone has told ye, I will love ye. And I will care."

Katja peered over her aunt's shoulder, across the snow, wind-swept into fantastic drifts sparkling in the light, where Freki frolicked. Warmed by her aunt's words and unconditional love, Katja's heart began to heal.

* * *

It was quiet. Too quiet. Calder struggled to wakefulness, a shaft of unexpected light blinding him. Realization struck. The storm had passed.

Jerking to his feet, he wrapped his plaide about his hips, securing it with his worn leather belt. Flipping the bulk of the wool over his shoulders, he bolted out the door of the tiny room and into the clear sunshine of morning.

Noises of the busy docks rocked him on his heels. Seagulls screeched overhead, vying for position on the ships' masts and rope lines, demanding to be fed. Shouts rose, one over the other in a raucous clatter as men prepared the ships for early morning departure, a nautical race to be out of the harbor and on the open sea while the weather held. Feet pounded the docks, wide brooms sweeping trampled snow and ice from the boards.

Dodging the busy lads, Calder wove to the nearest ship. "I am looking for passage to Lerwick," he shouted.

A man cut a brief glance in his direction. "We have room for a paying passenger. We will lay by in Stromness first and leave for

Lerwick tonight."

"I have a horse," Calder added.

The man frowned. "We have no provision for a horse. If ye bring him aboard, he will be yer responsibility. And must be kept out of the way. If he falls overboard, none will help ye."

Calder nodded. "When do ye leave?"

The man glanced at the sky then at the general chaos around him. "We will cast off within the hour. Dinnae be late."

Thus dismissing Calder, he strode across the deck with a shout to a dock hand who struggled beneath the weight of a wooden crate. With a glance to the sky, Calder retraced his steps to the ancient stable where Armunn waited, warm in his stall.

The horse pulled hay from the remnants of a manger nearly non-existent after years of worry by uncounted equine teeth. Dry flakes drifted around him as he shook his head, separating the stems into tiny pieces.

"We are finished here, lad," Calder said as he opened the creaky half-door. "Time for the next leg of our journey. How does an afternoon in Stromness sound to ye?"

Armunn snorted, spraying chipped bits of hay and moisture in Calder's direction. Calder laughed and dragged the bridle over the horse's head. Armunn shook his entire head and neck, settling his mane with a click of the bit against his teeth. Calder hefted the saddle and blanket, pulling the girth snug. With only token resistance, Armunn followed Calder into the winter sunlight.

Hope rose in Calder's chest, lightening his step as he returned to the ship.

One day—one more day and I will see Katja. His heart burst with the things he'd tell her, the words that would win her heart and prove he'd meant to keep his promise to her.

Ye will never have to look over yer shoulder again, Katja. I will always be there to protect ye. Impossible as that was, he was determined to ease her worries at all cost.

I will cherish ye, give ye bairns and a family. His family—not the cowards her da had raised who feared caring for their sister.

Armunn snorted as if he'd heard Calder's words. Calder jiggled the reins, tossing away his agitated thoughts.

"Aye, the lads arenae exactly *cowards*, but it sticks in my craw that my wife fended much for herself. We will protect her. We will see to it she never doubts she is loved."

They slowed, careful of a misstep on the lingering ice, mindful of the bustle around them. Reaching the ship he'd procured passage on, he led his protesting horse over the loading ramp. Calder tossed a coin to the first mate who caught it with the ease of long practice and, with a jerk of his chin, indicated a small open area on the deck.

Calder laced Armunn's reins through a rusted ring on the wall and settled in for the trip to Stromness, refusing to consider anything less than Katja's open arms.

Chapter Eighteen

Katja stared at the gossamer halo around the moon as she opened the door to admit Donnan into the house.

"Mayhap ye can sleep a bit in the morn," she noted in sympathy for the lad's dragging steps.

He sent her a disbelieving look. "Yer uncle requires me up before the sun," he sighed, collapsing to the floor beside the hearth. They were alone in the small front room, the rest of the family quiet in their own late-evening pursuits.

Freki thumped his tail on the rug and crawled the short distance between himself and Donnan on his belly. He nudged the lad, ears flat against his skull, tail wagging faster as Donnan fended him off with playful clouts and shrill cries designed to draw the dog into a frenzy of tussling.

Katja smiled indulgently at the pair as they wrestled on the floor. After a moment, Freki leapt to his feet and dashed about the room, returning to nose the lad into shrieks of laughter before darting away again.

Finally they settled, tongues hanging out as they panted, curled together on the floor.

"Ye must learn to watch the sky as well as listen for my uncle's orders," Katja chided gently. "There is a ghostly shadow about the moon this night."

Donnan raised up on his elbows. "What does that mean?"

"'Tis called a *moonbroch*," she replied. "A sign of bad weather ahead. With luck, it may result in an extra hour of sleep in the morn."

Donnan cocked his head, considering. "That is a verra good thing to know. Thank ye." He leaned back on his elbows and lowered his gaze.

"Ye seem to feel better, Katja. Are ye well?"

Amusement tickled one corner of Katja's lip. "I will survive," she drawled. "How are ye faring at the hands of my hard-working uncle?"

The lad regarded her. "He is no worse than those I've worked for before. And he will teach me to build ships—not simply give me a few errands and kick me aside."

The reminder of Donnan's life only a week previously sobered Katja.

"I am verra glad we met, Donnan."

He grinned. "I am, as well." He jostled to a seated position, a hand in Freki's fur. "And I want ye to tell me if he comes around."

"Who?" she asked.

Donnan scowled. "The man who made ye cry."

Katja blinked. They hadn't spoken of the reason for her travel to Lerwick, only that she was committed to the travel—so much as to hire a pick-pocket lad as her companion.

"Thank ye, but I dinnae believe ye need to fash over him. We needed a bit of time apart, is all."

Donnan lifted a brow. "Ye dinnae cross the North Sea in winter for *a bit of time apart*," he replied, mimicking her drawl perfectly. "I dinnae have many years, but I do know when a man has made a woman cry. I will help yer uncle keep ye safe."

"Och, Donnan! Ye are such a braw lad! I will give ye a shout if I need rescuing."

He scowled. "I know he abandoned ye to those in his clan who dinnae like ye and tried to kill ye."

"How do ye know that?" Katja asked, puzzled at why her uncle would give the lad such information, and knowing her aunt had very little chance to speak to the lad—and wouldn't have betrayed her confidence.

He shrugged. "Yer uncle dinnae tell me—exactly. People dinnae always notice me when they speak." His eyes blazed. "Dinnae have a soft heart, Katja. Dinnae listen to his false words."

"If he comes here, I will listen to him," she stated, giving Donnan a look that laced his brows together, but cut off his arguments. "'Tis unlikely he will arrive before the spring, if at all." She gazed out the heavy glass-paned window. "There will be few crossing the sea before then."

"Ye needn't go with him, Katja," Donnan wheedled. "Ye can stay here. I know yer aunt and uncle will allow it. And ye looked happy earlier. Ye havenae been happy since we met. Not truly."

"I've a lot to think on," she murmured, rising from her seat. Gliding to the window, she closed the solid shutters against the cold night air. "I appreciate yer concern, but I have much to consider."

"Was he brutal to ye?" Donnan angled his head to see her face. "Did he black yer eye?"

"Donnan! That is enough. 'Tis time ye were abed. Uncle Lund will want ye about as soon as can be on the morrow." Katja's lifted chin brooked no disagreement and Donnan scooted to his feet. Freki rose and padded to Katja's side, shoving his nose into her hand.

"I willnae let him hurt ye again," Donnan muttered.

"Away!" Pointing to the door, she motioned the lad from the room. Runa entered, passing Donnan in the portal.

"He is filling out nicely, but he's so tired he slumps," she noted as the lad disappeared down the hall.

"He is upset with me," Katja replied with a shake of her head.

"With ye?" Runa lifted a skein of woolen yarn from a basket and sank into her chair. The wooden knitting needles remained silent in her lap.

Katja sighed and spun slowly about. "He somehow overheard Uncle Lund speak of Calder and some of the things that have happened since my marriage." A strained smile tugged the corner of her mouth. "Calder will have to gain Donnan's approval if I am to return to Fairetur."

Runa peered at her niece. "Do ye wish to return?"

Katja dropped into her seat. "I dinnae know what I want. Other than to have this child." She wrapped her arms about her waist. "I scarcely know the bairn is there, yet I cannae imagine not holding him in a few months."

"'Twill seem like more than a few," Runa laughed. "Women always complain the final month lasts a year."

"Tell me more about my mother," Katja wheedled. "Sometimes I miss her so terribly."

Runa leaned back in her chair, gaze on the ceiling. "She was two years younger than I, and so bonny. Her favorite flower was the hawkweed. She embroidered the tiny yellow flowers on linen squares until I swore she must go blind."

Katja's heart stuttered. "She embroidered bluebells for me. I still have one of her handkerchiefs. Sometimes I think I can still smell . . .."

Tears welled as Katja soaked in the memories, faint though they were after so many years. She drew a stuttering breath and offered her aunt a ghost of a smile. "She wore their scent, and though it has been too long for it to linger on the cloth, I carry the handkerchief with me. To keep her close."

"Oh, Katja. I miss her, too. She charmed each of us, and I will be the first to admit she was spoiled. But such a sunny lass! Ye couldnae help but love her."

Runa picked up her knitting needles and settled in her chair, the *click-clack* following the movements of her hands. "Da couldnae bear to think of his Elke marrying, leaving us to start a family of her own. He sought a man worthy of her—though I daresay there were none." A smile lit her voice. "A man offered for her—och there was more than one, but this one was persistent. Da was opposed at first. The man had little wealth and dinnae live on the isle. 'Twas a love match on his side, though Elke took no notice of him, and no one spoke to her of his offer."

She sighed. "The Earl of Caithness had caught her eye. I will admit he was a striking figure—intense, muscular, charming. It wasnae until much later that we realized how manipulative he was. And by then, 'twas too late."

"How odd to think of ma as having a suitor before da," Katja remarked. "I wonder what became of him."

"He was laird of a small holding near Thurso. After Elke married, we never heard from the man again. Though he was verra fashed to learn of the betrothal. Enraged, to be precise."

Runa's knitting needles stilled. "He was once a fairly frequent visitor—though usually in da's office. Elke and I were only in his presence once or twice, but he clearly took notice of her. Though his clan was quite small and scarcely known, he was developing a sea trade—and showed great promise."

Katja released her breath slowly, eager to hear the next words. Runa remained silent, thoughtful.

"Well?" Katja prodded.

Runa shook her head. "He was the one who brought yer da here when his ship needed repairs. They had a shared venture . . .." Her voice trailed off, and she stared into the flames in the hearth. After a moment, she shrugged. "I seem to recall they dissolved their business after that. It wouldnae surprise me—he was that angry. This is the first I've thought of him in a verra long time."

"Poor Ma," Katja said. "I wonder how different her life would have been if she'd married him. He seemed to be in love with her."

"Obsessed with her, possibly," Runa interjected with a snort. "I cannae say that is healthy between a man and wife, either."

"He could have been kind," Katja insisted, reluctant to let go of the idea. "If only *Afi* had let them meet, had let him court her."

"Your grandfather would have left no stone unturned to bring yer ma home had he known of yer da's treatment of her," Runa replied crisply. "She rarely let the truth slip, and I wish she had confided sooner in me."

"I wonder if the man ever came to Ruadhcreag," Katja mused. "Anything to distinguish him, Aunt Runa? How odd to think I may have seen him."

"He was average," Runa replied. "Black hair, brown eyes—I truly dinnae remark the man." She dropped her wool into her lap. "His name was unusual," she said, drawing the words out, processing the memory. "'Tis the only thing I can think of."

"What was it?" Katja asked, excitement growing.

"I remember because it sounded much like *gjarn*, our word for eager—which he was." Runa smiled at Katja.

"Gair. His name was Gair Orrock."

* * *

He was not a sailor. Not in his wildest dreams, or in his lazy days as a lad floating on Loch Beaggorm, had he imagined such waves. Calder stared dizzily at the flap of tattered sail dangling in a forlorn manner from the single mast overhead. The wooden planks were slick with ice, and eddies of sea water lapped about in slushy puddles in the worn portions of the deck.

Armunn stood next to Calder, legs braced wide apart against the roll of the ship. His head hung between his knees, ears drooped with exhaustion.

"Sorry, lad," Calder murmured, patting the horse's shoulder. Muscles quivered beneath the satin hide. "I will see ye get an extra bag of oats once we're settled ashore. I dinnae look forward to the return trip any more than ye do."

The first mate had warned Calder of the possibility of a rough crossing to Lerwick. It was apparently to be expected in the winter, though this was a bit early for ships to remain at berth, wintered in for the season. Still, the *moonbroch* had indeed been a warning of the storm, though the captain had not wished to remain in Stromness, preferring to take his chances on the open sea to reach his destination.

They'd made it to Lerwick, but it had been a near thing.

They limped into harbor amid the cold, wet mist, emerging like a wraith, backed by the thin, dawning sunlight. Startled gulls screeched a welcome as they leapt into the air, black shadows against the gray sky. Activity on the docks was light to Calder's mind, though deckhands moved lively enough at the captain's call. Heavy ropes thudded to the deck as the ship drew into its berth. It waddled drunkenly on the swell against the dock, but sailors leapt about undeterred and unhampered by the toss.

Gripping the leather reins below the bit, Calder led Armunn over the planks to the dock. Scant attention was paid him as he set a careful pace over the slick surface. He stopped a lad, yawning as he scurried along in the early morning light.

Wary eyes rounded as the lad came to a halt.

"I seek Lund Sjoberg," Calder said.

With a jerk of his chin, the lad indicated a tall, muscular man not far away, his blond hair nearly white in the rising sun. "That is him. He is verra busy this morning," he added with a scowl.

Calder hesitated, observing the man who, wielding an axe in one hand, could be easily mistaken for a Viking warrior. With a steadying breath, Calder noted the man appeared to be a mature version of Christer—whom he liked, he reminded himself sternly. There was no reason to balk at this juncture.

"If ye're still here when I return, I'll introduce ye," the lad quipped, his cocky attitude goading Calder into action.

With a jerk of his head to send the lad on his way, Calder stepped through the growing crowd to Katja's uncle.

Calder ran his fingers through his hair, the drag of sea water thickening and matting the strands. He settled his plaide about him with a shrug of his shoulders, then gave up other attempts to make himself presentable. He was doubtless not the first weary traveler Lund Sjoberg had ever seen. But he hated making a poor impression on Katja's uncle when he wished to present himself as a competent laird and husband. Especially when he knew the man was a prosperous ship builder who was unlikely to simply hand his niece over to a man who looked like an unkempt, fortune-seeking *mumblecrust*.

He sighed. *A beggar I may yet be, and unkempt, but I at least have all my teeth. I will simply have to convince Katja's uncle I am no fortune-hunter.*

He paused a few feet away from the man indicated by the lad as Lund Sjoberg. Lund cut a glance his way, but finished his discussion with the other two men present and sent them on their way before beckoning to Calder.

"What can I do for ye?" he asked, his manner not quite brusque enough to indicate Calder was wasting his time, but enough to let Calder know he didn't engage in idle talk.

The crowd awaiting Lund Sjoberg's attention grew. Calder shifted his feet, thought better of his prevarication, and took a step closer. The man's gaze swept him from head to toe. He frowned.

"I dinnae wish to take up yer time, but my name is Calder MacGerry. I seek my wife—yer niece, Katja Sinclair."

* * *

Lund's jaw clenched tight. His gaze narrowed on the slender yet sturdy man before him. Lad. He was but a lad. Small wonder he'd been neglectful of his wife.

Tattered cuffs on sleeves short enough to be practical, not fashionable, framed hands used to work. A worn plaide draped the lad's hips, cinched with a leather belt tied in a supple knot, the strap thin from years of use. Dark stubble framed a square jaw, echoing the stains of exhaustion beneath his eyes. Yet his stance held steady, his back straight, his gaze true.

Against his better judgment, Lund motioned Calder to a door at his back. "Go inside. I will attend ye shortly."

With a nod, Calder tied his horse to a nearby rail, close against the building and out of the worst of the wind, and slipped inside the room that served as Lund's office at the dock.

Lund stared at the door as it closed behind his niece's husband, then turned abruptly to the men who awaited his next orders. With a snap of his fingers, he brought his assistant, Arn, to his side.

Lund's eyes flicked to the three men waiting patiently. "See to their needs and finish preparing the berths. I will be unavailable the rest of the morning."

Arn drew the men away, greetings and assurances falling drone-like on Lund's ears. His attention completely diverted, Lund followed Calder into the office.

He lifted the latch and stepped inside, recalling the sizzle in his blood at his wife's recitation of Calder's offenses. How dare this—

this *lad*—leave his *niese* to face the hostile MacGerry clansmen? What could possibly be more important than seeing to the girl's tender heart? He'd better have compelling reasons for his actions. Convincing him, Lund, of the reasons for his neglect might save his marriage. And his life.

* * *

Calder resisted the impulse to spin about as the door opened. He'd been caught staring at the shelves and bins lining the walls, evidence of the purpose of the small room. A large table took over nearly half the room, its surface laden with rolls of parchment and scattered with small rocks to keep the flattened pages in place. Quills, their nibs neatly sharpened, lay in a row to one side.

Books, such as Calder had never seen, were arranged on the shelves, their bindings of leather and wood—most plain, but a few tooled with elegant carvings. *She is out of my reach*, Calder thought—and not for the first time. *But she is my bride, and I will do my best to make amends.*

He reached a finger reverently to a fat tome laying cornerwise on a shelf . . . and nearly jumped out of his skin when Lund entered the room.

"Ye are the reason my *niese* risked her life to come here?"

No greeting. No offer of hospitality. Lund's words fell more like an accusation than a question seeking confirmation.

"I am her husband, aye. But I would never knowingly put her in danger. I realized the enormity of our difficulties far too late."

"*Our difficulties*?" Lund raised an eyebrow, narrowing his gaze until Calder had to fight the impulse to squirm. The air in the small room, only warmed slightly by a small brazier in the far corner of the room, grew close, heavy with unspoken threat. And scorn.

Lund broke his gaze and stalked to the large chair behind his desk. In stark contrast to his work bench, the surface of his much smaller personal table was clutter-free. Cloak billowing, Lund dropped into his seat, ignoring Calder's comfort, and leaned back, fingers gripping the chair's arms, his bulk no less threatening for his sudden loss of stature.

"Tell me why I should take ye to Katja," he invited, his words a verbal spar as though he'd clearly relish a more physical sorting of Calder's past actions.

"Katja and I married abruptly—at her da's insistence. I had no thought to gaining a wife, and I am certain she'd not considered a husband, either. We met at the altar and returned to Fairetur—my home—that day.

"Our clans have been enemies for many years, and though I'd hoped my people would welcome her as a hope for prosperity and peace, there were those who chose to hate her.

"To my shame, I paid little attention to her in the weeks after we wed. My clan is poor, but Katja's dowry gave us a chance to not only survive the winter, but to prosper—but only if put to proper use quickly."

Calder shifted his feet, feeling the weight of Lund's stare to the very pit of his stomach. "I chose clan welfare over that of my wife. I left her to manage the clan in my absence. I was an idiot."

"That ye are an idiot is yer best defense?" Lund crossed his arms over his chest, clearly distancing himself. A flash of panic swept over Calder, mingling with the heat of discomfiture rising in him. Exhaustion beat at him, along with the certainty he was no match for Katja—or her uncle.

"I want . . .." Calder flinched and swore under his breath at the words that would not rise to his lips. Gripping the tattered remnants of his pride, he steeled his gaze.

"I want her to know none of this is her fault. 'Tis mine. If for no other reason than to clear things between us, I want her to hear this from me. And, if she'll consider being my wife, I will do my best to keep the promise I made her the day we married."

Lund nodded. "I suppose that is a start," he allowed. "But ye best polish yer words, lad. She will be a lot harder to convince than I am."

The lad Calder had spoken to earlier slipped into the room, first an inquisitive nose, followed by rounded eyes sparking with indignation. When Lund merely lifted an eyebrow in query at him, he stepped inside, closing the door behind him.

"This is him?" he asked, cutting his gaze to Calder with a flash of anger. "Ye arenae thinking of taking him to her?"

Lund's bland gaze hardened perceptively, and Calder wasn't certain if his displeasure focused on the impertinent waif or if he agreed with the lad and reconsidered his decision.

"I wish her no harm, but intend to speak with her," Calder stated, irritated by the weight given the insolent lad's opinion.

"Ye dinnae deserve to speak to her," the lad shouted, jabbing an accusing finger at Calder. "She could have died running from ye! Ye arenae fit to wipe her arse!"

"As true as yer first two observations are, I dinnae believe ye are privileged enough to comment on the third," Calder remarked chillingly.

Eyes narrowed, the lad simmered beneath the rebuke. Lund cleared his throat.

"Come with me, and I will take ye to Katja," he said, rising from his chair. He gave the young lad a quelling look. "Though the lad has yet to make apprentice, I dislike blood on my floor."

Chapter Nineteen

To ask for another day as beautiful as the previous one would be too much, especially on the heels of the storm that crossed the ocean during the night. Impressed with her weather lore, Donnan had pressed her for more, and they'd ignored the rising wind as she teased the scamp into soaking up more knowledge than he realized.

Katja patted Skündi's nose, checked his water bucket and mound of hay in his trough, then whistled for Freki. She bundled her cloak about her and braced for the cold walk to the house.

"'Tis a *snell* wind," she remarked to Freki as a biting lash snatched at her hood, peeling it from her head. Grasping the edges of the wool more tightly, she ducked her head and quickened her steps, ignoring the strands of hair that leapt about her head. Startled to hear voices, she halted. Two men, one distinctively Uncle Lund with his broad shoulders and wealth of white-gold hair, handed their horses to a stable lad. The second man stepped from behind Uncle Lund, his dark green and blue plaide whipping about him in the wind. Blue, pink, and purple lights swirled about him. *Uncertainty. Love. Guilt.* What did it mean?

Katja's heart lurched as the man faced her as if sensing her presence, his bright, MacGerry-blue eyes piercing her soul. He took a half-step toward her and she opened her mouth to speak, though she couldn't for the life of her think of anything to say.

Why did ye promise me yer love then betray me? Is there more I should have done? Why can I not breathe?

She wanted him. She wanted him to hold her and tell her everything would be well. She wanted to toss him over the cliff where waves crashed below. Then race to his side and . . ..

Something tugged fiercely at her cloak and she motioned with a hand for Freki to cease.

"'Tis me, Katja!" Donnan hissed, tugging at her cloak again.

Startled, Katja pulled her hand away from the patting motion meant for Freki's furry head. She glanced at Donnan's face, eyes wide, mouth scrunched in a scowl. His arms crossed his chest as he jutted his chin in Calder's direction.

"He's here," he muttered, his voice hostile.

"Yes," Katja murmured, her attention drawn back to her husband. Calder tilted his head, questioning silently. "Thank ye," she added absently. Freki leaned his support against her hip on her other side.

Donnan hissed and snatched her cloak again. "He's no good for ye, Katja. Dinnae listen to his lies."

"I will speak with ye later, Donnan," Katja replied, giving her voice enough strength to quell further warnings from the lad.

Lund caught Calder's look and turned to Katja. He gave her a reassuring nod and stepped to her side. "Do ye wish to speak with him?" he asked, indicating Calder. "It isnae required of ye if ye dinnae wish it."

"He has never wished me ill, Uncle," she demurred, wiping a strand of hair from her face. "Mayhap we could step inside, out of the weather?"

"Take the front room. Yer aunt will bring drink and mayhap a bite. Though I willnae swear his willnae be tainted."

Lund's subtle humor grounded her, brought her feet back to earth where they belonged, and eased her racing heart. She realized she gripped her uncle's arm—tight. With a rueful look, she released him. "Aye. I imagine she will at least care to look at him. Hopefully 'tis all."

"Dinnae fash, Katja. Should young Calder make a misstep, the lad will champion ye."

"I daresay he will listen at the door." Katja offered a small smile. "Thank ye, Uncle. I will hear what Calder has to say." *But I willnae offer him my heart again.*

* * *

The world around Calder vanished. Katja was more beautiful than he remembered, her hair the color of the pure morning sun as it burst through the fine clouds in summer. She was radiant, her cheeks rosy from the wind, her eyes sparkling—though he suspected that was from the wind as well, for he could not imagine her shedding tears of joy in his presence.

He yearned for her to welcome him in more than simple hospitality. It would have sent him to his knees if she'd opened her arms to him, but he would have survived. For now, he'd settle for polite acceptance, her agreement to speak with him in private—and a bit of humor. Though he didn't welcome the abbreviated distraction attached to her side as surely as her dog.

"Will ye come?" Katja asked, her voice soft, low. He could glean no insight from the sound or inflection. She led him inside the house, shedding her cloak, dog, and two-legged protector at the door as they entered a comfortable seating area. She motioned him to a chair, and seated herself opposite.

"There is no need to close the door," she noted with a small shrug. "Everyone wishes a look at ye, and until Aunt Runa brings drinks, we will be interrupted anyway."

It was both a curse and a blessing. He'd sought her for well over a week, terrified at the tales he'd heard of her along the way. Afraid she'd be taken by the next man who saw her, mortified he was not there to protect her.

But now—now he was with her again, and he didn't know if he wanted to swear or shout at her. If he'd rather kiss her or hold her so tight she'd never get away from him again. His hands twitched, his arms trembled. What did Katja *see*?

There were eyes at the door, holding him motionless as nothing else could. The hair on the back of his neck prickled, but he refused to give indication he knew someone was there. It was likely the lad—Donnan, Lund had called him—whom Katja had befriended in Thurso. It was also likely Calder would owe the lad his thanks for keeping Katja safe on her journey from Thurso to Lerwick, but he would think about that later.

A tall, slender woman glided into the room, directing the placement of a tray on a small table at Katja's elbow as two young women arranged a pitcher and mugs and a plate of bread and cheese. She waved the lasses away and faced Calder, her gray eyes and strong chin an exact match to Katja's. Calder needed no introduction to know she was Katja's aunt.

"Ye have a lot to answer for," she said. "I will tolerate no intimidation or false promises."

"Thank ye for protecting Katja," Calder murmured, inclining his head respectfully. "There have been too few people in her life for her to rely on." He met her gaze. "It is my fervent wish to become one of those people. The decision, of course, is hers."

The woman gave a curt nod and, placing a hand reassuringly on Katja's shoulder, hesitated only a moment before leaving the room, closing the door behind her.

Calder glanced back at his wife. Her chest rose and fell with long, deep breaths, as if she tried to steady herself. Her cheeks, still tinted pink, provided a splash of color against her now pale skin. Fingers pleated the thick wool of her skirt.

What did she fear?

Calder leaned forward, resting his forearms on his knees. "Katja, ye dinnae know how glad I am to find ye well."

She glanced up, cool eyes boring into his. "Ye dinnae think I could take care of myself?"

And why would he not? Hadn't he left her alone with a strange clan who boasted any number of people who hated the fact she was a Sinclair? Why hadn't he worried about her then? There was no good answer to her question, and he let it pass.

He considered a different approach. "Are ye well?"

Her skin blanched further. "Well enough."

"Are ye injured?"

This time she tossed her head. "Do I appear injured?"

The obvious answer was no, but before he could reply, she brushed his words aside with an impatient gesture.

"Calder, I dinnae know why ye came. Yer clan needs ye. There is much left to do so everything is prepared for spring."

"But I need ye, Katja."

She bit her lip and dropped her gaze. "Ye need my dowry."

"I stand by my words. I need ye, Katja."

"Why?"

"Is baring my soul not enough? What do ye want from me?"

Her eyes leapt to life, sparkling with either anger or agitation, he could not tell. He wanted neither.

"I want be allowed to live my life quietly here. I long for a simple life, one of peace and being satisfied with myself and my labors . . .."

She bit her lip again and looked toward the window.

"What is it, Katja? Why do ye wish to shut yerself away here?"

"What do ye see in yer future, Calder?" she asked, not answering his question. He struggled to allow her to guide their conversation.

"My life changed drastically the day my da died. I was never meant to be laird, but it happened. I'm a hard worker, but I've shouldered too much responsibility in the past month, and there are capable men I should have allowed to help me. I would like to spend time getting to know ye. Learning what makes ye smile, laugh. I want to create a family, to have children and watch them grow."

Katja sprang to her feet and paced to the small shuttered window. She fingered the latch, then released it to pull the boards aside, letting thin silvery sunlight into the room.

"I am not the person ye seek. I dinnae belong in yer clan. No matter how ye try, I will always have to watch my back, inspect my food, pull the covers back at night before slipping into bed." She sent him a look over her shoulder. "Go home, Calder. I willnae contest yer right to keep yer leman. Ye would be free to adopt any child she gives ye."

Her jaw clenched and he could tell the words hurt her. He rose slowly, hands spread low, unthreatening. "What would ye get from such an arrangement, Katja?"

"Freedom. Release from the expectations of too many people who wish to control me."

"I have already sent Lorna away. She agreed to marry a man who fulfills the manrent on your dower lands." He stepped closer, studying her face, the startled blink of her gray eyes.

"There will be no base-born bairn to adopt. So, tell me. What would I get from yer arrangement?"

She stared at him, clearly at war with herself. Calder waited patiently, giving her space to breathe. Her hand drifted to her belly.

"Ye would get this child."

No air remained in the room. His lungs heaved, his muscles trembled as though he'd just run a great race. It was impossible to hear above the roaring in his ears. Calder stared dumb-struck at his wife, her trim figure showing nothing to support her claim.

"When did this happen?"

"Ye were there, or do ye not remember? 'Twas clearly more memorable to me than to ye." Katja's eyes flashed, the downturn of her lips outlining her hurt.

"St. Andrew's—" Calder raked a hand through his hair. "That isnae what I meant."

"The bairn is yers and willnae arrive until early summer."

Calder wanted to take her in his arms, reassure her he knew she'd not played him false. He longed to hold her against him, feel the bairn move inside her, though he rather suspected it would be some time before that occurred. It took all the strength he could muster to keep his arms at his side.

She twitched her skirt aside as she passed him. "If the bairn is a lad, 'twill be his right to train as the future laird of the MacGerrys. I will see that he knows who he is and has a sword in his hand before he walks. As much as I dislike war, I am not so foolish as to wish my son to be at a disadvantage. And when he is of an age, we will come to ye."

Crossing to her in two quick steps, he wrapped his fingers around her upper arms, surprised once again at the firm muscle beneath the gown's cloth. A warrior's arms. The arms of his wife.

"Ye and the bairn are mine! I willnae allow ye to shut yerself away like this."

"Ye think to possess me?" she tossed at him, a look of scorn at his hands. She sighed. "Ye and my father, cut from the same cloth. In yer own way, ye each seek to own me, use me for yer ends."

She had no need to fight him. If anything could have induced him to release her, the idea she placed him on level with her da made Calder's blood run cold. He loosened his grip and stepped back.

"I have followed ye for most of a sennight. I am exhausted and unable to think clearly. Mayhap a bath and rest is in order."

Without waiting for her response, he pivoted on his heel and left the room.

* * *

Katja dropped into her chair, unable to remain on her feet an instant longer. She gripped the front of her dress so tightly she thought the cloth might rip, but she was powerless to release it. She closed her eyes as a moan died in her throat.

Runa hurried into the room and slipped to her knees next to Katja, gripping her hands in sympathy.

"He sent Lorna away?" Katja choked. "But I heard him—he *bragged* about keeping her close to hand. Refused to let Robbie gainsay him." Or had he? It had been the final straw. She'd gone to him, glad he was home. Willing to give their marriage a chance. Only to snatch her hand from the partially-open door as his words burned through to her soul.

She'd not waited to confront him, hadn't wanted to see the beautiful colors of her new husband muddied with the brown of dishonesty, the red of lust—for another woman.

"I wanted him to be the man who made me forget everything. The husband I could trust, who would give me companionship, consideration."

"And love?" Runa asked gently. "Did ye expect him to fall madly in love with ye and never a cross word between ye?"

"Why not? Is there no other man like Uncle Lund who cares for his wife? Are all men like my da?"

She stormed to her feet, ignoring the incredulous snort from her aunt. "I've seen enough of the baser nature of men living under my father's roof. The gray aura of dark thoughts, the dark green of jealousy and resentment. The red glow of lust, the purple of guilt and shame. Is this all they are capable of?"

She flipped a hand into the air, cutting off Runa's words, working herself into a fine temper. "I willnae open my heart and my legs for a man, only to be cast aside when my use as a broodmare is over." Katja whirled. "I want more! I deserve more!"

Calder strode through the doorway and stood before her. He took her hands, though she scarcely felt his touch.

"In the presence of God and before these witnesses I promise to be a loving, faithful, and loyal husband to you for as long as we both shall live. I ask ye to be nothing other than who ye are, for I love what I know of ye, and I trust who ye will become. I will always respect and honor ye. No one will ever come between us."

Too stunned to pull away, Katja did not resist when Calder placed a gentle kiss on her brow. "I want only to protect ye enough that ye are free, and give ye moments that take yer breath away."

She closed her mouth with a snap, aghast to find it open like a landed fish.

Lund took his wife gently by the hand and led her to the door. "I told the lad to polish his words."

* * *

At first, he'd spoken to her of his accomplishments at Fairetur, and of Torri and Beitris and Robbie. Surprised to discover how much she missed the people she'd come to know in her short time there, Katja listened eagerly. The sound of his voice, so earnest and caring, soothed her. He wrapped her in his arms as she told him of her journey to Lerwick, buried his face in her hair as she recounted the danger she'd put herself in. He did not rebuke her, but settled a lingering kiss upon her lips as a prayer she would do nothing so foolish again.

The water in the tub had cooled and the candles had burned low by the time they adjourned to the room Runa'd had prepared for Calder. Katja heated more water and lingered to assist her husband's bath.

Katja discovered she liked the feel of her husband's skin beneath her hands, and if his lack of notice of the less-than-hot water was to be considered—and the increasingly red aura surrounding him—he liked her hands on him as well.

"Ye need to know something about me," Katja began cautiously, needing to tell him of her *sight*, yet unwilling to spoil their new accord.

"I want to know everything about ye, lass. Finding new things to love about ye is becoming my favorite pastime."

Feeling brittle and uncertain, she returned his gentle smile. "I hope that remains true," she said.

Calder rose to his feet in the tub, water sluicing off his skin flashing like rivers of diamonds over polished bronze. Katja blinked, the memory of their joining weeks earlier suddenly hot beneath her skin. With a flutter of breath, she handed him a piece of linen. He grinned and raised his arms, inviting her to dry him.

She swallowed. *How can this be more difficult than fighting two men who wish to kill me, or crossing the North Sea in a storm?* The absurdity struck and she stepped close to Calder, breathing in his scent, buffing his skin to a warm glow, completely aware of what her actions did to him—and to herself.

He didn't move. His fingers twitched and his breathing deepened, but he otherwise didn't move. Katja trailed her fingertips down the rippled muscles of his arm, the touch vivid with the last time he'd held her. Loved her.

He loves me.

She flattened her palms to his skin, glided across his shoulders, down his back to his narrow waist. Warmth rolled off his skin. Fine hairs glowed in the light. Pink and red burst around her as she pressed her cheek to his shoulder, leaned closer. She closed her eyes and ignored her sight and chose to listen to her heart.

I love him.

She slid her hands around his belly, up his chest. He leaned into her embrace.

"It was good, wasn't it, Katja?" he murmured. "So verra good."

Katja nodded briefly, drowning in the need to feel her skin against his. To remember, to know how good they were together. She would no longer compare herself to her mother . . . or any other. Her need for Calder was inexplicable, all-consuming, unique.

She opened her eyes as he faced her and framed her cheeks with his hands. "Trust me, Katja. I never meant ye harm. I promised to protect ye, and I failed. 'Twas never yer fault. Mine alone."

"I dinnae trust ye . . .."

"Ye can," he insisted.

Katja laid a fingertip against his lips. "Ye need to know *why* I dinnae trust ye. I *see* things. Auras." She searched his face for the shock, dismay, outrage sure to follow when he realized what she meant. An evil man would delight in her unearthly ability. A righteous man would consider it blasphemy.

Calder was not an evil man.

He nodded. "I know. Yer brother told me."

"Which brother?" she stammered, taken aback.

Calder ran the pad of his thumb over her cheek. "Christer. Though he was fairly put out with me at the time." He kissed the tip of his nose.

Katja blinked. "Ye arenae disturbed? Upset?"

"Aye," he admitted with a half-shrug. "What man likes to discover his wife can tell more about him than his words suggest? Though I believe men find it always so, even without the *sight*," he replied, his grin widening. He settled his forehead against hers.

"Sweetheart, I care not that ye see auras. 'Tis yer gift, and yers alone to do with as ye please."

"It doesnae serve me well," she whispered, hollow to realize the part of herself she'd relied on so fully had betrayed her just as much.

"How so? Ye have relied on it these years to keep ye safe."

"Safe. And apart. Isolated." Katja sighed. "I have discovered auras tell me much of a person, but mayhap not everything. My aunt had a dark red aura about her, which means anger, but she wasnae angry with *me*. With things to do with me, but not *me*. Had she not said so, I would have assumed she not only was angry, but had ceased to love me."

Calder edged half a step back. "Look at me, Katja. Tell me what ye see. Tell me everything."

She studied his body, drew her reluctant gaze to the lights wavering about him. "The silver tells me ye are strong physically. And the sparks of purple and red show a bit of guilt, and more than a hint of lust." Heat flooded her cheeks. "There is also the pink of love, and the soft blue of uncertainty."

"All of this is true. My guilt is for what I dinnae do, not for anything I plan to do to ye in the future. Ye cannae miss my lustful thoughts and hardly need to check my aura when ye can verify that by peeking a bit further south, aye?" He laughed. "I do love ye, Katja. But I am uncertain about our future. Will ye have me?"

Chapter Twenty

Katja answered him with her heart. She pressed against him, wrapping her arms about his neck, stretching up on her toes.

"Can ye unlace me?" she whispered.

Calder replied with a short bark of laughter. "I dinnae know. Ye have suddenly given me *gawky* hands." He reached behind her and, dragging her braid over her shoulder and out of his way, felt up and down her back for her laces. With a grin of triumph, he pulled them free, and Katja wiggled her shoulders as he worked the gown loose. He dropped a kiss to the bared skin, then hesitated as the heavy cloth slipped past her breasts to the floor.

Her breasts showed clearly through the sheer muslin of her chemise. The nipples beckoned dark pink, a dusky valley between. Calder took his time, cupping them in his hands, running the pads of his thumbs over the sensitive tips. Katja leaned into him with a soft moan. She tilted her face up and he lowered his lips to hers, hungry and eager.

Katja untied the bow at her neck and brushed the chemise to the floor. With a sigh that was a mixture of relief and insistence, she set her skin against the length of his. And felt welcomed.

Home.

"My beautiful Katja," Calder murmured. Sliding one arm behind her knees, he lifted her. Crossing to the bed, he settled her there, cradling her against him as though she were infinitely fragile. Priceless. Precious.

He took his time awakening her desires, though she twisted

beneath his hands, urging him on. By the time he entered her, they were both slicked with sweat. He groaned, fighting his release, but she burst beneath him in a cry of pleasure, her nails biting into his skin, legs wrapped about his waist so tight he could scarcely move. Her hips jerked again, and he was undone, uniting with her in the brilliance of their joining.

They curled together, touching each other through the lazy afternoon, loving when passion roused them yet again. Even in the aftermath, when they sought respite in cool air on their skin, he kept the fingers of one hand twined with hers.

"I am sorry I dinnae understand things," Katja murmured late in the night. "I should have asked . . .."

Calder kissed her temple. "Ye shouldnae have had to ask. I shouldnae have given ye reason to doubt."

"Lorna is truly gone?"

"I never had plans to keep her around. Even before ye and I wed, Lorna and I were only occasional comfort to each other. But I couldnae simply cast her out. Giving her a position as wife where she is needed pleased her."

"It pleases me, too," Katja admitted. "Now. But I heard ye say ye'd set her up in a cottage nearby. I immediately assumed ye would continue to visit her."

Calder's arm tightened about her. "I am verra sorry, love. The men in yer life never gave ye much reason to trust them, but I hope to prove different."

"Ye are. My heart trusts ye." Katja tucked her cheek against his chest.

"And I had no idea Auld Liam would go to such lengths . . .." Calder's chest shuddered and he brushed the hair back from her cheek. "I am so glad ye are strong enough to protect yerself."

"I had never faced a man in mortal danger before," Katja

admitted. "But my brothers and Ranald—doubtless knowing the type of men attracted to my da who would visit Ruadhcreag—were relentless in teaching me to defend myself. I dinnae wish to do it again, but there are now fewer scoundrels around who wish to take advantage of women."

Calder gave a soft laugh. "Aye. And if tales of Katja and Her Mythic Beast grow apace, mayhap a few more will think twice before accosting a pretty lass on the road to Thurso."

"Mythic Beast?" Katja cried. "He's a sweet lad. And I truly wouldnae be here were it not for him."

"He may have my portion of roasted meat for his reward," Calder teased. "And I believe we have another lad who has decided to champion ye."

"Donnan? He has had an unfortunate past, but mayhap faces a better future."

"He doesnae believe I am worthy of ye." Calder frowned. "I believe he mentioned I am not fit to wipe yer arse. I wonder where he learned such words."

"The imp!" Katja laughed. "I have spoken to him about his language. 'Twill be Uncle Lund's problem once I am gone."

"Are ye truly coming home with me, Katja?" Calder asked.

She wiggled in his arms until she could look at him. "Aye. I believe I can go into this marriage with different eyes, different expectations. I will compare ye to no others. And I will learn to ask if something is unclear."

"I now know what a treasure I have, and will risk it no harm. Love is to be tended, not put on a shelf once won. And I will make certain all at Fairetur know who their mistress is. The wrong I have done ye was from ignorance, not intent. Thank ye for opening my eyes."

* * *

Katja and Calder were enjoying mugs of heated cider when Runa entered the kitchen to begin the morning meal. A sleepy maid waved her to a chair and placed a mug before her.

"Already have the servants up?" she noted with a smile. "I'd have thought ye the last up today." She took a sip of her cider and sighed. "Though we saw little of ye yesterday and I imagine ye are starved."

"Aunt Runa!" Katja protested, her cheeks hot with embarrassment. Calder laughed and patted her hand. *He is my husband.* The words were both shy and proud and Katja ducked her head to hide her smile.

A freshly scrubbed Donnan darted into the room ahead of his master, claiming the end of Katja's bench from where he sent Calder a murderous glare.

"Dinnae listen to yer aunt, Niese," Lund rumbled as he plopped down next to his wife and thumped the table for his mug. "She is still vexed to hear she has the husband other women wish for."

Runa rolled her eyes. "For the love of—can we not lay it aside?" She canted her head at Katja. "I agree he is a rather singular man, and often thoughtful—mayhap no more than vexing on most days. But yer words have gone to his head and he reminds me of my good fortune in landing such a spectacular catch a bit more oft than is good for his health."

Calder buried his laughter in his mug, pulling his elbows from the table as the maid laid an enormous bowl of porridge on the table. Donnan dove for his bowl and spoon but managed to remember his manners an instant before Runa's ladle forced his attention. He settled to his seat, hands folded in his lap, as she served the table.

At last, everyone had a steaming bowl of cooked oats topped

with milk, honey and butter, a chunk of bread, and a mug of mulled cider before them. Lund brought his hands to the table and everyone hesitantly joined hands.

"*Deg, Gud, til ære.*"

Everyone mumbled after him, "To God the honor."

Donnan cast a look at the others, then grabbed his spoon, shoveling in his porridge at an alarming rate. A mild rebuking glance slowed him down, but he was well into his second helping as Katja finished her first.

He tugged her sleeve, leaning into her to keep his words from being heard. "Come help me with the horses," he hissed.

Katja stared at him. "Is aught amiss?"

Donnan shook his head. "I know Skündi misses ye. And Freki needs exercise." He peered around Katja to Calder and frowned. "And I need to talk to ye."

Katja nodded. "Let me speak to Calder—"

"Can ye not act without askin' him?" Scorn rolled from his voice, though he kept it soft, careful not to risk Lund's disapproval.

"Ye're a bold lad," Katja drawled, pulling her chin back as she raised her brow. Donnan flashed her a look and drew an impatient breath.

"Will ye come?"

Katja paused then nodded. "Away with ye. I will finish my porridge in peace and come to the barn after. Make sure Skündi has fresh hay in his stall when I get there."

Donnan nodded jerkily, snatching up a double handful of bread as he climbed to his feet. He bobbed his head in Lund's direction. "I'm to the barn, sir. I've stalls to clean." At Lund's silent nod of dismissal, Donnan bolted out the door.

Katja leaned against Calder's arm, propping her chin on his shoulder. "Donnan wishes to chastise me for falling so quickly for what he imagines to be your non-existant charms. He cajoled me into meeting him at the barn by calling into question my concern for my animals' well-being."

Calder grinned. "Shall I meet him behind the barn to repair my reputation—and yers as well?"

Katja laughed and landed a swift peck on his cheek as she rose to her feet. "Nay. I doubt I've faced a man more fearless—for all his lack of years. But I shall prevail. Feel free to check on Armunn in a bit should it cross yer mind."

Calder caught her wrist and pulled her close for a hard kiss on her lips before he let her go. "I will," he promised. "Dinnae let the lad disturb ye."

Lund glanced up from his steaming mug. "And see to yer beastie. He pined something terrible for ye whilst ye gave yer attentions to yer husband. I sent him to Skündi's stall rather than force him to the kennel like an ordinary hound." He cocked an eye at Calder. "The dog, that is, nae yer husband."

She laughed and gave them an airy wave as she stepped from the kitchen. Stopping at the front door, she checked the blades sheathed at her forearm and at the nape of her neck. Calder had teased her when he caught her strapping on the dagger at her thigh, but she'd not been without these three in too many years to count. Truth was, on a normal day, she'd count no fewer than six or seven blades, but this was no normal morning. This morning she'd woken in Calder's arms. And in her uncle's house, she felt safer than any place she'd ever been.

Wrapping her cloak about her, she opened the door and stepped outside.

The sun, streaming through the feathery clouds, caressed her skin with luminous warmth, as though lighting her from within. Face to the sun, Katja strolled down the walk to the stable, humming happily. The never-ending breeze caught at her braid, her cloak, her skirts, giving them a playful tug. The yard was quiet save for the occasional harsh whistling call of a curlew. Their long bills tapping the ground for deep-burrowing prey, the birds scattered about the nearby meadow.

With a hard yank, Katja dislodged the stubborn side door to the stable and blinked in the sudden gloom, her eyes taking a moment to adjust after the bright outside light. The door creaked closed behind her and she inhaled the air redolent with fragrant hay, the musk of manure, and the sharp tang of urine.

Good lad! Already hard at work. She smiled again as she glanced about the barn, its roofline low to hold in the heat, the stalls deep in fresh straw, piles of soiled straw in the center aisle awaiting the cart.

Barking erupted from Skündi's stall and Katja laughed as the wolfhound's head poked over the top edge of the open half-door. Freki flattened his ears against his skull and wagged his entire body in enthusiastic greeting. Before Katja could open the door, Freki sailed over the top, landing gracefully in the passageway. He whined excitedly as Katja ruffled his fur, his paws dancing on the packed earth.

"Did ye miss me, lad?" she teased, thrilled to see her dog again. It shocked her how focused she'd been on Calder the day before, but she knew Freki had been in good hands despite her lack of attention. She hugged him close.

"Never again," she whispered. "Ye are free to sleep in my room. Though I may need to fix ye yer own bed by the hearth."

Freki cocked his head, seemingly aghast at her suggestion. Katja laughed. "I dinnae think Calder will take kindly to a beast yer size taking up space in his bed, but ye are welcome to find out."

"No!" Donnan cried, pelting his way down the stable aisle. "Ye cannae go with him. He's no good for ye." He skidded to a stop a few feet away, hands fisted on his hips. Leaning forward, he pinned her with a glare.

"He's only going to break yer heart, Katja," he insisted. "Ye arenae so daft as to fall for him again, are ye?" He shot a glance over his shoulder and lowered his voice. "He could have an accident, ye know."

Katja held her ground against his angry challenge, though she had to bite her lip to keep the smile at bay. It warmed her heart to have such a champion, but knew he would not take her dismissal of his concerns lightly.

She folded her hands before her and nodded slowly, giving his words the attention they were due. "I understand ye have reservations, Donnan. I would clearly be daft if I dinnae have concerns as well. And whilst Calder could easily become lost in a *haar* early one morning as it rolls in from the sea and tumble over one of the cliffs, I think we'll give him a second chance."

Donnan scowled and scuffed a toe in the packed dirt of the passage. "I wouldnae truly hurt him. But I could scare him plenty!"

"I know ye could, and whilst I dinnae believe that is the right thing to do, either, 'tis good to know ye care about me."

Donnan folded his arms over his chest and hung his head. "Ye are like my sister," he muttered. "I dinnae have family—and now I willnae again."

"Och, Donnan!" Katja cried, her heart twisting in her chest. "Ye are the best brother ever. But families separate to begin new families—it doesnae mean we'll never see each other again." Though she knew life as an apprentice left no time for the days it would take to visit her at Fairetur.

"Uncle Lund and Aunt Runa are yer family, now," she soothed.

"Yer uncle is my master," Donnan growled.

Katja propped her hands on her hips. "And who has been fattening ye up?" she demanded. "And slipping ye sweets to take with ye nearly every morning?"

The reminder of sweets snatched a smile from Donnan. "Ye knew?"

Katja gave tiny shakes of her head as she smothered her laughter. "Aunt Runa is the most soft-hearted person I know. Though she'll deny it and have my hide for suggesting it. She slips sweets in Uncle Lund's pockets as well."

Donnan's grin drooped. "Ye are leaving?"

"Aye."

His voice dropped to a bare whisper. "Ye're going to have a bairn?"

"Aye. And I will tell him he has an uncle named Donnan who wants to meet him some day."

A smile quivered at one corner of the lad's mouth. "Even if 'tis a lass, I'll still be her uncle, aye?"

This time, Katja laughed. "Even if 'tis a lass," she agreed.

"I'll miss ye and yon dog," Donnan said, drawing his shoulders back as if to shake off his moment of weakness.

Katja mussed his hair. "And Freki and I will miss ye, too. We wouldnae be here if not for ye. I will always remember it."

He shrugged nonchalantly, as if rescuing damsels in distress were an everyday occurrence for him. But color tinted his cheeks and Katja knew her words pleased him.

"*Ek ann þér,* Donnan. Ye are part of my family now. That will never change."

Donnan ducked his head and blinked hard, and Katja wondered if anyone had ever told him before that he was loved.

"When will ye leave?" he asked a moment later, his voice rough.

"As soon as possible. There willnae be many chances to cross the sea once the winter storms come."

His eyes widened in shock. "Ye mean they will get worse?"

Katja laughed. "Aye. They will get worse. And ye will ask my uncle for a heavier coat and mittens, and Aunt Runa will knit ye a scarf. In fact, it wouldnae surprise me if she wasnae doing that now."

"They're good people," Donnan noted. "They dinnae have to take me in."

"Ye will prove yer worth, lad. Dinnae fash."

* * *

Calder paced the front room, the hearth fighting a losing battle against the bitter cold as a winter storm raged without. Three steps cold, three steps back to warmth. Turn and go back. He dragged himself to a chair next to the fire and collapsed into the seat.

How long can a storm possibly last? Nearly a sennight has passed and nary a glene, much less enough of a break to book passage to Thurso. He burrowed deeper in the chair cushion, stretching his toes to the fire, seeking other distractions to his worry.

A bairn. The thought never failed to astound him. His body, tense from his inability to change the weather to suit his needs, went slack. A smile tugged at one corner of his mouth.

I cannae believe I will soon be a da. A shiver shot up his spine. Responsibility crashed over him, threatening to swamp his previously avowed good intentions. He forced a deep breath. *Can I be someone my child respects? Someone he can trust and rely on? Will the bairn be a lass or a lad?*

Suddenly his fingers itched to create something for the bairn. Something to make the tiny bairn he wouldnae see for seven long months more real. A toy sword? A wooden doll?

Gentle hands slid over his shoulders, smoothing the returning knots of worry. The subtle scent of lavender captured his senses a second before the instinct to leap to his feet crashed through him.

"I know ye are fashed about the weather," Katja murmured. "Uncle Lund says 'twill be another day before the wind settles, but it should be a fine day for sailing after that. He suggests ye both ride to the dock tomorrow and discover who will be sailing soonest and place coin with them." She kissed the top of his head. "'Twill be a cold and windy ride."

He patted her hand and leaned into her caress. "I dinnae believe waiting will do more than bring us worse weather. And if we linger through the winter, 'twill not be safe for ye to travel."

Calder grasped her wrist and pulled her to his lap, cuddling her close. "And I wouldnae consider risking ye or the bairn."

"Aye. I would enjoy visiting longer with my aunt and uncle, but soon the journey home will be too dangerous."

"I wish I could send a message for us to be met at Thurso. I would feel better to have guards riding with us."

Katja chuckled. "I can fend for myself, husband," she reminded him. "I meant the ice and snow."

Calder shook his head. "I dinnae like the thought Gair Orrock holds a grudge against ye."

"I doubt he likes that I bested him and killed his men. And we know what my da did to him and his clan. But how will he know I have returned? Few people risk the seas this time of year. We will travel swiftly once we leave Thurso, and I will dress in trews and wrap in a cloak and we will travel as two clansmen, not a woman alone. How could he possibly recognize me?"

Somewhat mollified, Calder's attention diverted to the pleasant weight of Katja in his lap. He brushed his fingertips over her cheek and down the long column of her neck. Slipping his fingers inside the neckline of her gown, he reveled in the satin smoothness of her skin.

"I have a mind to take my wife to bed before her uncle drags me into the cold. What do ye think of that idea?"

Katja slipped from his lap and, taking his hand, drew him with her through the door.

Freki stretched his long limbs and followed them from the room.

Chapter Twenty One

Parting from Lund and Runa had been difficult, filled with tears and smiles and promises to visit. Katja regretted losing the precious family tie, knowing it would be months if not years before she would see them again. Sadness warred with the excitement of beginning life anew with Calder—and their bairn.

As Lund predicted, the weather cleared spectacularly, giving them beautiful skies to pair with the choppy passage.

"Ye are greener than a wily toad," Katja teased Calder as the ship approached Thurso.

He groaned. "I love yer aunt and uncle, but let's allow them come to us for the next visit."

Katja tightened her grip on his arm in sympathy and anticipation, turning her face into the sun as gulls swarmed overhead. The flap of the sail merged with the shouts of men on the docks as their ship came to rest against the wooden planks. She and Calder moved quickly to the loading plank, leading the weary horses, Freki at their heels, and stepped ashore.

She scanned the sea of faces around her and noticed Calder did as well. Freki strode between them, avoiding the seething mass of bodies that wove in and out on their innumerable errands.

"We'll stay here the night and be on our way at first light," Calder said.

Katja disagreed. "I would rather ride to Hacraig and stay at the inn there. 'Tis only a short journey and it would be good to stretch our legs."

"I saw Orrock at the inn, there. I dinnae think that is a good choice."

"Ye saw him here, as well. Thurso is a verra busy town. 'Twill be easier to spot him in the village."

She knew he didn't like it. He scraped a hand through his hair, frowning. Lines creased his face, and she realized how tiring the crossing from Lerwick had been for him.

"Och, ye're right. 'Tis growing late, and we shouldnae be on the road after dark." She slipped her hand in his. "We will find a private room before they are all spoken for and put some warm food in our bellies."

Calder opened his mouth to reply, but she gave him a slanted look. "My belly needs extra nourishment, husband."

With a nod of decision, Calder led her to an inn near the outskirts of town.

The following morning crept along, swathed in fog. Thick, damp leaves deadened the sound of the horses' hooves. The air was cold and sharp, and the trees glistened with frost.

Katja blew a breath into the air, watching it mingle, cold and gray, with the heavy mists. The inhale seared her lungs, but she grinned, her Viking heritage exhilarated by the biting cold. The road ambled along the river where fog hovered a foot or so above the water. Trees hugged the banks, giving her and Calder some protection from the bitter wind.

Freki flushed a rabbit from a bit of underbrush and he raced off in pursuit. His head lowered, eyes on his target, the rabbit no match for the wolfhound's ground-covering dash. Catching his prey in a half-dozen strides, he settled down near a boulder to dine.

Katja shook her head. Had she sent him on the hunt, he would have brought the rabbit back to her. But she and Calder had broken their fast at the inn, and a full-grown wolfhound needed plenty of sustenance.

"The ride to Hacraig isnae long. Shall we make a short day and rest there before continuing to Fairetur? Or push on and risk a night in the open?"

Calder tilted his head, musing Katja's question. "I hesitate to halt whilst the sun is up. But I dinnae think we should sleep without shelter."

"I agree. 'Tis cold, but I see no storm clouds. It appears we have traveling grace for another day at least."

"'Twill be good to be home and before a roaring fire. I know Beitris and Torri have missed ye."

"I have missed them. It was nice to have a sister."

"Even one who chatters as much as she does?" Calder teased.

"She's spirited," Katja laughed. "I dinnae mind."

They rode over a small hill, closer to a bend in the river, where trees crowded together and frost hid from the sun. Katja turned in her saddle.

"Where has Freki gotten off to?" she mused.

Calder glanced about. "Likely chasing down another rabbit," he said.

The sound of branches cracking and hooves pounding the frozen ground turned their attention from the road. Before Katja understood what was happening, Calder drew his sword and used the flat of the blade to slap Skündi on the rump.

"Run!" he shouted. Skündi squealed, pinning his ears back as he leapt into a panicked gallop, clumps of snow and earth churning from beneath his hooves.

It took several moments for Katja to recover from the shock of Calder's actions. She wrestled Skündi under control a short distance down the road and shot a glance over her shoulder. Three armed men converged on her husband while two others chased her, all astride stocky Highland ponies. Anger seared her gut and fired the

Viking blood in her veins. She drew her sword and wheeled Skündi about to face the approaching threat.

Her sword held aloft, she screamed her battle cry, her voice ringing in the clear air. *"Freki! Ganga at!"*

Realizing the odds of Calder surviving an attack from three outlaws were slim, she steeled herself against the outcome and urged Skündi forward to intercept her first pursuer.

The battle tactics Ranald and her brothers had drilled into her rose to the fore. Hoping these were common thieves, not warriors, she positioned the nearest rider between her and the next, sending Skündi slamming into the pony, his well-muscled chest overwhelming the smaller, slighter horse. Its rider gripped his shaggy pony's mane with both hands, struggling to stay mounted. With a shriek of anger, Katja brought her sword down on the man's head. He dropped to the ground and the riderless animal careened down the trail.

With the second pursuer almost upon her, Katja reined in Skündi, sinking him deep on his haunches.

"Lofta," she commanded.

Her destrier rose on his rear legs, steel shod forefeet flailing as the next outlaw closed on them. The man gaped at her in shock as he sawed at his pony's reins, attempting to avoid the larger horse's powerful attack, but both rider and pony fell, bloodied and broken beneath Skündi's hooves.

Her path cleared, Katja turned her attention to Calder as he gamely held off his attackers. Armunn held firm, biting and kicking when a pony drew too close, but the bravery of both horse and rider were overwhelmed. Calder bled from two wounds Katja could see. Her husband was dying before her eyes.

Drawing the knife from the sheath at her nape, Katja rose in her stirrups and hurled her blade, striking the flank of the nearest horse, causing it to buck and squeal in pain. Freki's tawny form streaked from the underbrush in a rush of power and sound, snarling as he savaged the hock of another horse. The pony screamed and launched a lightning-fast kick, unseating its rider and striking Freki in the head. The force threw Freki into a tree where he crumpled in eerie stillness.

Katja ignored the pang in her chest at the sight and rammed Skündi into the pony she'd struck with her blade, blood streaking its dun-colored hide. Off-balanced, the rider fell to the ground, but rolled to his feet. From the advantage of her mounted height, Katja struck the man's shoulder with her sword, knocking his long dirk to the grass and the outlaw to his knees. Crazed with the fire of battle, Skündi rose and fell, crushing the man's skull beneath his deadly hooves.

Calder remained locked in battle with the final outlaw. A crimson stain bloomed from a cut on his chest, his off-hand barely grasping Armunn's reins as blood flowed from a deep gash on his forearm. Using his knees to guide his steed, Calder wheeled Armunn in a quarter turn to place his opponent on his right.

Unwilling to watch further, Katja spurred Skündi forward with a scream of challenge. "MacGerry!"

Skündi rammed the outlaw's mare, sending rider and horse in a tumbled heap to the ground. The man rose gingerly, grasping ribs likely broken, blood streaming from a fresh wound on his forehead.

Katja blinked, startled as the man lifted his scarred face, hatred spilling from his eyes. A sulphur-colored aura of pain warred with the thick black cloud of long-lasting unforgiveness and the muddied red of anger.

Gair Orrock.

* * *

Calder stared at Katja through eyelashes partially matted with congealing blood. His chest heaved with exertion and his heart raced with battle-lust. The pain from his wounds a mere tingle, held at bay by the rage sweeping through him.

Gair Orrock.

He'd known he was wrong to leave the man alive when he left Thurso. He'd pitied him for what he'd suffered at the earl's hands, but in his heart, he knew the man would ever be a threat. Weakness? Or justice?

The man faltered, weaving on his feet. He cried out and collapsed to his knees. Slowly crumpling forward, he braced himself with one hand on the ground as a stream of blood spewed from his lips. A deep cough racked him, and he wailed pitifully, holding his arm over his chest.

Calder and Katja exchanged glances. Katja nudged Skündi closer but did not dismount.

"Ye will need care to survive that wound. Will ye accept our help?"

"Yer da's help put me in the hell I've lived the past twenty-six years," Gair spat.

"'Twas my father—not me," she stated.

"Leave him," Calder rasped. "'Tis better than he deserves."

"He is injured—" Katja began.

"He could have killed my wife and bairn!" Calder lashed, furious.

"And he came close to killing ye," Katja acknowledged. "Yet because he once loved my mother, I will offer him mercy."

Gair cocked his head, his gaze sliding over Katja, coming to rest on her face. "Ye are like Elke," he whispered. "She was young and spirited—and kind." He closed his eyes. "She never noticed me.

And when yer da decided to marry her, 'twas too late."

"My aunt said ye loved her—my ma."

Gair's breathing changed, shallow and fast as he fought for air. "I was . . . no match . . . for the rich earl."

"Had she known ye, 'twould not have mattered."

The light in Gair's eyes dimmed then was gone, and his body slackened against the ground. Calder swayed in his saddle and Katja's gaze darted immediately to him.

"Can ye ride?" she asked, worry on her face.

"Aye," he breathed as pain washed over him, dimming his vision. He felt more than saw Skündi's frame next to him, Armunn's reins sliding from his hands as Katja fisted them in her free hand. He saw her dismount, but could force no protest from his lips. She quickly bound his arm, pulling a strip of cloth tight over a pad made from the remnants of his tunic sleeve. Her fingers pressed against his other wounds as she staunched the bleeding, leaving bandages tied hastily in place.

She disappeared from his view, but returned moments later. Or perhaps longer, as Calder's world existed only in pain and mind-numbing cold. She mounted behind him, settling her arms about him protectively as she urged the horse forward. Calder slumped forward and was lost to the darkness.

Chapter Twenty Two

Katja checked Calder's bandages again, scanning the long length of the wound on his forearm for signs of infection, the streaks of redness and heat that would indicate the beginning of a losing battle for Calder's arm—and maybe his life. The healer in Hacraig had lingered long hours over Calder's wounds, rinsing them again and again with an herbal solution before she stitched them closed, a procedure of which Katja heartily approved.

The flesh puckered between the heavy stitches, but not angry, and she replaced the cloth, pleased to see no discharge on the bandage. A smile quivered on her lips as she ran her fingers gently through his hair, rubbing the pad of her thumb over the rough stubble around the gash in his scalp.

He willnae like the way we trimmed his hair, but 'twill grow back. Her breath lurched in her chest as she considered the length of time since he'd lost consciousness, two long days previous. She squatted on her heels, weary and disheartened.

"Ye should eat, lass. I will sit with yer lad."

Katja turned bleary eyes to the innkeeper's wife, casting a disinterested look at the tray resting on the unsteady table. Her stomach growled, but she could scarcely summon the strength to eat. She picked up the tray and crossed the tiny room to the blanket by the hearth. Freki lifted his head, his tail beating a gentle tattoo on the packed earth floor.

Bite by bite, the two shared the meal. Making sure a dish of water was close at hand for Freki to drink, Katja curled next to him, letting the warmth from the fire soothe her aches.

She must have fallen asleep. The door opened and she stared groggily at the dark figure silhouetted in the portal. It lingered a moment, staring at Calder's form on the narrow bed. Freki whined low, but did not rise. The man at the door shifted his gaze to the dog—then to Katja.

"Are ye well, lass?" He stepped inside and closed the door.

"Uncle Finn?" Katja blinked rapidly, feeling wooly-headed after her nap. She made an abortive attempt to gain her feet and Finn clasped her elbow to assist her. She flashed him a smile of gratitude and crossed to Calder's side where the innkeeper's wife regarded Finn with a dubious look.

Katja dropped gentle fingers to Calder's forehead. His eyelids fluttered and for the first time in nearly three days, she saw the glimmer of MacGerry blue eyes regarding her.

Relief so profound it nearly sent her to her knees washed over her, driving away the sadness and anger. She smiled, choked back sudden tears, and smiled again as tears spilled down her face.

"Welcome back," she whispered.

"I'd think I was in heaven . . . were it not . . . for the *trow* . . . over yer shoulder." Calder's eyes tracked Finn who loomed over Katja.

Katja hiccupped over her snort of surprise. "Yer uncle isnae a troll," she chided gently, delighted to hear Calder's banter, weak though it was.

"Dinnae fash, lassie. Being called a troll is better than facing what I feared."

With a bleak nod, Katja agreed. She stared at Calder, his breathing shallow but firmer than it had been, the gleam of his eyes sparkling behind narrowed lids.

She sought refuge from her emotions by discussing Calder's injuries.

"He has a gash in his scalp," she said, brushing the shaggy locks away from the roughly shaved area.

"'Tis a good thing our lad has a hard head. 'Twill give him fortitude when he sees the state of his shorn pate." He chuckled. "Thinking of joining the church, lad?"

Katja hid a grin at Calder's scowl. "Be off with ye, auld man," he rasped. "I can do without . . . yer humor."

"He's healing well," Katja hurriedly interjected, not wishing to exhaust Calder should he and his uncle begin a bantering spate. She motioned to his chest. "He took a scrape here and an ugly strike to his arm. The healer did a good job sewing him up. And none of the wounds fester."

Finn peered closely at the wounds and nodded his head. "A right fair job," he agreed. "'Twill give ye character to have a wee scar or two."

His gaze met hers with a meaningful glance at Calder's wounded arm.

"How bad?" he murmured.

Katja smoothed Calder's cheek. "Can ye sip a bit of weak ale?" she asked him. The innkeeper's wife brought the flask from the table and poured a mug. Finn carefully raised Calder's shoulders enough to allow him to drink and Katja held the mug to his lips. He managed several swallows before he groaned and settled back onto the bed. Katja tucked the blanket around him and kissed his forehead before she turned to Finn and his question.

She waved at him to be seated by the hearth. The innkeeper's wife gathered the tray and bustled from the room, leaving them alone.

"The wound is verra deep, but it bled clean and I dinnae believe he has lost the use of the arm. Howbeit, it will heal with much scarring and he must use it, not coddle it, if he wishes to regain full use. 'Twill take time, and 'twill be painful. I have seen this sort of wound once before."

Finn nodded. "And the rest?"

"The rest should be of little bother to him in another few days. Tender, mayhap, but the chest wound was a clean slice. We will continue to watch for dizziness and such. He took a hard blow to the head."

Suddenly her composure left her and she fisted her hands, pressing them deep into her lap to still their quaking. Finn offered her a mug of ale and after a moment she took a sip, managing to keep it from banging against her teeth as she drank.

She set it aside and sent Finn a tiny smile.

"Thank ye for coming." There was a wealth of words she could not force herself to say. Of the deep fear as she rode behind Calder to the inn at Hacraig, his body slack in her arms, barely able to keep him on Armunn's back. The hollow feeling of being lost, adrift as the healer set herself to her job, the utter uselessness carving a hole in her heart. Finn had apparently ridden hard from Fairetur, for she'd not expected him for another day at least. And for that, she would be eternally grateful.

The sedative effect of relief settled over her and she relaxed in her chair. "Are ye alone?" she asked.

"Nae. I've three lads with me, but they're warming their bellies in the inn. Robbie will likely send a few more in a day or so. A proper escort for ye."

He leaned forward, forearms propped on his knees. With a glance to Calder, he looked at Katja. "Will ye tell me what happened?"

She nodded cautiously, unsure of her ability to recount the tale. "We sailed from Lerwick and arrived in Thurso after a long trip. Calder wasnae feeling well—a wee bit seasick—and we stayed overnight in Thurso.

"'Twas a bright morning, and we chatted . . . Freki chased a rabbit or two." Katja glanced at the dog, still lying on his blanket, head on his paws, eyes closed.

"We knew a man named Gair Orrock could be waiting for me. My da did some terrible things to him and his clan and he hates all Sinclairs." She wrung her hands. "I was beset by two of his men on my way to Thurso a month ago." She slowly lifted her gaze to Finn. "I killed them both. Gair arrived only moments later, and Freki attacked him. Regardless of fault, Gair hated me, too."

Katja took a calming breath and waited until her heart regained its normal beat. "Gair lay in wait for our return. I suppose he had a spy in Thurso, watching for a woman with a large dog. Calder and I were taken off-guard. He tried to send me away, but two men followed me. They scattered as they chased after me, and I was able to kill them one at a time. I then returned to help Calder.

"Freki downed one horse. It struck him with a hoof, and I thought the blow had killed him. Freki is very unsteady and willnae use one front leg. I am hoping he recovers.

"The last outlaw was Gair. Skündi sent his mare to the ground. She rolled on Gair and I think his broken ribs pierced his lungs. I dragged Freki atop Skündi and rode behind Calder to keep him on his horse. When we left the clearing, Gair was dead."

* * *

"'Tisnae dignified," Calder grumbled. He glared at his wife, but she sent him a merry smile.

"Ye would look even less dignified were ye to fall from yer horse."

Shock burst on Calder's face. "I havenae fallen from a horse since I was a lad!" he objected. But his limbs quivered from the exertion of moving from his bed at the inn to the litter constructed for him. The litter dipped as Freki limped onto the frame and settled next to him. Liquid brown eyes stared at Calder and he scratched the furry head.

"Would ye rather stay here until ye are stronger?" Katja asked, lowering her voice. She touched his face, concern in her eyes, and his mood softened immediately.

"Nae. I'm ready to go home," he replied, careful to keep the grumble from his voice. "Have I told ye today I love ye?"

Her smile returned. "I am obliged to tell ye of yer negligence on the matter. I could be persuaded to overlook it this once—for a small penance."

"I am yers to command," he replied.

She leaned over him, her braid swinging across her shoulder to brush his chest. "I will require a kiss."

He tilted his chin, lifting his lips to hers. He sighed as she closed the gap between them on a breath of warm air. The tip of her tongue traced his lips, and his mouth opened, welcoming her.

"Ye be certain to let us know when ye are ready to leave, Laird," Finn called. The other men hid their guffaws behind their fists.

"Dinnae mind them," Katja said as she straightened and strode to Skündi. Settling into the saddle, she sent Finn an enchanting smile. "I'm ready to go home."

Epilogue

Rain pattered on the roof and dripped from the eaves in a steady flow. The sky was a gloomy blend of gray skies and scurrying clouds, but the laird's chamber was cozy with a single shutter open to allow fresh air and a crackling fire on the hearth. Katja breathed deep of the scents mingled in the air. Rain mixed with the familiar odor of damp earth rising from the ground below. The tang of wood smoke as tendrils escaped the draw of the chimney. And the sweet, sweet scent of the bairn asleep on her chest.

"Would ye like me to lay the wee imp in her cradle?" Calder asked, his voice a low whisper to keep from waking her.

Katja glanced at the nearly white curls dusting the child's head and the rose-tinted, round cheek. The bairn's mouth was slightly open and her tongue pushed forward twice as if nursing.

"Nae. She isnae heavy and I like to watch her sleep."

Calder dropped to the cushioned bench next to Katja, curving himself against her. He dropped a kiss to her cheek, then to the bairn's head. "I like watching her, too," he admitted, wrapping an arm about Katja's shoulders and drawing her close.

"I cannae believe she will be a month old soon." Calder rested his cheek atop Katja's head.

Neighs and the rattle of harness drifted up from the bailey.

"Boar's bollocks," he muttered. "Who would travel on such a day?"

Katja rested a hand on his arm in mild protest when he drew away to stand. "Let Robbie handle it. 'Tis likely a peddler or a minstrel. Someone who requires shelter for the night."

"They tend to have enough sense to linger with their host in such *dreich* weather," Calder muttered. But he sank back next to Katja and the bairn, though Katja knew he had one ear on the commotion in the bailey and expected an accounting from his brother shortly.

She shifted the bairn slightly and tugged the edges of her bodice together. Calder's hand drifted up to cup a full breast. Warmth hummed deep inside her, heavy and insistent after the constraints following childbirth. Katja murmured her approval as his fingers stroked her through the cloth of her gown, his palm weighing the heaviness of her breast.

A knock sounded on the door. Calder's eyes met hers in a promise before he yielded to the necessity.

"Enter."

The door swung open and Katja gasped in surprise to see her aunt and uncle in the doorway. Donnan winnowed his way between them, eyes on the bairn.

"Am I an aunt or an uncle?" he demanded.

Everyone roared with laughter, waking the bairn. Katja rose to her feet, jostling the baby who wailed and stuck a tiny fist in her mouth. Runa flew across the room, enveloping Katja and the bairn in a hug, at last drawing back enough to peer at the tiny face.

"She has Calder's eyes," she said. "Never mind most bairns have blue eyes. Hers are quite a startling shade." Runa gave Katja another hug. "And her hair will be a true Norse gold." Her voice dropped to a whisper. "She looks just like yer ma."

"We named her Elke," Katja said. "Did our letter reach ye?"

"A few days ago," Runa admitted. "Lund dropped everything as soon as it arrived and made arrangements for our passage here."

"I spared no expense or effort to see the woman who appreciates my finer qualities," he grinned, peering over Runa's shoulder at Katja and the bairn.

Runa sighed and rolled her eyes. "He is truly insufferable, Katja. Ye have created a monster even our Viking ancestors couldnae conceive of."

Lund planted a kiss on his wife's lips, his eyes sparkling with good humor. He reached between the women and plucked the bairn from Katja's arms. Cradling her carefully in the crook of his elbow, he and Elke stared at each other. Elke waved a small fist and clucked her tongue.

"Ye are a beauty, lass. There will be none like ye."

"Ye spoil her, Lund," Runa chided, but her voice held no censure. She deftly scooped the bairn into her own arms and rocked her gently to and fro.

"What a clever lass to take after yer ma," she crooned. Elke gurgled.

"I have a present for her," Donnan said.

Everyone looked at the lad. His cheeks reddened, but he reached in a large satchel hanging from his shoulder. It squeaked.

"Let it out, lad," Lund commanded. "Dinnae take all day."

Freki's ears perked forward and he rose cautiously from his bed. He strode toward the lad with a gentle limp, his head tilted to the side.

"He only has partial sight in that eye," Katja murmured. "But his lameness is much improved." She smiled. "He went afield with me last week and caught a rabbit."

Freki sniffed the satchel as Donnan plunged both hands inside and brought forth a plump puppy, its coat a shade darker than Freki's.

"Uncle Lund said I could pick one for the bairn. 'Tis only just weaned, and I named it Geri—for Odin's other wolf. 'Twill be like Freki—except 'tis a lass."

"He did a fine job of caring for the pup on the trip," Lund added with a nod of approval. The lad ducked his head, but his grin betrayed his pleasure at Lund's words.

"I am pleased beyond measure, Donnan," Katja said. "What a fine gift, and one that will grow with Elke. Thank ye."

The bairn mewled and Katja took her from Runa's arms. "She is hungry," she explained, warmth in her cheeks at the overcrowded state of the room.

"The men will be pleased to retire to the hall for refreshment," Runa announced, shooing them to the door.

Katja laid a hand on Donnan's shoulder. "It would please me if ye would care for the pup whilst ye are here. And mayhap play a bit with Freki as well?"

Donnan nodded. "Aye. I can do that. Uncle Lund lets me care for the dogs at home."

"Thank ye, again, Donnan. Ye are a thoughtful lad."

He turned to follow the others from the room, the pup tucked under one arm, his other hand buried in Freki's ruff.

"Oh, and Donnan?"

He glanced over his shoulder, pausing at the door.

"Ye are an uncle."

~The End~

A NOTE FROM THE AUTHORS

Thank you for reading Katja Sinclair's story. We were inspired to write *The Highlander's Viking Bride* after Anna's story in *Highland Escape* was so wonderfully received. Readers appear to appreciate strong heroines as much as we do, and after DD's years of training with tough women in a variety of dojos in several states, characteristics of these women were combined to create the heroines for the Hardy Heroine Series.

The Highlander's Viking Bride takes place in an era when Viking influence was still strong in the Orkney and Shetland Islands, which were not a part of the Highland clan system, and retained many of their Viking customs.

The Earls of Caithness are real people, though our story takes place between Walter, 1st Earl of Atholl—who lost the title when he was executed for high treason in 1437—and Sir George Crichton, who gained the recreated title in 1452. The strong influence of the Sinclairs in the northern regions of Scotland gave us the impetus for our heroine's conflict with an impoverished Scottish laird who, under normal circumstances, would never have been considered a matrimonial match for her.

MORE BOOKS by CATHY & DD MACRAE

BOOKS IN THE HARDY HEROINES SERIES

Highland Escape (book 1)
The Highlander's Viking Bride (book 2)
The Highlander's Crusader Bride (book 3)
The Highlander's Norse Bride (book 4)
The Highlander's Welsh Bride (book 5)
The Prince's Highland Bride (book 6, available 2020)

by DD MacRae

The Italian Billionaire's Runaway Bride

by Cathy MacRae

The Highlander's Bride Series
(books 1-5)

The Highlander's Accidental Bride
The Highlander's Reluctant Bride
The Highlander's Tempestuous Bride
The Highlander's Outlaw Bride
The Highlander's French Bride

De Wolfe Pack Connected World
The Saint
The Penitent
The Cursed

Mhàiri's Yuletide Wish (a Christmas novella)

The Ghosts of Culloden Moor series
(with LL Muir, Diane Darcy, et al)
Adam
Malcolm
MacLeod
Patrick

About the Authors

Cathy MacRae lives on the sunny side of the Arbuckle Mountains where she and her husband read, write, and tend the garden—with the help of the dogs, of course.

You can visit with her on Facebook, or read her blogs and learn about her books at www.cathymacraeauthor.com. Drop her a line— she loves to hear from readers!

To keep up with new releases and other fun things, sign up for her newsletter! There's an easy form on her website. (You'll find DD's news there, too!)

Other ways to connect with Cathy:
Facebook: Cathy MacRae Author
Twitter: @CMacRaeAuthor
Pinterest: AuthorCathyMacRae
Instagram: Cathy MacRae_Author

DD MacRae enjoys bringing history to life. Research is one of the best things about writing a story! And with more than 35 years of martial arts training, DD also brings breath-taking action to the tales.

You can connect with DD through www.cathymacraeauthor.com. It's always exciting to hear from readers!

Acknowledgements

We'd like to thank our fabulous critique partners, Dawn Marie Hamilton and Cate Parke for their unstinting work on The Highlander's Viking Bride. They saw the story in its infancy and helped guide it to the full-fledged book it is today.

A special thanks to our editor, Liette Bougie, who loves to chase down time-honored words and phrases that make writing historical novels so much fun!

And a round of applause to our beta-readers who always see the book for what it is, but more importantly, for what it can be. Thank you, Raine, Donna, Cathy, April, Sharon, Valerie, Barb, and Ann!

A huge thank you to Dar Albert who created the beautiful new cover!

~ Cathy & DD MacRae

Read an excerpt from The Highlander's Crusader Bride

CHAPTER ONE

The Holy Land
County of Tripoli, 1221

The pungent smell of burning pitch and the screech of steel on steel dominated the afternoon. Crouched behind a merlon, Arbela MacLean took aim at the siege tower inching toward the castle and launched another flaming arrow toward the lumbering wooden target. The poorly constructed battlement was in danger of being consumed by fire. The men pushing it crouched behind shields to avoid arrows, stalling their advance.

The group manning a battering ram at the gates fared no better. Screams pierced the sounds of battle as a cauldron of heated sand tipped, pouring its burning contents through a chute built into the barbican, showering the men below. While enemy shields deflected much of the sand, Arbela knew it didn't take many grains to slip into clothing, searing skin as if on fire.

"Remember Jerusalem!"

Her father's men repeated the oft heard battle cry from atop the wall. Ever since Saladin had retaken Jerusalem and slaughtered all the inhabitants, this had become the call to arms of all Latins in the Levant.

"Arbela!" her brother Alexander shouted, drawing her attention from the gates.

He and Philippe de Poitiers fought several Turkish warriors

who had scaled the curtain wall, a ladder propped against the top. Arbela pulled four arrows and placed them in her right hand for rapid firing. Drawing her bow, she hit the enemy atop the ladder under the arm as he reached for the wall, sending him tumbling backward, disrupting his follower's ascent. She fired the next three arrows in rapid succession, striking an equal number of warriors, her movements fluid and deadly. Alex and Philippe finished off the remaining invaders who had made the climb.

Alex offered her a brief salute of thanks, then used his war hammer to shatter the top rungs of the ladder. He, Philippe, and two other men pushed the ladder along the wall until it fell, its occupants plummeting to the rocky ground below. As Arbela fitted another arrow and sought a target, the Turks abandoned their tower, fire consuming it as they fled. She turned to the gates and struck down the few remaining fighters. Their tenacity was to be lauded—their tactics, however, were not.

In the distance, the remnant of the invading army withdrew over the hills, likely headed from whence they came. After four days of attempting to breach the gates and walls, it appeared they'd given up the fight. This marked the third such attack they'd endured this year, each more desperate than the last. The Turks seemed to grow over-confident and more numerous as the months went by.

Alex removed his helm and coif, a triumphant grin beaming across his face. His black hair and deep brown eyes sparkled. As twins, he and Arbela shared the same coloring and similar features.

"I look forward to a hot meal and soft bed tonight, sister mine."

Philippe strode toward them, sword in hand, enemy blood spattered on his tabard. "Aye, 'twill be a welcome change to a cold supper and keeping watch on the wall."

"I long to trade my haubergeon and gambeson for a long soak in a hot tub." Arbela pulled the short mail shirt and padded jacket, wet with sweat, away from her skin. She led the others down the stone stairs of the outer wall toward the keep. As soon as her feet touched the baily, two dogs, one black, one sable, tackled her.

"Off! Ye two beasties! Leave off!"

Philippe and Alex laughed at her as they left her rolling on the ground with the dogs and strode toward the hall.

"Toros, Garen, sit!"

The two dogs dropped their haunches in obedience, tongues lolling, anticipating her next command. Arbela rose and dusted herself off.

"Come." She snapped her fingers and each dog took up position beside her—Toros on the right, Garen on the left—nosing her hands. Each dog's shoulder reached just above her knees, their furry tails and bodies wriggling with delight. Thus flanked, Arbela made her way toward the chapel where she would pray for the dead and ask forgiveness for taking life. She prayed to never grow so callused that killing—even in self-defense—would become commonplace. After cleansing mind and soul, she rose to do the same for her body.

"You look lovely, milady, considering you've spent the past several days fighting the cursed Turks. I prayed for your safety daily, and the Almighty saw you through the siege without so much as a scratch."

The older woman crossed herself then finished braiding Arbela's hair and affixed her hijab. Arbela, dressed in a flowing thawb, the one-piece garment commonly worn by both men and women, and loose salwar pants, sat patiently on a cushioned stool. Her clothing, constructed not of linen or cotton, were of embroidered silk, marking her as nobility.

"Thank ye, Aunt Zora. Ye are a treasure."

Arbela flashed a smile to her mother's older sister. After Arbela and Alex's mother passed, Zora had offered to live with them and provide female guidance to Arbela. The thought brought a smile to Arbela's lips. She had spent most of her childhood chasing after her brother, the two of the making a goodly amount of mischief. Aunt Zora had the patience of a saint, though at her age, Zora was more grandmother than aunt.

After finishing Arbela's ablutions, the two women descended the stairs, the noise from the hall expanding with each step. Supper in the great room carried a joyful mood as the residents of Batroun gathered to celebrate their victory. Donel MacLean, Baron of Batroun, had ordered sheep cooked on a spit and a cask of his best wine to be served to all, as each played an important role in repelling the infidels.

Her da occupied the central chair at the high table with Alex seated one side, and Farlan, his captain, on the other. Philippe, the third son of Bohemond IV, Prince of Antioch, Count of Tripoli, and her sire's liege, sat next to her brother. He had fostered with them for years, growing up with Alex, the two of them inseparable. Truly, Arbela viewed him as a second brother, though not as close as her twin. He was a good man and a good knight.

Arbela sat at Farlan's side as her sire stood and raised his cup. The hall grew quiet in anticipation.

"To victory!"

"To victory!" the people roared.

"A MacLean!" Gordon, one of her father's knights toasted. The cheer was chanted thrice by everyone in the hall.

Her da drained his cup then sat and turned to his captain as the crowd returned to their festivities, disquiet etched on his face. "The attacks grow bolder."

Farlan paused before answering. "We protect the pass of Saint Guillaume. It's worth is well known to both pilgrims and traders."

"Och, 'tis plain enough why we attract attention from the Turks. The question is, who is behind these assaults, and why do they keep coming?"

"Likely a nobleman wishes to make his reputation as a powerful caliph. By attacking holdings in the region, they may find a weakness and draw more followers with their success, no matter how small. Papal attention remains on Egypt and ridding the Iberian Peninsula of the Moors. This is widely known, so there is no expectation of another crusade on this soil in the coming year."

Donal scratched his whiskers, dark red now peppered with gray. "Aye, but with each attack, Batroun's reputation of being impenetrable grows."

"Begging yer pardon, laird, but no fortress is impenetrable."

The baron grinned widely. "Agreed. But the Romans knew what they were about when they laid the foundations for this keep. Sheer cliffs on all sides with a small approach from the east gives the advantage of spotting any enemy well in advance, with only one option for entrance. 'Tis mayhap a wee barony, but we have the most secure holding in the Levant. Only size limits how much food we can store over a long siege."

Arbela entered the conversation. "Who fancies himself the next Saladin?"

The older men turned their attention to her question, a frown marring her father's face.

"Mayhap the better question, daughter, is who among the Turkish leaders *doesnae* wish to emulate Saladin by driving out all Latins from the Holy Land?"

Firm in her da's confidence of her logic, Arbela met his gaze. "Aye, but all three attacks have been undertaken by the same leader."

Her sire's dour expression gave way to a knowing grin. "What makes ye say that, lassie?"

Arbela nodded at his challenge. "Each attack learned from the previous. The men we faced in the past few days did not make the same mistakes the others did, nor did they use the same tactics. The important question is, how will this leader continue to draw followers to his cause if he continues to be defeated? I would think this aspiring warlord will pick lower hanging fruit for his next attack. Mayhap a holding further inland."

Donal clapped Farlan on the back. "Now ye see why I need to find her a husband. When Prince Bohemond realizes her worth, he'll replace me with my daughter, here."

Arbela dropped her head to her hands and groaned aloud. "Marriage again? I do not wish to be married, Da."

"'Tis a woman's fate to marry and breed sons, Bela." Alex sat upright, arms folded, his smug expression telling the story they'd had this argument before. Arbela narrowed her eyes at him, wordlessly threatening retaliation. Philippe remained quiet, taking neither side, though his lips twisted in a partial smile.

"And who would have guarded yer back today, dear brother?" Arbela quipped. "The Prince and Clan MacLean would be in mourning this eve had I not been ready with a bow to even the odds."

A knight in her father's service approached her da from behind, missive in hand, interrupting any further talk of marriage and women's duty. The baron broke the wax disc and opened the parchment.

"My sire's seal," Philippe observed.

Donal nodded agreement as a frown replaced his previous mirth.

"What does the Prince say, Da?" Alex leaned close to get a glimpse of the message.

"It says we are to leave for Antioch on the morrow. Philippe is to be wed and the Prince seeks my counsel on a matter of some importance, though what, he dinnae say." Donal lifted his head and called to another of his men. "Amhal!"

"Yes, *Albarun*?" Her da's dark-skinned castellan bowed briefly before receiving his orders.

"Sir de Poitier, my family and twenty knights are to depart for Antioch at first light. See to the preparations at once."

"As you wish, *Albarun*." With a turn, Amhal shouted orders in rapid Arabic, putting all servants within hearing into motion. Though an Arab, Amhal was Coptic rather than Muslim, and had proven his worth a thousand times over, easing the way for her father to hire people to work the land and to establish local connections for trade. They now turned away people seeking work due to her da's reputation, as not all Latin nobles treated their servants as well.

Donal's pronouncement muted the celebration as news of Philippe's nuptials spread, and speculation about the Prince's summons began.

Arbela rose from the table. "Da, might I be excused?"

Her sire stood and waved for everyone to continue, then gestured for Arbela to follow him. He escorted Arbela to his solar on the second level. He gestured to a chair and poured them both wine while she sat, arms crossed, preparing for the lecture certain to come.

"Arbela. Ye know ye are as precious to me as my next breath. After yer ma was cut down by a Turkish sword, I swore I'd never allow ye to be helpless. I've encouraged ye to train alongside yer brother. Ye take to the training like a hawk to the wind. Ye've a keen mind for logic and tactics. However, 'tis time ye considered yer future, and 'tis not as one of yer da's men at arms. Yer brother and Philippe both earned their spurs this year and will soon go their own ways. 'Tis time for ye to seek a husband."

Arbela twisted her archer's thumb ring and calmed her breathing as she attempted to push emotion aside and gather her thoughts. "Aye, Philippe and Alex earned their spurs, and were I a son instead of a daughter, I would have earned them as well. I am better with a bow and dagger than either of them, and have skills they know nothing of."

Donal shifted uncomfortably in his chair and ran his fingers through his thick silver-shot auburn hair. "But ye arenae a man, ye are a woman. No matter how much ye wish otherwise. Dinnae remind me of the Hashashin training ye received from yer ma's kin. Had I known yer uncle practiced the black fighting arts, I wouldnae have allowed ye to spend so much time with them."

"What need do I have of a husband, Da?" Arbela asked, attempting to distract her da from his speech against training she'd found fascinating. "What have I to offer a man? Do ye think any husband will allow me to fletch arrows? Lead the hunt? Sharpen his sword or mend his armor? I cannot embroider, nor can I weave." She knew she was running out of time before her sire lost his temper and ended her conversation.

He dismissed her arguments with a wave of his hand. "Ye have followed Amhal about since ye were a wee lass. He has taught ye all ye need to know to run yer own home. Ye love Farlan and Elspeth's children like they were yer own."

Arbela shook her head and opened her mouth to reply, but her da halted her with a lifted forefinger.

"I may have been a poor younger son of a Scottish laird when I took up the cross and followed King Richard, but I am now a baron of a small but important holding, serve a powerful lord, and have made a fortune twice over in trade. Ye have blue blood from yer ma's side, and a very large dowry to ensure ye are considered by every nobleman's son in the Levant."

The look in her father's eyes and the determination he wore marked her defeat. She would have to have to consider another strategy. "My dowry will ensure men will see only what they stand to gain, and ignore the woman." Melancholy filled her voice.

"Ye are ten and seven summers, daughter. 'Tis past time for ye to marry. I will find ye a husband who willnae try and break yer spirit, but ye will obey me. I will seek the Prince's counsel on the matter and see ye married before the year is out."

Arbela rose, made her curtsy, and quietly left her da in his solar. She padded down the hall to her chamber, Toros and Garen in her wake, her heart throbbing painfully. Marriage would mean she'd have to give up the life she loved and submit to a man who cared naught for her—only for the color of her da's coin. Briefly, she considered running away to her mother's people, but knew they would allow her fewer choices than her da had. Misery threatened to settle like a shroud. The journey to Antioch she'd greatly anticipated only an hour before, now loomed like a trip to the gallows.

Printed in Great Britain
by Amazon

40269948R00169